LEGENDS OF THE
NIGHT

Other books by
Stephen Mark Rainey

The Last Trumpet
Balak
Dark Shadows – Dreams of the Dark
   (with Elizabeth Massie)
   HarperEntertainment, 1999
Fugue Devil & Other Weird Horrors
   Macabre, Inc.; 1993

LEGENDS OF THE NIGHT

STEPHEN MARK RAINEY

WILDSIDE PRESS
Doylestown, Pennsylvania

Legends of the N ight
A publication of
Wildside Press
P.O. Box 301
Holicong, PA 18928-0301

www.wildsidepress.com
FIRST EDITION

Table of Contents

Before the Red Star Falls

Dedicated to H. G. Wells

"Show me what you have brought."

"It's this," Melbury said, raising the glittering object in front of Cedric Hayward's eager eyes. "I had a rather dotty old uncle die, and this was among his property left to me. I fancy it must be worth a pound or three."

"I should say!" Hayward exclaimed, his luminous blue eyes widening with excitement. Graeme Melbury had journeyed here from Woking this morning with his newly acquired artifact and now sat in front of the large hickory desk, across from the jeweler. An early afternoon sun streamed in through the windows, turning the ivory walls a warm shade of bronze. Though not inordinately hot, London, during August of 1894, was humid and uncomfortable.

"I've never seen stones like these before," Hayward murmured. "Not in all my days in South Africa. Blast, the whole item is quite curious! Your uncle wasn't particularly wealthy, was he?"

"Hardly. A modest man, if ever there was one. Difficult to imagine him having this hoarded away."

The item in question was a spherical, metallic device about the size of a cricket ball, studded with faceted crystals of uncanny size and brilliance. The stones resembled intricately cut diamonds, but their pulsing, reddish hue seemed to suggest that, inside the sphere, a powerful energy seethed in vain attempt to burst its container.

"My God, it's heavy," Hayward remarked with surprise, as Melbury placed it in his hands. "It must be filled with solid gold!"

Melbury nodded, tweaking the tip of his long moustache. "So, Hayward. How much do you think such a thing could be worth?"

The jeweler snorted. "You must be joking. I wouldn't hazard a guess without an in-depth study. I'm not even sure if these stones are diamonds. And this metal — I've never seen anything quite like it. I don't see how even solid gold could weigh this much. Must be close to four stone. And look at this colour: coppery, with a bluish tinge. But it shines so!"

"I believe it's hollow."

"Impossible," the burly man said with a scowl. "To weigh this much it must surely be solid."

"I would agree with you. But look here." He pointed to one of the sparkling crystals. "Look deeply into the gem. If you hold it just so, you can see right into it. I'm sure it's no illusion."

Hayward lifted the sphere — not without some effort — up to the golden sunbeams firing through the open window. Turning the object as Melbury had suggested, he peered at the flattened crown of the largest stone, indeed seeing what appeared to be the encased tips of the stones on the opposite side of the sphere. When he passed his hand between the light and the object, the gems blinked out.

"Remarkable," Hayward breathed. "But I do believe you have a point. Tell me. Did your uncle ever show this to you or discuss it with you while he was alive?"

"Never. But in his office safe where he kept this thing, he left a letter for the heir of his estate — which happens to be me, since my nephew's sad bout with the grippe; God rest his soul. Anyway, there's no clue as to what the thing is. But the letter describes a long history of Melburys, all of whom have owned it. Quite a mystery, actually."

"Yet, you are here with your strange prize. Do you intend to sell it? Do you need money?"

"It's not that," Melbury said with a shake of his head.

"Needless to say, my curiosity's been aroused. According to the letter, this thing has existed for a staggering number of generations — dating back at least 500 years."

Hayward blew a harsh lungful of air through pursed lips. "Impossible. Patently impossible. The craftsmanship. . . ."

"Naturally, I cannot prove it. But the family lineage documented in the letter has been verified by the College of Arms."

"An amazing tale," Hayward said, offering Melbury a conciliatory nod of his balding head. "Well, let us have a look." He took from his desk a jeweler's loupe and screwed it gently into the hollow of his eye. Then, moving the sphere onto his cleared desk, he focused on the largest of the sparkling gems, watching the spectral array unfold before him in a dazzling rainbow.

"My God, it's incredible!" he blurted. "The colours! My dear Melbury, the thing you have here. . . !"

He did not finish his ecstatic exclamation, for at that moment the cloud concealing the sun went about its way, admitting a new cluster of rays through the window. The crystal beneath Hayward's scrutiny flared with supernal brilliance, and with a deafening *crack*, a blinding bolt of energy darted straight into Hayward's loupe. He cried out in shock, falling backwards as the bolt arced from the lens into his client's incredulous, gaping face. As if guided by an intelligence, the ray found Melbury's unprotected eye, then flashed out of existence as the room dimmed to its normal state.

"By the saints!" cried Melbury. "I can't see! I'm blind!"

"I, also!" came Hayward's tortured voice. "Wait . . . no, my vision is clearing. Thank God . . . we're all right, Graeme. We're going to be all right!"

Melbury rubbed at his burning eyes, fearing that they had melted in their sockets. Scalding tears poured down his face, and despite Hayward's comforting words, he could see only a white-hot field dotted with black stars that swam erratically like maddened fish in a churning ocean. Then. . . .

Relief! The negative starfield began to fade, and normal colours broke through the taut fabric of his blindness to swirl slowly into recognizable forms — so he thought.

As his vision returned, he realized that, while he had not gone blind, he must have surely gone stark, raving mad. For he and Hayward no longer occupied a comfortable London office; instead, as if borne on an ethereal wind, they saw a great tableau opening before them, in which they were not participants, but distant, disembodied observers. . . .

*I*t was a long, rolling countryside, bisected by a swiftly flowing, crystal blue stream that wound down from a steep, grassy knoll far to the right. Toward the northern horizon, atop a stepped mound of earth, the black, towering mass of the castle Bannockburn loomed against the deepening, violet sky like a giant vulture surveying its realm for carrion.

Just ahead, a long pit filled with pointed wooden stakes barred passage to the castle; beyond this, as yet unseen, lay many more such trenches.

The thunder of horses' hooves was deafening in Sir Thomas Melbury's ears. His own steed, Firebrand, sensed the danger ahead and hesitated, snuffling uncertainly at his master's lack of rein. Melbury took heed and slowed his mount, raising an arm to signal a halt. A dozen knights had ridden with him to scout the perimeter of Robert Bruce's defenses, in advance of the 500 footsoldiers camped a league to the rear. Already, a hundred knights and at least 5,000 soldiers had lost their lives in this struggle to annex Scotland for King Edward II. The evidence of such unspeakable slaughter was clear, for as Melbury approached the pit, he found that dozens of bodies, most already picked clean by scavengers, hung impaled on the stakes. And what he had taken to be stones in the heather ahead could now be identified as the ravaged bodies of fallen men.

Bruce had overwhelmed the northern reaches of England, burning everything; killing men, women, and children alike before turning and securing himself at Bannockburn, in the hills northeast of Glasgow. England's former ally openly intended to rule an independent Scotland; during the long ride from York to join with King Edward's forces, Melbury had learned that the Scottish peasants considered Bruce a great patriot.

More a butcher, Melbury thought, having witnessed first-hand the brutality of Bruce's knights. And now, approaching the castle of his enemy, he could only wonder if *devil* might not be a more appropriate term. For the "patriot" Bruce must have surely made a pact with Satan and gained the power to conjure demons. Melbury, and all his men, had seen the fire in the sky two nights prior: a huge, blazing mass of brimstone that trailed sparks and green smoke as it hurtled earthward. A fantastic concussion had then rocked the countryside, and for the rest of the night, a demoniac, greenish glow tinted the sky above the Comyn Forest, to the west.

Since then, no trace could be found of Lord William Camden and his men, who had been advancing on the castle from the west. Nor had a one of Melbury's runners sent to investigate ever returned. If Camden's force had been completely wiped out, then the English had lost a full quarter of their numbers. The prospect was unthinkable; yet Melbury could deny neither the evidence of his senses nor the fact of his vanishing runners. Surely, it was witchcraft!

The day was growing old, and the company had fallen far short of their hopes for reconnaissance due to a skirmish with a band of Bruce's men during the afternoon. Melbury had been victorious, having lost only one knight – Brüch, the Hun, a loyalist from Monmouth. The rest had come away with minor wounds. But at the cost of time.

Melbury's trusted squire, Simon, a sturdy, blond youth of sixteen, now rode up on his mount – Firebrand's own sibling, a charcoal-coloured stallion named Greysmoke – and pointed to the west. "Sir Thomas! Do you hear? Strange sounds in the forest! The clashing of metal!"

Melbury could scarcely hear a thing above the din of the horses and their riders drawing up behind him. But straining to listen, he at last discerned the faintest hammering sound, like a sledge striking a giant anvil. Strangely, along with the noise came the cold, grim feeling that its source must be something so terrible as to threaten to the Almighty Himself. Then, shrugging off this unseemly mood, he nodded to his squire and said, "I hear it. But I am loath to send another man to a virtual certain end." Turning, he regarded the dozen knights and their squires clustered aft, all studying the terrain attentively. He shouted, "Wycliffe! A moment, please!"

From the rear of the ranks, an onyx stallion rode forward,

carrying a proud figure in polished silver armour, the crimson dragon on his shield and breastplate spitting a great gout of fire. Like Melbury, Sir Roland Wycliffe carried a well-used mace and a dagger at his right side, with his sheathed sword at his left. His squire rode a horse's length behind.

"Have you heard the sounds from the forest?"

"I have," Wycliffe said. The knight's chiseled face dripped with sweat that glistened in his blue-black moustache and beard. "It is the sound of the Devil's own smith."

"Indeed. I will send no more men into the forest. However, night will fall soon. We must secure a place for our encampment. At this distance from Bruce's keep, we can risk no fires."

"I understand."

"I want to press a little farther and find out how many more lines of pits the scoundrels have dug over the next half league or so. Ride close with me. I need your keen eyes and ears. Something about the forest troubles me greatly."

"Aye, my lord."

Melbury gazed toward the distant treeline, then toward the castle on the horizon, feeling a tremor of apprehension. Over the last few days, King Edward had lost untold numbers of men making direct assaults on the keep. Robert Bruce himself was rumoured to have slain hundreds of Melbury's countrymen, while the Scots had lost only a token few. Even the King's celebrated longbows, catapults, and Chinese blasting powder had failed to shake the scoundrel from his stronghold.

Sir Thomas turned to face the rest of his knights, who regarded him expectantly. The nearest, a stout Welshman named Colwyn from Caernarvon — the King's own birthplace — held up his lance as a gesture of readiness, his dark, rather brutish mien haggard but alert. Melbury gave him an approving nod and then called out, "Let us ride. Sunset will be upon us all too soon."

He spurred his horse, and Firebrand took off at a trot, paralleling the stake-studded ravine, followed closely by Simon, Wycliffe, and the rest of the company. These traps had cost the King dearly as his columns marched in strict formation, while the Scots charged like madmen, forcing hundreds of English soldiers into the pits beneath the sheer weight of the onslaught. Having learned from the costly mistakes of his predecessors, Melbury had wisely chosen a less obvious approach.

As they drew nearer to the edge of the dark forest, Melbury's anxiety increased. Although no sounds crept from its eerie depths at the moment, the trees bore a distinctly sinister aspect. The wood had swallowed too many men and all-too-recently voiced the presence of something within that he was certain had no place in God's creation; a fact all the more troubling because he had hoped to use the forest as a means of concealment. The open spaces leading directly to Bannock-burn could easily mean death for such a small company as his, should Bruce dispatch scouts from his castle. And the already fatigued horses could not possibly carry their riders all the way back to the main camp without a reasonable period of rest.

Ahead, a cluster of large rocks marked the end of the first stake pit. Only a narrow path between the boulders and the treeline allowed passage beyond. And it was as Melbury began to lead his knights up the path that he heard the clamour to the rear. Drawing quickly to a halt, he turned to see a trio of horsemen galloping furiously toward him, waving the banner of the King and shouting his name. He recognized the leader as Master-of-Arms Holmworthy, and there was blood on his pain-racked face.

"Sir Thomas, the Scots have sent a column over our guard! They've overrun the camp and are moving this way. They mean to pinion us between them and the castle."

"That devil, Bruce," Melbury growled. "How for the love of Christ did we not encounter the column ourselves? What manner of witchcraft concealed them?"

"They moved in from the east. They must have proceeded along the River Forth and come out this side of Clackman-nan. It's a rout!"

As if on cue, a distant roar echoed toward them across the fields. And then, to Melbury's shock, from a glade just beyond the stream behind them, scores of dark silhouettes in the shape of men magically appeared, lining up just south of the first pit. Only a few hundred yards stood between them and the small English band.

"Damn them!" cried Melbury. "We'll have to fight."

"Into the forest with you!" cried Holmworthy. "There is nothing noble about their brand of slaughter!"

Melbury, a man of strict honour, could never justify running from a battle. However, the fight was now unavoidable, and knowing the Scottish guard would pursue them without qualm, he nodded to the Master-of-Arms, then called, "Simon! My helmet!" The lad tossed him his heavy iron headpiece, which he caught easily and tugged down over his head, lifting the visor so he could be heard. "I do not know what we will find in this place. But we will ride in 400 yards and dismount. We take them on foot. They outnumber us at least ten to one, so we must fight well. Fight well for the King!"

The knights raised their lances and their voices in response. In counterpoint, the Scotsmen's own voices rose in a cacophonous roar, and, as one, the line charged. Melbury turned his steed and dashed into the darkness of the trees, his men following faithfully behind. The last remaining sunlight gave up the ghost as the larches and oaks closed in around them, the branches whipping defiantly at Melbury's armoured limbs. He was forced to duck low several times as branches thick enough to take off his head appeared out of nowhere. All he heard now was the heavy beat of his horse's hooves, the clanking of his armour and weapons, and the rapid thudding of his heart. Firebrand maneuvered through the underbrush with the surefooted grace that Melbury had trusted for many years, but it was difficult to count the horse's paces on the erratic course he was forced to take. When he reckoned they had ventured in a good 400 yards, he reined the stallion to a stop and quickly dismounted, simultaneously drawing his blade, which he called *Sanguinaire*: an irreverent nod to the French, many of whom had met death at its bite. He saw Colwyn materializing out of the darkness to his left, and, just to the right, his faithful Simon was dropping from Greysmoke's back and drawing his own heavy sword from its scabbard. Melbury felt a pang of regret, realizing that this was certainly to be the lad's final battle. It was honourable to die here, he told himself; but so much a pity that the squire would never live to see knighthood.

The Scots roared as they poured into forest. Melbury clumsily ran to his right, motioning for Colwyn and his squire to take up positions among the nearest trees. He saw two steeds bolt and gallop away at their masters' goadings, while the knights — Sir Drake of Devonshire and Sir Allard of Warwick — took up their heavy maces and readied themselves to meet the charge. The trees, rising like basaltic pillars around them, would slow the Scots enough so that Melbury's men could draw the first blood. Then, the fighting would begin in earnest.

He could see a cluster of silver ghosts appearing amid the black towers, and the heavy tramp of hooves loosed a shower of dying leaves upon on his head. Firebrand reared, steam spurting from his flaring nostrils, and Simon moved to calm the horse. But Melbury shook his head, and said, "Let him go. I shan't be needing him now. Prepare yourself, lad."

Simon's eyes widened momentarily, but his muscles tensed, and his sword rose to salute his master. Melbury's men lay in wait along a hundred-yard-long line, and if this were to be their final battle, then it would be at a very high cost to the northern land's "great patriot." For a moment, Melbury thought he heard a distant clang of metal against metal somewhere behind him, and remembered the horrid glow in the sky from two nights before. Glancing back into the pitch darkness, he saw nary a threat, but felt a quick fluttering in his stomach at the thought of the sorcery that must have been Lord Camden's final bane. He immediately turned his attention back to the approaching horde; only seconds remained before the first blows were exchanged.

The thunder among the trees took on the sound of an avalanche; and then Scottish armour was bearing down on the English, the red and blue-striped seal of the Bruce family shining from every shield and breastplate. A plume of steam was the first thing Melbury saw of the lead horse, as if its nostrils spewed dragon-flame; then a tall, black stallion, mane flying, leaped a fallen larch, its rider hunkering down in the saddle to avoid the branches overhead. Sir Thomas Melbury's sword swung upward in a broad arc, to crack loudly against the shaft of the warrior's giant battle axe. The heavy axe-head tumbled to the ground, and the rider cried out in a loud voice, "Ye Sassenachs a'hae! Hae!"

Melbury did not pause, but struck again, aiming his blow at the knight's arm. With a sharp clang, the blade connected, and a pained cry escaped the rider's lips. The horse spun to avoid a tree, and with a swift movement, Melbury grabbed its flying reins and pulled, the horse's own momentum throwing it off balance. The stallion went down with a shriek, toppling its master, who landed on his broken arm. Melbury heard a muffled grunt, and knowing that he had several seconds before the knight could regain his balance, he turned his attention to the next marauder.

They were swarming now, and the harsh ringing of blade against shield pealed endlessly through the darkness. A huge mass zoomed past Melbury's head, and he swung blindly; Sanguinaire's sharp edge cut into the hindquarters of a steed. The horse stumbled, its armoured rider lurching from the saddle with limbs flailing. Now, Sir Thomas turned back to the first man, who was sluggishly attempting to regain his footing, left hand fumbling for the dagger sheathed at his hip. His right arm hung uselessly, the bone having been shattered by Sanguinaire's furious blow. Sir Thomas hesitated just long enough for the knight to draw his knife; then he struck with all his strength. The pauldron — the protective metal covering between the arm and shoulder — shattered like rotten tree-bark beneath his blade, and the knight's left arm took its leave. The limb fell to earth and jerked once, as a shrill scream of horror and agony erupted from behind the visor of the stricken man's helmet. A rich spray of blood jetted from the socket, and the body pitched forward to land facedown in the dirt. Instinctively swiveling to address his second foe, Melbury brought his blade up with a smooth motion, catching the rising man beneath the chin, twisting his head around, and cracking his neck. The body dropped like a sawn oak.

Scotsmen poured through the black forest like a tide of vermin. One horseman was lifted from his saddle by a low-hanging limb, back snapping with the sound of a powder blast. By now, most of the attackers had realized the futility of a mounted assault and were beginning to dismount to engage their enemy on foot. Already, some of Melbury's knights faced three, four, or more foes, yet it was mostly

Scottish blood soaking the ground. He saw Colwyn's mace swinging at lightning speed, making contact with a helmet, smashing it inward with a sickening *clang-thunk* as bone collapsed beneath metal.

A blue and red shield rose up in front of Melbury, and a huge wooden mallet swished perilously close to his head. Backstepping, he suddenly found himself overbalancing and falling to the ground, dragged down by his own heavy armour. Above him, the Scot raised the mallet to strike again, and all Melbury could do now was roll sideways in attempt to avoid certain death. But in a flash, a lithe silhouette bounded in front of him, only to take the vicious blow directly in the chest. *Simon!* The lad's breath whooshed through his lips as his feet left the ground and his body crashed down atop his knight.

Through a red mist of pain, Melbury saw Sanguinaire lying only inches beyond his reach; he kicked himself forward, and his fingers closed around the haft. But a pair of iron-shod feet suddenly appeared before his eyes, and he knew now the killing blow was about to land.

Then, a tremendous *crack* shattered the air. In its wake, an unearthly silence fell. Englishman and Scotsman alike froze in mid-strike, and even the wails of the dying were hushed. Somewhere in the distance, a heavy thud broke the stillness as a great tree struck the ground. Then a piercingly loud, musical wail split the night, rising up through the forest and outward to the stars, as if in supplication to Lucifer himself:

Uullaah!

A brilliant flash of white light transformed the forest into a weird chiaroscuro, followed by a concussion louder than any powder blast mortal ears had ever heard. Just in front of him, an invisible blade cleaved a white oak, its upper portion crashing down upon several frozen Scots. And the pair of armoured legs that belonged to Melbury's would-be killer toppled over — severed above the knees. The ruined stumps were charred black, laced with streams of molten metal.

No trace remained of the rest of the body.

An acrid stench assailed Melbury's nostrils: the odor of scorched wood and roasted flesh. A cloud of smoke rolled over him, and he coughed painfully, trying to heave the weight of his squire from his back.

He heard a quavering moan.

"Simon! Are you badly injured?"

"Can't . . . breathe."

"Let me up!"

Obediently, the wounded youth slid onto cold earth, allowing Melbury to rise to a crouch. Gazing into the green haze several hundred yards away, he saw something moving against the backlit trees and heard the crack of limbs and trunks being smashed as if by a great weight. Another white flash stung his eyes, and this time, to his right, as if a gigantic, invisible scythe had swung through the forest, row upon row of trees split just above the heads of the transfixed warriors, the boughs bursting immediately into bright, roaring flame.

"Mary, mother of all saints," whispered Melbury, now as transfixed as the rest. For the first time in his life, he felt his heart stutter with pure, childish terror. The monstrous cry rose again, as if from the throat of some unearthly bird of prey: *Ullaah! Ullaah!*

The moving shape drew nearer, pushing down trees as if they were twigs: a mighty behemoth, or the Devil himself, marching toward them with two fiery eyes focused upon the knights. The pounding of its feet against the earth sent cold waves of nausea through Melbury's bowels. He tightened his grip on his sword, desperately fighting the instinctive urge to flee. He dimly heard a scream, and out of the corner of his eye, he saw a man stagger out of an inferno, his helmet gone, hair and beard ablaze. He fell seconds later, to jerk pathetically on the ground with a last agonized sob.

That poor Scot, Melbury thought, might be the luckiest man on the battlefield tonight.

A tree crashed down 20 yards to Melbury's right. Now, even young Simon, clutching his chest, rose to his knees, eyes as big as saucers, to watch the spectacle unfolding.

With a mechanical whine, the thing strode into clear view: a monstrous insect, so it seemed, stalking purposefully on three segmented legs, moving with a rhythmic, loping motion. But the body, Melbury saw, was a glittering engine of bluish metal, its underside high enough to pass above the head of even the tallest man. Several snakelike projections hung from its lateral and ventral surfaces, and these whipped back and forth as if questing for prey. Translucent, pupil-less eyes glared from beneath an arced metal carapace, and for a moment, Melbury thought he saw a dark, bulky silhouette moving behind them. Below the glassy orbs, a long, tubular snout protruded ominously, like a mosquito's stinger, seemingly designed to draw the lifeblood from a man with a single, quick stab.

But a second later, Melbury realized his error, for the tip of this projection flashed brightly, and again, a swath of trees and men were cleared by an invisible force which sent up new gouts of flame and smoke, accompanied by the shrill screams of burning men.

"This cannot be the work of that bastard Bruce," he muttered, for most of the victims of this Satanic eidolon were themselves Scots. But Sir Drake had also gone down under that last terrible volley, Melbury realized as he saw the emblem on one of the shields that littered the ground.

A new sound took over the forest: the panicked cries of men whose nerves had been shattered. No longer transfixed, knights, footsoldiers, and squires were bolting blindly before the advancing monstrosity, their iron wills reduced to slag.

Then, a strange thing happened. The monster swiveled with uncanny quickness, its snout angled toward a point a few hundred yards beyond the retreating warriors. The tube flashed again, and a wall of trees collapsed in flames, so that the left flank of the retreating body was now cut off. The tripod then began a quick, deliberate stride southward, cutting across the course of the retreat, again creating a barricade of shattered trees and rising flames. A number of lucky Scots had already made it past the fireline, and Melbury found himself wishing them godspeed. But another odd event now occurred: from behind the carapace of the stalking horror, a barrel-shaped cylinder zoomed aloft with a sharp cracking sound, blasting its way through the upper branches and hurtling skyward, trailing a plume of thick black smoke. Half a minute later, from somewhere out in the meadow, came the deep, thudding crash of its impact.

There followed a chorus of frightened cries from the unseen escapees. And within seconds, they fell silent.

The monster had now turned the retreat from east to south, and with amazing quickness, the giant tripod turned to intercept the fleeing Scots, unleashing another invisible, fiery tongue ahead of it. The thing had successfully blocked all avenue of escape, except to the west — the direction whence it came, where the sky had been tinged with green on the night of this horror's birth.

Where Lord William Camden and his army must have surely met their doom.

A groan rose from close at hand. Melbury saw a bloody face that he vaguely recognized; it was Colwyn, somehow still standing, his cleaved breastplate leaking blood. He shambled to Melbury's side and placed a hand on his shoulder for support.

"Armageddon," he whispered. "This is the end of the world."

"It destroys Scots and the King's men alike," whispered Simon. "It is the Devil himself."

"It is an engine," Melbury said. "Made of metal. Perhaps there are men inside of it."

Colwyn spat. "Men! Who? The French?" He laughed spitefully, then broke down into a fit of pained coughing.

Heavy footsteps approached from the left. Sir Roland Wycliffe stepped into view, his helmet gone; a long scar drawn down his right cheek leaked blood freely. "It will be back upon us in a minute," he said. "And the bloody Scots will trample us in their panic."

Melbury smelled smoke. The fire was creeping closer. "We must either retreat to the west . . . or make a stand here."

"Melbury!" cried Wycliffe. "Those men will crush us before we can land a blow to that devil! And do you mean to fight it with these?" He held up his sword. "Pah!"

"Sir Thomas," said Colwyn, his voice thick with pain. "May I suggest . . . an honourable retreat?"

The din of the approaching stampede rose with each passing second. With a reluctant nod, Melbury called out, "Into the forest, then, though we may well come upon the lair of this demon!" He glanced around and saw a couple of horses tramping nervously in place nearby. He sent Colwyn's squire after them, with orders to assist his injured master into a saddle. Then, to his amazement, he saw that, in the glow of the creeping blaze, Firebrand had materialized as if by silent command. A wide smile broke out on Melbury's face as he ran clumsily to the horse and grasped its reins, stroking its muzzle soothingly.

"Simon, into the saddle with you," he ordered, leading the stallion back to his injured squire. "You shall ride."

"No, my lord. He us . . . yours!"

"No longer," he said. "And argue not!" Then, helping the young man to his feet, he hoisted Simon into the saddle. He patted the leather bags draped over the horse's crupper armour. And then, a tiny light of hope flashed in the darkness of his heart.

"Come on, then!" he called. "Death is close at hand!"

The remnant of Melbury's company — six knights, five squires and the three horses — broke into a run, the knights clumsy in their heavy armour, slowed further by various wounds. Melbury didn't hold out much hope for Colwyn, and he feared for young Simon as well. For that matter, it would be blind luck if the panicked horde hurtling toward them did not mow them down before they could even reach the demon's den.

The underbrush grew thick and tangled, and men constantly fell and picked themselves up, occasionally discarding shields, helmets, even gauntlets. The clamour from behind kept pace with them, gaining very slowly, if at all. But a few of the Scots' horses caught up with them and passed them, some with riders, some without, none paying the Englishmen a moments' heed. Old enmities were forgotten under the threat of a soul-damning death approaching from beyond this world.

An untold distance from the scene of battle, disoriented and ready to drop from fatigue, Melbury now caught a glimpse of greenish light ahead that sent a thrill of fear up and down his spine. His legs, propelled by momentum, were slow to obey his mental command to halt. But a cluster of chalky-looking boulders loomed ahead of him, and he aimed himself directly toward the nearest, extending his arms to absorb the shock of impact. As he careened into the natural barricade, he collapsed against the cold stone, barely able to keep from falling onto his belly. The company drew to a stop, some by simply dropping to the ground.

All panting and near fainting, each man fixed his gaze on what lay ahead. From behind, the sounds of screams tore through the wood, and the monster's thudding footsteps could again be heard as well, for it had gained considerably upon its prey. The horses danced in agitation, their nostrils flaring, their eyes bright with terror.

"Trapped," muttered Sir Roland, gazing hopelessly to the rear. "Fire to the north and south, Hell and the Devil to fore and aft. Herded here like sheep!"

Melbury was about to relate his plan, when suddenly, Colwyn's squire, a lad of fifteen, shrieked like a girl whose belly had been slit. Turning, he saw the youth's body lifted from the ground and pulled quickly over the top of the boulder. A split second later, Colwyn himself let out a yell and fell from his saddle, landing heavily in a heap upon the stony earth. His horse reared and broke, disappearing in a thunder of hooves. And before Melbury's shocked eyes, the knight was dragged into darkness, where he loosed a pitiful, resigned cry that was then silenced forever by something that uttered a harsh, gurgling cough.

"Christ!" screamed Wycliffe, reaching for the mace at his right hip. But his fingers never closed on its haft, for his legs were torn from beneath him by something that wormed its way past the nearest boulders and encircled his ankles. Then he, too, was dragged out of sight, screaming.

Without thinking, Melbury leaped for his steed, fingers working at the straps that secured his leather-wrapped bundles. At the periphery of his vision, he glimpsed a pair of luminous disks the size of wagon wheels, then something incredibly strong wrapped itself around his waist and pulled him away from the horse. Firebrand let out an almost human screech of terror and bolted, to be immediately swallowed by the depths of the forest. Melbury's feet left the ground, and his back brutally struck the boulder he had used to brake his mad flight.

But he still held his precious bundles. He hugged them to his chest as if they were children, refusing to let go, no matter the force that gripped him. He saw a dark, leathery cord around his waist, pulling him backward over the rocks and along the mossy earth, toward a dark mass he thought was a mud-encrusted boulder.

But the boulder suddenly grew huge, shining eyes that gazed incuriously at him, and he heard a bear-like grunt issue from the half-seen shape.

"Good Christ!" he shouted, releasing one of his packages to fumble for his dagger. "Good Christ!"

As he took hold of the haft and ripped the blade from its sheath, he heard a shrill scream close by; he thought it came from Sir Allard. But he could spare no attention to the death-throes of another. With all his strength, he plunged the dagger into the leathery tendril that encircled his waist. A greenish fluid sprayed into his face, burning his skin like acid. And a high, demonic screech drilled into his brain, issued from a gaping orifice beneath the eyes of the thing that held him.

The next sound he heard was his own scream, blending with the voice of the monster, rising toward the heavens in dirge-like harmony. Green light washed over him in heatless waves, and he caught a last glimpse of the saucer-shaped eyes glaring at him with the fires of Hell burning in their depths.

Then, he knew nothing more.

*H*e woke to a leaden sky and the sounds of strange hammering echoing from a distance. For several moments, he had no idea where he was or what had happened; he was mainly conscious of a sharp pain in his temples and a pressure behind his eyes. An acrid, smoky odor drifted on the cold morning breeze, and he heard a low, agonized moan come from somewhere nearby. He turned his head to search for the source, only to feel a white-hot stab of pain in his neck and shoulders.

Then, remembering last night's slaughter, he forced himself to remain silent and motionless. He was lying on his back in a clearing of some sort, for the nearest trees looked to be 20 to 30 yards away. Glancing toward his feet, he saw that his body was intact, still armoured, but weaponless.

His powder bags were gone.

Then he became aware of a deep, throbbing noise rising from somewhere nearby; not loud, but low and powerful. And then, most horrible of all, came a series of garbled grunts and thick muttering sounds, articulated with the cadence of a language — but spoken by no human tongue. Turning his head ever so slowly, he sought the origin of this devilish utterance.

And when his eyes beheld the sight, he had to bite back a scream, for a lingering shred of sanity assured him that releasing it would sign his death warrant.

Three bodies hung upside down from tethers connected to a strange, metallic gibbet; bodies that were missing heads and portions of limbs, all gutted like deer following a successful hunt. One of the heads — Sir Colwyn's — rested on a silvery pedestal, the crown of its skull shorn away to expose a hollow cavity. And close to it, strapped to a metal litter by leathery bindings, Sir Roland, naked, the muscles in his arms and legs straining, the cords in his neck standing out in stark relief as he struggled to escape.

And beyond him, three great masses of glistening, wet leather, possessed of piercing, luminous eyes, their filthy grey bulks girdled by arrays of long, crinoid arms that waved in the air like sea-stalks in a strong current. The tips of several tendrils were coiled about evil-looking, glittering devices, their functions made hideously apparent by their long, curved blades and barbed hooks. The three demons gurgled and whistled to each other in their own Satanic tongue, their attention focused solely on their task; they paid no mind to Melbury or any of the other prone men who lay scattered around the encampment — whether living or dead, Melbury could not say.

Beyond these monstrosities, the engine that had wreaked havoc among the knights stood motionless near the treeline, beside the walls of what appeared to be a great, circular crater, at least 50 yards in diameter. This, then, was indeed the domain of this horror from the skies, these emissaries of Satan who appeared to operate without favouritism toward either Robert Bruce or the crowned King of England. It was from the machine that the low throbbing sound arose.

He suddenly heard a hoarse curse from Wycliffe's tongue

— then a small, childish sob. Looking back at him, Melbury saw one of the infernal devices in a coiled tendril lowering slowly to Sir Roland's chest; and a high-pitched scream exploded from the knight's mouth with enough force to ruin his vocal cords, for from then on, his mouth gaped and tongue spasmed, but no sound came forth other than a whisper of breath. The second of the three monsters, the vivisectionist, moved closer to peer into the crevice slowly opening in Wycliffe's chest; one of the other arms lowered a tool which suctioned away the purple blood raging from the wound. Another arm inserted a shining, glass-tipped rod into the chest cavity, and Melbury saw a flash of light and wisp of smoke rise from the body, which continued to jerk and writhe in its constraints.

Mercifully, after only a few more seconds, Sir Roland's struggles ceased. Only a reflexive jerking of his fingers indicated that life had ever coursed through the obscene slab of meat secured to these butchers' table.

Melbury's own chest felt as if it had been savaged. God, the cold-bloodedness! Never could he have envisioned such brutality, not from the most ruthless human foe! Would that all the men under Robert Bruce's command descend upon this place and wipe every trace of it from existence. Surely, the very presence of these things was an abomination, an affront to God. At the cost of his life, he must attempt to expunge these monsters from the land!

But how to do it? Any movement he made would likely alert his captors. And none of the men lying on the ground appeared to be in any condition to assist him. His eyes desperately searched the clearing for any sign of his powder bags. They, surely, represented his only hope against these devils. But he had lost them somewhere, very likely back in the trees.

Melbury saw one of the metal devices lower into Sir Roland's opened chest, to emerge with a deep red, dripping organ dangling from one pincered end. The eyes of the beasts seemed to study the heart curiously, as if such a vital organ might be inconceivable to their demoniac brains. Another tool began its exploratory penetration of the body with sickening, wet crunching sounds, and Melbury turned his eyes away, afraid of attracting the monsters' attention by voiding his stomach.

Then, a movement at the edge of the clearing caught his eye. He dared to lift his head, ignoring the pain in his neck and shoulders, and suddenly his heart leaped. Simon! His squire, still alive, though obviously in great pain, slowly crawling across the mossy earth toward him!

And slung over Simon's shoulder, one of Melbury's precious bags of blasting powder.

Blessed Saviour! Melbury glanced at the monsters, who were still engaged in their work to the exclusion of all else. Knowing now what he had to do, he slowly rolled onto his belly, cursing the clatter of his armour, alert for any sign that the devils had taken notice of his movement.

For now, they showed none. Melbury slowly, as silently as possible, crawled forward to meet his squire, praying only for enough strength to fulfill the new purpose for which God Himself had commissioned him.

*I*t took nearly fifteen minutes to cover as many yards. He moved as slowly as the sun passing overhead, his armour still occasionally rattling frightfully; but if the monsters took any notice of him, they gave no sign. Perhaps they realized that their captives posed no threat and were content to allow them certain minimal movements. But Melbury could not bring himself to rise or increase his speed, for a single mistake could result in his sharing Wycliffe's fate so much the sooner.

As he reached Simon, he whispered, "The bag. Pass me the bag."

His squire was surely just this side of death. His face had gone pale, almost ghostly, his eyes shrunken into their sockets. A thin black line of blood dripped from his lower lip and down his chin. But Simon carefully pulled the leather bag from his back and slid it into Melbury's waiting hands.

Glancing toward the great tripod, Sir Thomas saw his opportunity. Beneath the belly of its arachnid-like body, a darkened portal to its interior hung tantalizingly open. The beasts were so massive, so heavy-looking; surely they could not intercept him before he reached their machine. Indeed, as the monsters worked, their bear-sized bodies quivered and pulsated but remained rooted to their spots, as if their great weight rendered them almost immobile. Only their multitudes of tentacles displayed quickness and agility.

He began a somewhat faster crawl toward the tripod, protectively cradling his powder bag. But then he discovered how wrong he had been about the devils' apparent incognizance. Before he had gone another yard, one of the beasts emitted a deafening, bird-like whistle, and three pairs of huge eyes rolled to regard him with unmistakable fury. With a sickening rustling sound, one of the bodies began to slide toward him, propelled by a set of thicker appendages low to the ground. Its charge was hardly lightning fast; yet it moved with ominous purpose and more quickly than Melbury would have expected. He realized now that, weighed down by his armour, he would not be able to gain his footing and reach the engine before the thing was upon him.

"Sir Thomas!" cried Simon, somehow rising to his knees. "Give it to me! Quickly!" He reached for the powder bag without waiting for Melbury's assent, and ripped it from his grasp.

Then, by some miraculous strength of will, the injured youth struggled to his feet and stumbled toward the tripod, clutching his burden for the sake of his life. Melbury had gotten as far as his knees, and the weight of his armour threatened to topple him. Then, one of the advancing monster's tentacles rose, brandishing a transparent tube that ended with a jewel-studded, metallic sphere. Inside the tube, a light quickly flared, transforming the sphere into a brilliant, miniature sun. A sharp pain suddenly exploded in Melbury's head, and his body was rendered utterly immobile. He heard a low buzzing sound in his ears, and he feared that his brain had begun to boil. His senses suddenly felt ravaged, and something — an unknown, vital piece of himself — seemed to be ripped from him as mercilessly as Wycliffe's heart had been torn from his chest.

Just shy of fainting and shocked by the sudden, strange emptiness inside him, he managed to turn his eyes back to the machine. Simon was staggering, but wearing only chain mail, he was able to move with greater speed and agility than an armoured knight. The other two devils were now charging at him with surprising speed; but they were too late. The squire fell against one of the machine's legs, reaching into his hip pouch for his flint. Melbury's heart soared, though he realized that only moments of life now remained for both himself and the lad.

The arrogance of the devils had sealed their doom. Simon painfully heaved himself through the gaping hatch into the tripod's belly. For a moment, Melbury feared the squire was going to lose his grip and fall to the ground. But again, determination overcame his pain and fatigue. He disappeared in the dark opening only seconds before his pursuers reached the engine.

Melbury was now forced to turn his attention to his own attacker, which now brandished another horrible, bladed weapon. Still frozen by the fiery sphere wavering before him, he took a deep breath, and prepared himself for the deadly blow surely about to strike him down. The demon's eyes focused coldly on him, transmitting a loathing and hatred as deep as his own.

Then, as if in slow motion, the huge bulk was swept away by a roiling burst of flame, and Melbury's eardrums shattered with the sound of the explosion. He felt a hot wind roasting his exposed flesh and saw a multitude of brilliant golden tongues lapping at his armour. And he was tossed backward with such force that his feet were torn from his boots. He hit the ground on his back, all the wind driven painfully from his lungs; his field of vision became a black sea dotted with white stars that reeled before him at nauseating speed.

When his sight returned, it was to see a smoking ruin where the monstrous engine had stood; its legs had been blasted from their mounts and were now only twisted pieces of metal wrapped grotesquely around the neighbouring trees. The spiderlike body lay on its side, its "eyes" completely obliterated, the portal that Simon had entered now three times its former size, edges jagged and curled outward.

Of the three monsters, only one of them remained even partially intact — the one that had attacked Melbury. It lay in a heap several yards to his left, gushing yellow-green ichor, its eyes crushed and leaking thick, steaming fluid. Its remaining tendrils quivered and jerked like those of a broken insect, and its ruined body continued to pulsate weakly for several endless minutes. Finally, with a wet, gurgling hiss, the mortal thing expired, its grey-brown skin turning quickly black as if a torch had been applied to it.

Melbury drew a long sigh of relief, though the effort hurt him to his soul. Poor, brave Simon! The youth had died a knight, the best and Godliest of them all. Somehow, he told himself, he had to live, to escape the remains of this evil lair so that Simon's story might be told.

He managed to roll painfully onto his belly and saw that his right hand was nothing more than a blistered, reddened mass of useless flesh. His sword-wielding days had come to an end. His feet, thank God, remained attached to his legs, and while he felt no pain as yet, he could not even guess at the damage done to his body. He hoped that, someday, he might be able to walk again.

A glimmer of light to his left caught his eye. Turning painfully, he saw, embedded in the ground near him, the strange, metallic sphere studded with brilliant, pinkish gem-stones that had capped the evil tube. Melbury reached for it with his better hand and tried to grasp the curious object. Alas, the thing was of incredible weight, for all he could do was fumble it toward him across the ground. But this, he swore, would be his prize, his reminder of the Lord's victory over Satan, and a symbol of Simon's ultimate sacrifice.

A talisman to be preserved forever.

He did not hear when the trio of knights — the remnant of his army, whose encampment had been decimated by the Scots — staggered into the clearing and found him lying facedown on the mossy earth, only to believe him dead. Their faces fell aghast when they saw the remains of the great machine, the ruined corpses of countless men, and the blasphemous pile of blackened flesh that oozed greenish blood. Only when Sir Thomas Melbury groaned in the throes of some dream or memory did they realize that human life remained anywhere in this forest.

"*M*y God!" exclaimed Hayward, gazing in supreme shock

at his ashen-faced companion. "Oh, my God!"

"We saw it. *You* saw it, didn't you?"

Graeme Melbury nodded slowly, staring at the spherical horror resting innocuously on Hayward's desk. "They came from another world . . . another dimension. This thing cannot belong to our planet!"

Outside, night had fallen. They had been under the spell of this infernal device for several hours!

"What does this mean, Melbury?" Hayward whispered. "What is it telling us?"

Suddenly, an emerald light filled the room, and both men rushed to the window to peer outside. High above, piercing the veil of night like a flaming spearhead, a brightly burning mass sped across the sky, descending steadily as it neared the western horizon. Shortly, a green flash like summer lightning briefly banished the darkness, and several moments later, a deep concussion shook the walls of Hayward's office, tilting the portrait of his grandfather that hung above the desk. As the flare diminished, a pale swash of green-tinted light painted the horizon, somewhere in the vicinity of Woking — Melbury's own home!

"It will be different this time," Melbury whispered. "Before, they came here to learn. What *have* they learned during all these years?"

Hayward shook his head, and the question remained unanswered. But Melbury knew that the answers would be forthcoming soon enough, and he dreaded them. For now, he knew he had to return home; his wife and their son Nathanael would be there alone, and God only knew how near the thing had fallen to his own neighbourhood. Already, she would be wondering what could have become of him.

He hurried away, taking the evil eye of the monstrous machine with him, intent on casting it away, for fear of what other dreadful power the thing might manifest.

Before Melbury's carriage even left Hounslow, the crowds of people who had gathered in the streets had begun to whisper the news about the cylinder that had landed in Horsell Common.

Stalker
of the Wild Wind

*M*y name is Klaus Von Moltke. In September of 1918, toward the end of the Great War, I was a Rittmeister, or Captain, in the German Imperial Air Service's Jagdstaffel 15, stationed at St. Mihiel, France, several kilometers east of the German border and virtually within shooting distance of the bloody trenches of the Western Front. In those days, the time-honored traditions of warfare were undergoing dramatic changes, due to the development of such weapons as the machine gun, the tank, the submarine, and the aeroplane. On the battlefields, more men died in a single skirmish than in whole campaigns a few short years before. In those God-for-saken trenches of mud along the Front, hundreds of thousands of young soldiers from both the Allied and Central powers huddled with disease, rats, spoiled rations, and poison gas, ever obeying their commandants' misguided orders to charge valiantly into "no-man's land" — the scant hundred meters or so between opposing trenches — where they would be immediately cut down by machine gun fire and hand grenades, or entangled in barbed wire should they by some dark miracle gain the far side. Indeed, conditions in these trenches were so horrible that, in their hopelessness, men preferred death by bullet or bayonet to the slow agony of remaining in their strongholds.

So it was that those men such as myself who flew the new machines became a class unto themselves, an elite fighting force who filled the heavens with fire and angry sound, all with the hope that their efforts would help bring a swift end to the inhuman suffering below. Alas, while the aeroplane unquestionably altered the shape of the war, it was the unfortunate fact that Germany's initial air superiority only prolonged the struggle in the trenches, for the Allied machine would have otherwise decimated the Prussian infantry months or years sooner. In the end, severe shortages of equipment, poor judgment from the Central Powers' high command, and the threat of revolution at home finished the war both on the ground and in the air.

But it was on September 13, 1918, the day after the Allies began their offensive on St. Mihiel, that I flew my final mission, and since that day I have not and will not in any manner board an aeroplane. The fear might be called irrational by some, but to speak openly of its basis would place me at a handicap in the company of sane persons. Still, the fear exists, as certainly as the events I witnessed did exist, and no matter its irrationality, the fear of that *thing* is greater than any fear I might harbor of fighting in mud, or of dying in any fashion at the hands of men. Its history is relegated to this manuscript so that my lucidity may be acknowledged or discounted only by those who come after me.

On September 12, America made her first great offensive of the War, sending over 600 aircraft, including British and French planes, against St. Mihiel, outnumbering our air force, the Luftstreitkrafte, two to one. Their ground offensive commenced simultaneously, and our forces were crushed by the weight of sheer numbers. Even our superior aircraft could not withstand the onslaught, and I lost many friends that day. In my Fokker D.VII, I brought down four French Spad 13s and one of the new Sopwith Snipes, the British answer to the D.VII; but even then, the struggle was all too obviously futile. During a dogfight, I sustained a deep gash to my right cheek, whether from a bullet or flying shrapnel I never knew. The wound was painful and I lost a disturbing amount of blood, but it was not sufficient to stop me from flying. However, for the rest of that day, I managed only to elude enemy gunfire and avoid colliding with one of the hundreds of aircraft buzzing through a compact airspace. In the end, I retreated to our aerodrome at Metz, just across the German border, to regroup with other survivors, of which there were few, and hurriedly plot a last-ditch counterstrike for the following day. My fellow Rittmeister Erich Hoffmann and I divided the six remaining pilots of our squadron into two wings with the intent of launching a raid on the allied occupation force at dawn.

The morning of the 13th saw our small group joining up with the remnants of several other Jastas and Jagdgeschwaders (large hunting groups) who had also retreated to Metz following the previous day's disaster. All totaled, our number was 17, and of these, we lost two on takeoff, due to the damaged states of the aeroplanes. Hoffmann's group flew to a level of 6,000 feet, while I led my wing in vee formation up to 12,000, keeping the rising sun at our backs. The assorted pilots from the other wings, led by a young Oberleutnant named Reisendorf, flew to the northwest, their plan being to swing south and attack from the rear once we had engaged the enemy.

My Fokker D.VII was at that time the finest scout craft ever produced, and my own personal plane — awarded to me upon my attaining the rank of Rittmeister — had seen the downing of 19 enemy aircraft over the course of four months. Prior to that, during 1916 and 1917, I had flown Albatross D.IIs and D.IIIs, in which I brought down 26 enemy planes and a dozen observation balloons. By January of 1917, I had earned the Orden Pour le Merite award, often known as the Blue Max. During my career, I had been shot down twice: once without serious injury; the other, behind enemy lines and at the expense of two fingers of my right hand. That calamity, in October of 1917, very nearly took my life, but I succeeded in making my way back to our base at St. Quentin, and was returned to active duty a month later.

So you may see, my experience has been one of closeness to death; indeed, the pilots in my Jasta nicknamed me "Schwartzenkater," or "Black Cat," a tribute to my having cheated death on so many occasions. Accordingly, since, unlike their French and British counterparts, German flight leaders were allowed to paint their aircraft as they wished, I painted my D.VII black, with red wing tips and tailfin, in order to be recognized by friend and foe alike — much in the same way that the late Von Richthofen, the so-called "Red Baron," had painted both his Albatross and his Fokker Dr.I Dreidecker brilliant scarlet.

I must confess that on this last day I felt terrified, for I knew that the chances of returning from this mission alive were less than slim. The clearly imminent defeat of the Fatherland contributed to my feeling of despair, yet I still proudly considered myself a fighter pilot, an ace, and my own will to fight refused to desert me. I allowed none of my terror to affect the course of my mission; however, I recall that, as we flew westward high above the French countryside, I turned to gaze at the rising sun, feeling in my heart that this would be the last dawn my eyes would ever behold.

And then, moments later, I saw the first dark specks appear in the sky over St. Mihiel; only a small number, probably a single squadron, flying at about 10,000 feet. They would see Hoffmann's minor wing below well before they saw mine. I resisted the temptation to dive into an immediate attack and waited until the enemy fighters began to close on Hoffman.

Evidently, they must have expected my ploy, for half their number broke formation to attack Hoffmann; the rest began to climb, obviously without having yet seen me, but anticipating an attack from above. There were five of them, dark olive bullets with broad, bat-like wings, their red, white, and blue roundels flashing in the sunlight like defiant, fiery eyes. Spad 13s, I saw, probably piloted by Americans. They continued climbing past our own altitude, and I knew that they would attempt to circle to the northeast and hopefully snare my wing from behind. Giving my pilots the signal by waving my right arm up and toward the enemy, I throttled up and pulled back on the yoke, lifting my D.VII into a slow climb, anticipating an intercept at 15,000 feet, fortunately with the sun still at our backs.

The maneuver resulted in my flight positioning itself, undetected, directly in front of the oncoming fighters. When their leader saw me, I was already bearing down on him, tracers spitting from the barrels of my twin Spandau machine guns. I noted with satisfaction that a double row of bullet holes appeared in his engine cowl just before he roared past me. His squadron immediately realized its predicament and split down the middle, one pair veering to the left, the other to the right. I gave a last hand signal, directing my two wingmates to pursue the dispersing targets, while I banked sharply to the left to chase the flight leader. I caught a brief glimpse far below of a dogfight in progress — Hoffmann's wing had engaged the enemy as well.

The leader's plane was already smoking, but he had come about with amazing quickness and was heading toward me by the time I completed my turn. I saw his guns flashing, and heard the sharp *ding* of a bullet striking my left wing. This was an experienced pilot, I knew, for as he bore down on me, he did not so much as waver from his course. I opened fire at a hundred yards, but within two seconds, the Spad was behind me again.

The Fokker D.VII was the only aeroplane in the Great War that could climb vertically for a short distance, and complete several loops in succession. I throttled forward, pulled hard on the yoke and roared into a steep climb, until the plane was completely inverted, then rolled right-side-up, finishing a half-loop that put me above and in pursuit of the enemy. He had already begun to bank to his left, but now, with my advantage of altitude, I dove hard and caught him from behind, opening fire at point-blank range.

I saw the pilot twist around in surprise, no doubt shocked by the agility of my aircraft. He leaned into a sharp dive, but it was too late, for my shots rattled over his fuselage and I saw a flash of flame erupt from the engine. An accomplished aerial marksman, I attempted whenever possible to fire only into an opponent's engine, giving the pilot an opportunity to crash-land and possibly survive. But today, driven by desperation, I loosed another volley, and seconds later, the whole foresection of the fuselage was blazing angrily. The poor pilot, realizing he was about to burn, climbed from his seat and leapt into the air, to fall writhing beside his flaming ship. While balloon observers often escaped death via parachutes, fighter pilots had never been issued these lifesaving devices. The Spad and its doomed pilot fell quickly out of view, leaving behind only a spiral plume of black smoke that quickly dissipated in the wind.

I had only just glanced back for a sign of the remaining

enemy when a loud *thunk* shook me from behind. One of the
Spads had circled around and was gaining on me from
behind, machine guns crackling. I saw his wingman behind
him, banking to intercept me should I attempt to escape. I
twisted the stick hard to the left and then back, sending the
Fokker into a spiraling barrel roll that sent a dizzying rush
of blood into my head but succeeded in temporarily shaking
the enemy from my tail. I had gained a few seconds before
they were back on me, and having pushed my velocity to
better than 200 miles an hour, I again pulled up into a steep
climb, then applied the rudder hard to the right as the Fokker
began to stall. Now, pulling back on the stick, I spun back
into a quick dive and straightened out, a maneuver I had
learned from the ace Max Immelmann. The two enemy planes
were now zooming at me head-on, so I cut loose with my
Spandaus, to hear the gratifying *dings* of contact with one of
the Spads above the roar of my engines.

This victim was apparently a less hearty soul than his
unlucky flight leader. He peeled away to his left, cowl smoking, then went into a straight, shallow dive. I turned to pursue,
praying I had time to make a pass before his partner bore
down on me again.

I did. My target was steady and true, its pilot seemingly
unnerved by my first attack. He looked back and saw me
coming, and still did not take evasive action, merely increased
the angle of his dive, hoping to outrun me. But my Fokker
caught up easily, and I was now able to rattle off a volley that
went straight into the Spad's Hispano-Suiza engine. Its pro-
peller went whirling into space, and the plane arced into a
slow spin, but did not burst into flames. The pilot at least
had the presence of mind to recover from the spin and try to
glide his craft to a landing. The last I saw of him, he had
leveled his wings and was attempting to bring his nose up.
His descent was terribly steep.

I knew I still had at least one immediate enemy with which
to contend, and a second later, I saw him coming at me from
the right; the sun on his wings betrayed him, otherwise, I
might have been shot down by surprise. Forewarned, I turned
toward him and pushed over into a vertical dive that would
have torn the wings off of any plane but a D.VII. Cold wind

burned my face, painfully whipping at the wound I had received on the previous day. Within seconds, I had descended 3,000 feet, and found myself about to enter the thick of the battle raging between Hoffmann and his quarry. My Fokker screamed into a sharp bank to the right, leveling out at 8,000 feet, now bearing northward, toward Belgium. Glancing back, I saw my pursuers still locked on my tail but at least half a mile behind. I knew that if I could put some distance between the nearby dogfights and myself, I would be able to turn and attack the Spads without risking a collision with a fellow German.

But it was then that my fortune changed, for to my left, I saw a new squadron of planes coming up from St. Mihiel, and their leader, flying a pure white Sopwith Snipe, immediately homed in on my solitary aircraft. Now, close to 30 planes filled the sky as, to the east, Oberleutnant Reisendorf's two flights appeared to join the fray. I resolved to push ahead for another mile before swinging around to commence a new attack, thus taking advantage of the open airspace to gain altitude. I thought I could hold my own against the Snipe.

It was not to be. This new aircraft, almost a match for my Fokker, closed to within a hundred yards before I'd gone half a mile. I began to roll, dive and climb sporadically, hoping to throw the enemy off my tail. This pilot, a level-headed, cool Brit, hung back far enough to keep me in view no matter what maneuver I attempted, but was able to fire several volleys at me that made contact. With a loud *thwap!*, a bullet split one of the struts on my right wing, and a dense cluster of holes appeared in the wing disturbingly close to my cockpit. I executed a split-S maneuver – rolling inverted and diving into the last half of a loop – which sent me back in the opposite direction a thousand feet lower; I then repeated the diving turn to head north again at 6,000 feet.

But when I looked back, the Snipe was still there, and off to my right, the Spad I had previously engaged was closing rapidly. I dove again, hoping to coax even more speed from my ship, but the damaged strut began to quiver and groan, protesting that any additional stress might finally rip the wings from the fuselage. Adrenaline boiling in my veins, I desperately tugged on the yoke at full throttle, risking a fast climb, then a shallow dive, then another quick, shorter climb. I put a little distance between my pursuers and me, but I still could not achieve a position to engage them in battle.

The Snipe and the Spad continued to maneuver deftly behind me; each time, I managed to break free from their lines of fire and gain more altitude. But my crippled wing would eventually cost me a decisive move, and it seemed only a matter of time now before they had me. A couple of bullets zipped through my tailfin, one of them pinging off the metal rim of the cockpit so that I felt the heat of its passage. Somehow, I wrung more altitude from my engine without losing my lead on the enemy. The altimeter read 15,000, and the air had grown almost intolerably cold. Much higher, and my carburetor — and my struggling lungs — -would freeze.

Suddenly, I was enveloped by a bank of dark grey clouds that appeared out of nowhere. Moments before, the sky had been clear and sunny, but I had to consider the unexpected cover a Godsend, for here was my chance to escape my foes and perhaps turn the tables. More than likely, they would climb above the cloud layer hoping to catch me as I emerged. So, despite losing the advantage of altitude, I descended slowly, hoping to come out of the cloud well out of their sights.

But then, the veil abruptly vanished as quickly as it had appeared. I found myself flying over dark, rolling hills mottled with stands of twisted-looking trees, with no roads or railroads anywhere in sight. My compass assured me I was still flying north, and I knew I should now be over Belgium, with Luxembourg to the east. A silvery river threaded the highlands several miles to the west, which might have been the Meuse, but the countryside appeared totally unfamiliar. Far ahead, I could see shadowy, humped silhouettes along the horizon, which looked like tall mountains, but which must have been clouds, since no major ranges lay between here and the North Sea. Most disturbingly, nowhere could I see the first sign of human habitation — no town, nor house, nor church, nor farm.

I turned around to see if I had shaken the enemy fighters. To my surprise and dismay, I had not. Both the olive-drab Spad and the snow-hued Snipe cruised perilously close to my tail. Yet, the Allied pilots appeared as struck by the landscape below as I, for they were passing hand signals back and forth, both peering around and about them as if they, too, could not comprehend the transition into unknown territory. Furthermore, when I gazed backward, I received a violent shock, for my eyes beheld, not empty sky or even a solitary, drifting cloudbank, but a mammoth, grey wall of snow-capped rock crested by unnaturally regular, sharply-angled peaks, like the monolithic teeth of some continent-sized monster. Vertigo assailed me, for never had I seen anything so huge, not even the Alps. And worse, the sense of unreality that swept over me nearly caused me to lose control of my aircraft. I almost vomited.

The mountain range rose higher than my plane could ever climb, much less have already crossed.

Completely disoriented and shaking uncontrollably from the cold and the impact of this bizarre phenomenon, I merely nosed the plane down, feeling that, beneath this alien sky, I was exposed to some unknown horror that at any moment might lash out and strike me from the air as I would a fly. All thought of eluding my pursuers had vanished; instead, I found a strange comfort in their proximity, as if the fact that there were other human beings here served as a link to the familiar, however chaotic world I had left behind.

Neither of them made a move to attack me, no doubt sharing my disbelief and discomfiture. And now, to add to my already shaken nerves, I saw that great banks of dark, rolling clouds had begun to amass overhead, almost like living things converging from all points of the compass. The sun disappeared behind a huge, grey wall of vapor in the east, submerging the awry landscape in almost impenetrable shadow, while, to the west, quick flashes of brilliant yellow light began to pulsate within the hearts of the clouds, splitting that same shadow with questing, illuminating tendrils. A low, powerful rumble rose above the sound of my engine, gradually growing louder, like but yet unlike peals of thunder after a lightning strike. This sound was constant, never diminishing or receding, but possessing a weirdly modulated quality, almost as if the deep tones were becoming articulate.

Even had it been conceivable to return over the top of that

colossal range to our rightful airspace, I could not deny a strange, fear-tinged exhilaration, the thrill of having discovered some exotic new frontier, though quite unintentionally and with no earthly idea if escape were possible. I determined to press on while my fuel held out. Looking back toward the two enemy pilots, I wondered if they, too, felt the challenge of this newfound mystery. The Brit in the Snipe made eye contact with me and offered a respectful salute. I returned the gesture.

Then, my heart almost stopped, for in the distance ahead I saw those huge black masses coalescing like smoke from a vast kiln, slowly twisting and growing with the incredible illusion of sentience. I felt as if I were witnessing some sort of monstrous birth in the sky, for as the clouds began to take on a definite form, deep within their hearts pulsed bright yellow flashes of energy, accompanied by an increase in the rumbling I'd heard before.

To my complete horror, I saw that the amorphous shape in the sky had assumed the vaguest outlines of something manlike — a trunk, miles high, with two pairs of vaporous appendages that uncannily resembled arms and legs. And the head, if such it could be called — a domed nimbus of swirling smoke — was crested by spidery filaments of mist almost in the shape of a spiked crown — or the horns of a titanic demon.

I merely continued to fly straight, overwhelmed by the vast and incredible majesty of the thing striding across the sky. And stride it did, for those great bipedal columns billowed into slow, rhythmic motion, almost gliding, so it seemed, atop a layer of thin, flattened cloud. High above, from where one might expect "eyes" to be found, a bright, cyclopean ball of energy crackled and blazed, seeming to glare down at our mosquito-like aeroplanes with manifest intelligence.

Mesmerized by the unfolding spectacle, I had neglected to pay my instruments their deserved attention, and I was suddenly forced to take note when a cold blast of air reminded me that I had slipped into a steepening dive. I pulled on the yoke, climbing quickly, but losing airspeed. The Snipe pilot behind me, also focused solely on the phenomenon before us, reacted just in time to pull his aircraft away from a potentially deadly collision.

He waved an apology, which I ignored, my attention now demanded by this nightmarish stalker on the clouds. I quickly banked right, away from the Snipe, veering into a 90-degree turn that would carry me away from the stratospheric giant, but toward a dark, forbidding skyscape that no longer offered a horizon as a point of reference. I noted that, far in the distance, numerous tiny flashes of yellow light split the darkness, which for all I knew might suddenly generate new horrors of their own. Still, I had no choice in the matter, for it was clear to me that this impossible reality had become the *only* reality with which I could concern myself.

Glancing back, I saw that the Snipe remained close on my tail, but the mammoth stalker already loomed over the straggling Spad with obvious malevolent purpose. An arm of thick, roiling vapor rushed down toward the tiny aircraft, trailing tendrils of grey smoke; I saw the plane dive quickly, banking right at full speed, then hurtling earthward in a controlled spin. My heart swelled with hope as, for a moment, I thought the pilot might make good his escape. But then, his maneuver proved to be his own undoing, for with a sudden jerking motion, his wings snapped from their mounts, fluttering away like the torn wings of a butterfly, while the bullet-like fuselage began a long, arcing plummet toward the earth below. A bellowing roar of immense volume shook the air, a thunderous voice that echoed either triumph or fury at the death that might have been its own to impart.

The Snipe pilot must have crossed the brink of sanity then, for I saw him shouting inaudible curses at the monstrous thing on the clouds, and he swung around to attack. I confess that at that moment I shared his insane notion to take the offensive; my remaining hundred rounds or so of ammunition offered a small, illusory measure of comfort, for in the "normal" world, the hard reality of the gun meant that I was not defenseless. So, praying with little faith that the Snipe pilot might somehow survive his mad dash, I turned to follow him, preferring in my heart to die fighting rather than fleeing. But my immediate thought was: what possible effect might bullets have upon a cloud, living or otherwise?

The answer came soon enough. The Snipe climbed quickly toward the towering, spiked "head," its Vickers guns spewing lethal tracers straight into a vast, widening chasm that I took to be a mouth. From this gaping maw a brilliant bolt of white light flashed toward the Snipe, outlining it with a hot corona. I thought this to be the end of the brave Brit, but then I saw the plane bank sharply left, still under the pilot's control. He zoomed past me and circled to execute a second pass. Now, my turn was coming, and I tightened my grip on the stick as adrenaline exploded in my veins with a grenade-like burst.

The cyclopean eye of fire rolled down to regard me, and in that moment, I perceived a terrible cognizance, a passing of awareness between us. The stalker loomed larger and larger, its slowly converging "arms" threatening to engulf me as I zoomed into my attack. I pressed the trigger of my Spandaus, loosing a long, unbroken salvo of fire into the horn-crested mien, determined to empty my last round into it if for nothing more than to voice my defiance. I felt the air turning hot, and the apparition before me wavered as if through a heat-haze. The black nimbus and the burning eye grew to nightmarish proportions, and my gun choked to a halt, either empty or jammed. I practically tore the yoke from the floor as I pulled the Fokker into a vertical climb to keep from slamming into the onrushing visage.

Then, the sky was suddenly empty, for I had somehow crested the mountainous head. However, my overwhelmed reflexes were slow to react, and I suddenly found the plane shuddering to a halt, the engine groaning as I neared and reached stall speed. Then my left wing lost its lift, and the alien landscape suddenly appeared before me, spinning dizzily as my plane tumbled toward the earth like a bird in the throes of death. I barely had the presence of mind to push the nose down, waggle the stick gradually to the left and right, and pump the rudder pedals against the spin. I came out of the dive at 8,000 feet, headed south toward the gargantuan mountain range, leaving the behemoth behind.

Now, unable to attack with so much as a gesture, I resolved to take my chances and challenge the impassable peaks looming before me. It was this direction whence I had come, and this direction that I perceived to be my only chance at salvation. I looked back, wondering about the fate of the Brit in the Sopwith Snipe. For several moments, I could not see him — only the vast and awful silhouette of the cloud-stalker blocking the entire horizon astern. But then I saw a quick flash of white, and the Snipe appeared just to the west, high above and also heading south, his bravery now perhaps tempered by the wisdom gained following our ineffectual attacks. I began to ascend, only to find the plane's movement sluggish and bumpy, and I realized that the cracked strut had completely given way during my last panicked maneuver. The lower right wingtip, bent just this side of the strut, sagged at a dangerous angle, prompting me to hold the stick as level as possible; on my first abrupt maneuver, I *would* lose the wing.

I was suddenly swallowed by darkness. With a movement that defied the laws of physics, the stalker bore down on me with speed like the wind. From that wall of black cloud came a roar of exultation, and I realized now that the end must surely be at hand. Even had my wing been whole, there was no way I could outrun death thundering toward me on demonic wings. Having lived so close to the edge for the past few years of my life, and realizing now the inevitability of my fate, I found myself suddenly overcome by a feeling of calm acceptance. My proud, Prussian soul was prepared to take the final journey with honor. I began to very gradually bank my plane toward the great beast so that I might face it head-on.

Then, the most strange and wonderful event happened, one I recognized as a sign of the kinsmanship between those who flew in the service of their country, regardless of their respective state's politics. The pure white Sopwith Snipe circled near me, its pilot obviously aware of my aircraft's disabled state. As the plane passed close by, the Brit raised a hand in a final salute, and I saw his ship briefly nose down, then roar into a full-power climb, aimed directly at the burning eye of the monster. He sailed through space like a comet, and his last few tracers spat from his guns. I realized his intent, and shouted a vain plea for him to desist, for I could not imagine that such an attack might for one moment slow the momentum of the cloud-thing.

I recall the Brit's death as if it were a dream. The Snipe homed in on that cyclopean fireball with unerring precision, as if the pilot had by some preternatural instinct recognized it as not merely an eye, but a *heart*. I silently counted down the seconds to impact, and when I reached zero, I held my breath and wished my former enemy a quick and painless crossing of the threshold into God's house. Then, a blinding flash of light seared across my field of vision, followed seconds later by a reverberating *boom* of such force that I feared my damaged wing might be shaken to pieces. But it somehow held together, unlike – to my great elation – the stalker on the wind, whose cumulus, billowing form began to come apart before my eyes, spreading slowly and majestically into countless, seething masses that trailed thin streamers of dark vapor. These disintegrating components slowly unraveled like balls of gaseous fibers, swirling and blending with one another but failing to reshape themselves into their former state.

I think I must have shouted praises to the heavens then, though my memory of these moments is muddled due to the unchecked flood of adrenaline that coursed through my body. I somehow maintained control of my aeroplane, for the moment having completely forgotten about the impassable barrier that lay ahead of me. I was brought back to that terrible reality moments later, when I turned from the scene of death behind me and focused on my heading.

The mountain range was there, now partially cloaked by a thick veil of grey fog that seemed to grow denser even as I watched. My spirits, so heightened by the destruction of this kingdom's terrible monarch, plummeted abruptly with the realization that I must prepare myself yet again for a death that I had been temporarily spared. My Fokker had begun to shudder and lurch erratically as the integrity of the damaged wing diminished, and I knew that all hope must again be reluctantly abandoned. I resolved to merely proceed straight ahead with a flight that would end quickly and mercifully in a collision with the steep, almost vertical plane of rock that jutted cruelly into the sky.

Well before I was to reach that bitter end, my D.VII entered a thick bank of clouds that for many anxious moments I feared might prove to be a new, living extension of that thing I had left behind. But as I flew, the greyness began to brighten, slowly transforming into a white mist almost as pure as the Sopwith Snipe. Then, as if by divine hand, the clouds parted, and I found myself soaring over a wooded, rolling landscape, checkerboarded with fields and farmhouses, divided by the bright blue ribbon of the Meuse River off to my right. Far ahead, I could see a tiny blotch amid the greenery that I knew to be Tellancourt, and another farther east, which was Verdun. The aerodrome at Metz, from which I had taken off some unknown time before, lay about 40 miles ahead, and if God's hand held my wing together, I knew I might somehow return alive. I gauged by the sun that it was close to noon.

I landed at Metz, fuel tanks dry, and on touchdown, my damaged wing finally came apart. But I rolled to a halt outside a deserted hanger, finding no flight crew waiting to greet me. Apparently, none of my flight had survived — though I came to learn from observers on the ground that Rittmeister Hoffmann and Oberleutnant Reisendorf had met their fates bravely, both having taken down large numbers of the enemy. The Allies were now on the march, all resistance crushed. A few assorted personnel remained at the base, all busily packing what supplies they might, or destroying equipment that could not be evacuated — a category that included, to my utter dismay, my aeroplane. No one was at the moment interested in my ordeal, and had I related even a cursory account of it, my word would have ceased to have any credence among my peers, and surely, my superiors would have ordered a court-martial. So, without witnesses or evidence of my experience, which I knew and still know to have been as real as the war itself, I merely fabricated a story of having engaged the enemy and emerged victorious, after sustaining damage that resulted in the destruction of my aircraft. It was a story never to be questioned or even repeated, for just over a month later, Kaiser Wilhelm II fled to Holland and the war ended, as did my illustrious career as an aviator.

*E*xactly what happened — and where it happened — I have never learned and probably never will. In these days of widespread air travel, it seems inevitable that, at some point, another flyer, perhaps even in some other portion of the globe, might penetrate the same mysterious veil between worlds that I and two others did on that day so many years ago. Indeed, during the following World War, and all the conflicts since, where the skies have been filled with fighting machines as never before in human history, who is to say that some who left the earth in their ships, never to return, did not suddenly find themselves flying over an unknown land, only to hear the thunder of some impossible, monstrous giant on its way to deal in death?

While for all these years, as I have said, I have never again allowed my feet to leave the earth, I sometimes awake in the night and find myself reeling through a grey-hued, shadow-choked sky, hearing the pealing voice of the cloud-stalker, and I tremble with the knowledge that it must still exist somewhere on the fringes of our so-firmly-perceived reality. And sometimes, I see that anonymous face behind the helmet and goggles: that of the brave and noble Englishman who went to his death so that I, his enemy, might have a chance at life. Moreso than at the existence of that monumental horror, I have marveled at the way that man I never knew so willingly died, and his salute still haunts me. Every September 13 since that date, I have drunk a toast in his honor, and above all the men and women I have known in my life, somehow I feel that he was my truest friend.

I am old, and am not long bound for this earth. I hope that the keys to God's house will be offered to me at my time, and there, I hope to meet that pilot, that we may soar among the clouds together.

Something in the sky does call to me.

*M*anuscript discovered among the belongings of Klaus Von Moltke, who died at the age of 98, in Heilegenstadt, Germany. Found with the manuscript, an airline ticket in Von Moltke's name, dated the day after his death — destination unknown.

Gunhand

*T*he city bred strange things.

She saw the overcoat shuffling out of the shadowed alley across from her chamber window; stooping, picking something up, depositing it in a hidden pocket. The body within the coat looked bulky, lumpy, curiously proportioned, with long arms and presumably long legs, for the figure was very tall. The streetlights didn't illuminate the face beneath the wiry mane that sprang from the coat's broad collar. Looked like he had no face. A no-face under a tangle of rusty barbed wire.

She sipped wine, gazed out the window; an everynight ritual. Overcoat had appeared for many nights now, collecting things from the street. Maybe he collected people, too, she thought, watching the way the head twisted and turned, seemed to listen, to sniff, to taste traces of passersby in the air. But whenever someone walked past, overcoat faded into the recesses of nearby doorways, behind trash cans, always disappearing; becoming no one.

But she knew. She saw him. She watched him.

She was Francesca.

The figure crept to a storm drain, knelt, picked up what looked like piece of pipe. He held it up to unseen eyes, cocked the mane as if the inanimate object had spoken to him. Nodding in approval, he stuffed the pipe into his coat, then shuffled farther down the street, his quest for another evening begun. Francesca had never seen him return, even when she had stayed up all night watching. But he always appeared again the next evening, just as the shadows grew long. Always from the same alley.

Home?

At the street corner, the overcoat paused, backlit by neon and mercury vapor, face still a void as the head tilted back to regard her window.

What was this? Had he seen her? Did he know she was there? If he had ever been aware of her watchful presence, he had given no sign.

Something like an eye flashed in the blackness above the collar, but more like a tiny spotlight. A beam of pale yellow cut through the haze between the corner and her window, settled on the glass of wine in her hand, turning it bloody and alive. She lifted the glass to her lips. The light followed, touched her fingers, her face.

Heat!

Yes! Look at me! Let me see you. . . .

But then he disappeared, shambling off as ever, perhaps disappointed by what he had found. He simply expected anyone who would watch him to be more thrilling. She cursed, warmed by shame, anger, frustration. She was desirable. As if one such as he could spurn her!

She rose and found her black trench coat, pulling it around her shoulders with the arms hanging loose. Tossed back the last of her wine. Brazened by his affront, she could no longer be a spectator behind her glass wall; now, she would mingle with the night from which, in her haughty fear, she had always kept her distance.

How many times she had wanted to leave her rooms to explore the city labyrinth under the opaque sky, when the familiarity of sunlit streets yielded to a vaster strangeness that beckoned her to be its witness; yet always failed to draw her from her shielded throne. How uncannily simple, she marveled, to be impelled by the mere rebuff of a stranger (but *what* was he?) who had cast his light her way.

His brilliant, scrutinizing gaze.

Down the stairs and through the foyer, out to the chilly street, pounced upon by the harsh radiance of a streetlight that obliterated the world beyond its limited reach. She moved out of the frigid-hot arena and let her eyes adjust to the shadowed world that the overcoat secretly ruled. Why should she find the prospect of discovery so thrilling? He was surely no potentate, but a beggar, unsavory and perhaps lethal.

Her steps led her in the direction he had gone, into streets all but empty, the night glowering with disfavor on those who intruded upon its quiet dominion. From far elsewhere came sounds of human congregations; not all the urban veins had atrophied like this place. Certainly that other, brighter world laid claim to her, although incompletely. She lived on the labyrinth's edge, bonding with the unfamiliar, but only to the extent that her glass walls allowed.

Until tonight.

Something around the next corner clanked lightly, metal upon metal. She shrugged away the urge to return indoors until daylight again warmed this glacial corner of the city; and hearing again the soft metallic sound, she continued toward the next alley, sensing that he--*it*--must surely be near.

Then . . . yes!

The same golden beam that had found her earlier pierced the shadows like a silent drill, bouncing off the dirty brick walls until again it shone upon her face, where it stopped and held her in its unblinking glare. Something materialized at the other end of the beam, something terrible and dark, looming larger and larger until it hovered over her, clanging and muttering with the sound of an idling gasoline engine. She could not turn away. *It* lifted its arms toward her--a pair of long, jointed appendages wrapped in the sleeves of the ill-fitting overcoat, limbs that bent at inorganic angles.

Cold steel brushed her face as the arms embraced her; suddenly, her feet left the ground, and she was whisked into the darkness of the alley, so quickly that she didn't realize what had happened until she saw cracked pavement moving far beneath her and her trench coat being trampled and kicked into a dark, unseen corner. The thing had slung her over its shoulder and was now carrying her into whatever lair it claimed, its footsteps clattering and ringing in a syncopated, staccato rhythm. Her lips parted, trying to form the word "Stop," or perhaps, "Help," but only the softest hiss escaped, and she feared that even that much might cause her captor to silence her — for the arm around her waist pressed very hard, threatening to effortlessly crush her. Vaguely, she wondered how something so huge and lumbering could camouflage itself so perfectly on the city streets.

The thing veered into a pitch black opening in the alley wall, and its eyebeam flared to life; but Francesca could see only the dark path behind, the dim opening to the alley shrinking steadily until it vanished altogether. Ahead, the bass throbbing of heavy machinery pounded insistently, still distant but immensely powerful, growing louder with every clanging step, shuddering into her eardrums, her skull, into her bones . . . a deepening rhythm . . . like a giant heartbeat.

Light gradually filled her vision, pale electric blue, intensifying to violet, revealing purple brick walls to either side. Ringing tones rose around her, joining in a wistful harmony, mimicking human voices, but in doing so, emphasizing their alien source. As they wove into a chorus backed by the machine beat, the rhythm became erotic, filling her with an inexplicable heat--and an almost narcotized complacency, as if her will were being drained by either the thing carrying her or the sound itself.

Suddenly, she felt herself being unceremoniously lifted and dropped; she fell for a shocking distance before landing face first on a spongy surface, bouncing up and down several times before settling into a soft, warm, fleshy material. In the darkness, her eyes could not yet discern any details.

Gradually, she perceived herself to be within a broad, cylindrical chamber that rose to dark, unseen heights. In the distance above, frequent violet flashes and occasional golden sparks revealed that the shaft was not empty; *something* occupied the space up there: the originator, whatever it might be, of the deep, intense machine music.

Overcoat stood before her, studying her with its eyebeam, grumbling and muttering, adding its own low voice to the metal symphony. She pressed herself into the yielding material, which felt warm and alive, oddly comforting in the frigid darkness. Her blood raced hot through her body, her nerves strangely exhilarated by the cold scent of danger pouring from the figure looming over her. She saw its arms rise, tug at the buttons of its coat, and for a moment she felt a ridiculous twinge of embarrassment that, like a robotic flasher, this beast was going to reveal itself to her.

The coat fell away, and she gasped. Gold, violet and crimson flashes reflected on crazy, skeletal arrays of tubing and wire that wound in and among themselves, coming together in *something* resembling a human form, however superficially. Beneath the barbed wire mane, the eye beam peered from a cyclopean socket within a wedge-shaped metal plate; the head, such as it was, rested atop a cluster of twisted metal pipes, and as Francesca watched, one of the arms rose again, now holding the piece of pipe she had seen it pluck from the street. Grasping it in triple-pronged pincers, the thing placed the tip of the pipe at the base of its neck, driving it downward and in, then tugging it back far enough to lock the upper end into whatever served as its skull.

Great God, the thing is building itself!

"What are you?" she whispered. "What do you want with me?"

The eye flared, its hot beam falling upon her cheek just below her right eye. A grinding sound rose from the thing's torso.

"Where do you come from?"

The eye gazed at her impassively for several moments; then one of the arms lifted and pointed skyward. With a heavy clang, the shape took one step toward her. And above, a deep groaning that slowly grew louder indicated that whatever hid in the upper reaches of the cylinder was about to descend.

In the flashing light, Francesca now saw several flexible, silvery tubes wriggling down toward her captor, and as they drew near, they began belching powerful jets of white steam, bathing the naked metal beast in thick, roiling clouds. The mechanized chorus rose loud and long, and the thing's two arms extended to their full span--at least ten feet, she realized with alarm. An almost soothing violet glow appeared overhead, brightening as the music intensified, and finally the steam cleared, revealing the glittering metal being in all its naked splendor. Its every limb and organ was fashioned intricately from dissimilar metal scrap; from copper tubing, to lead pipes, to twisted plates of aluminum. Like thorn-skinned serpents, long strands of barbed wire wound angrily around the torso and limbs, sprouting Medusa-like from the crown of the silvery skull.

Something brushed her ankle--and looking down, she saw one of the snaking tubes from above encircling her lower leg, followed by another and then another, each caressing her body with sentient deliberation. The steel tendrils tightened around her, binding her arms at her sides, holding her helpless before the gleaming eye of her abductor. And one of its long arms now reached for her, the triple pincers grasping the fabric of her blouse and shredding it, tearing away the remains to expose her naked breasts. She gasped, not in horror, but in strange fascination--and desire. The heavy rhythm, the warm flesh in which she nestled, the cold steel restraining her limbs, the almost elegant form of the artificial but *living* construct looming over her . . . these had fired her blood to a raging boil, and even knowing that her last moments of life might be fast approaching, she felt a thrill of anticipation unlike any she had ever known with a mere man.

The claw-tipped arm reached for the button fastening her pants, deftly snipped it away, then closed on the zipper . . . slowly tugged it open, proceeding to pull her pants down to her knees. The pincers returned to clutch her panties, quickly slicing through one side and tearing them completely from her body. She felt her lower regions heating up, moistening, though somewhere in the far corners of her consciousness, alarms blared, warning her of the horror now surely impending.

No! she cried back. She could not resist; compliance was surely the only possible path to self-preservation.

The monster's other arm now came into view. Unlike the pincered tips of the first, this one ended in a long, blue steel barrel, like the muzzle of shotgun, which now waved slowly and tantalizingly before her widening eyes. Lust and terror mingled in a superheated brew, and as the gunhand lowered to brush her thighs, she released a long, plaintive moan that blended in low harmony with the chiming tones echoing from the upper reaches of the chamber.

The cold steel pincers tentatively touched one breast; she flinched as the sharp metal slid across her tender flesh, seemingly capable of tactile sensation, exerting pressure without slicing her skin. The muzzle of the long arm pressed into the flesh of her inner thigh, and her back arched involuntarily at its frigid touch. The single, radiant eye peered into hers, and Francesca could sense both satisfaction and curiosity in its cognizant gaze.

"You're not going to hurt me, are you?" she whispered.

Of course it spoke no word, but the thing began making a purring noise deep within its twisted torso, and the gunhand gently pressed forward, touching her clitoris, sending an electric thrill through her entire body; the barrel worked tight little circles around the lips of her vagina, and she felt herself moistening, preparing to receive him.

No, not him. *It.*

The muzzle hesitated only a moment, then pushed itself into her. She gasped in horrified ecstasy, wishing to both block out and fixate upon the incredible thing entering her body. The barrel twisted, then plunged deeper, causing her to cry out, not in pain or shock, but in disbelief--and unthinkable pleasure. Such an abomination taking her this way should send her over the sanity's brink, a fading voice warned her from somewhere inside; but she could only allow the colossus's scheme to play out, for anything else would certainly mean her death. Something she had seen in that brilliant eyebeam — something resembling humanity, she told herself--seemed to assure her that ending her life was not its aim.

The metal coils binding her alternately constricted and relaxed in rhythm with the gunhand's movements. Steam swirled around her, warm and wet, and beneath her, the unknown cushion of flesh seemed to knead and stroke her back, soothingly, adding its flavor to the melange of sensation.

The metal tendrils suddenly applied pressure--twisted--and rolled her onto her stomach, all while the gun muzzle continued pumping inside her. She heard a hissing sound above, and daring to crane her neck and look up, she saw a plethora of writhing tubes lowering toward her, filling her with the sudden dread that she had only imagined any reassuring warmth in the machine man's glare. But then, like gentle snakes, or a lover's fingers, these narrow, rubbery tendrils fell upon her back and softly brushed back and forth, caressing her, running from her neck to her buttocks. She felt a blunt tip slide into her crack, probing, sliding toward her anus--finally inserting itself, slipping in and out ever so gently, gradually increasing its force. Another slid in along with the first, and she moaned in unadulterated pleasure as together, the ravishing metal barrel and the flexible fingers touched the vital spot inside her, sending her into a hot, convulsing orgasm that went on and on, finally culminating in a long, animal scream as, for a moment, her rational mind departed altogether, broken by this perfect assault of demoniac hideousness and divine delight.

The flesh beneath her quivered, and the obscene gunbarrel withdrew from within her, admitting a swirl of cooling air that refreshed her like the juice of a cactus to a thirsty soul in the desert. The rubber tendrils continued to play over her body, but the steel coils relaxed enough so that she could again turn onto her back to face the metal giant still standing over her.

The gunhand extended toward her, its muzzle touching her lower lip, offering her the scent of her own musk. Something above drew her gaze upward, and now, within a pulsating violet wreath, she saw, high in the cylindrical chamber, the source of the multiple appendages that bound and stroked her body.

"Oh, my God . . . oh, my God."

Like a great metallic mandala, easily a hundred yards across and at least that far above her, a wheel within a wheel spun slowly and hypnotically, its axis connected with its rims by dozens of criss-crossing spokes. From the central hub, multiple clusters of steel arms dangled and waved like silvery tentacles questing for prey. She realized that *up there* lay the true source of her violation, if such it could be termed; the metal man was merely some pawn, something formed and directed by whatever intelligence resided in the slowly spinning wheels.

"What are you?" she whispered. "What is this place?"

Inside her body, something stirred, and the sudden realization that the gunhand had deposited something within her nearly caused her to retch.

"What have you done to me?"

Do not fear.

No voice had spoken, yet she knew that there had been a response to her question. Indeed, the machine, if machine it truly was, possessed awareness, the ability to touch her mind as well as her body.

"Where am I?"

At the heart.

"What are you? Where are you from?"

Far.

She swallowed hard. "Do you mean to kill me?"

No death.

The metal man's eyebeam blazed, touched her cheek. Hot. Inside her womb, pressure. Francesca raised an arm toward the beast; to her shock, she saw that her skin appeared discolored, the veins pronounced and dark. Her long finger-nails gleamed with purple light.

"What is happening to me?"

You into me . . . me into you.

More pressure. Pressure, but no pain. Looking down, she saw her ribcage disturbingly pronounced, the skin stretched taut over her bones. She tried to pull herself from the soft warmth around her, but she seemed weighted down, lethargic. Had she been poisoned?

She now saw that the spongy material around her was veined, alive, pulsating and writhing around her, pulling at her flesh. The skin of her fingers seemed to soften and melt, to flow into the organic mass in which she nestled. Still, there was no pain, no sensation that her body was coming apart; changing.

As her flesh slid away to join its host, her muscles hardened, took on the sheen of the metal man's skin. She lifted her right hand, marveling at the fully exposed, sparkling steel bone structure, the jointed appendages that had replaced her soft fingers. Her breasts became sleek, flattened cones of metal welded to an ornately curved steel rib cage that encircled bronze-tinted muscles and organs. Finally, the coils around her began to fall away, allowing her to move on her own. Heat surged through her veins; not just heat, but *power*, and she realized that, all along, she had had nothing to fear.

From above, the piping sounds rose in exultation, for something new was being born. Gunhand had been an earlier step in the evolution of the machine from beyond; she would be its next logical phase, the next link in the chain of its unknown destiny.

She stood, her body a gleaming, elegant construct of metal, casting away the remaining shroud of skin that had once enveloped everything she had been. Her human remains blended into those that had come before, partners of the whirling twin wheels overhead. Looking up, she saw the shape of her progenitor ascending into the highest reaches of the cylinder, which she now knew to be the subterranean lair of something wonderfully extraterrestrial; a chamber that must have existed here beneath the labyrinth for countless years as the machine being experimented and evolved, built itself into something new, casting parts of its being from the refuse of the human world and from humanity itself.

Gunhand knelt before her, recognizing her as both its offspring and its successor. For a brief moment, her past life attempted to reassert itself, to drag her back to mere human-ity, but the new power within her refused to yield. She dismissed all that she had been with a wave of her exquisite metal arm, and reaching for Gunhand, she bade him rise. The shape stood, extended a long, jointed arm, and with triple pincers stroked the regal mane of steel fibers that cascaded over her shoulders from her chrome skull.

She felt its touch with nerves charged by electricity, a wonderful, warm sensation that ran more deeply than any she had known as a creature of flesh and blood. She was truly beautiful now, the perfect hybrid of mortal and machine, yet more than the either. She could feel perfect satisfaction in the transmitted consciousness of the being above her, and she knew its mission, and accepted her new purpose without reservation.

Leaving Gunhand and her grandsire in the chamber be-hind, she stepped into the tunnel through which she had been brought those eons ago, her twin eyebeams cutting through the darkness as she made her way back to the surface--to begin her quest for the next link in the chain of destiny, over which *she* now held dominion.

Somewhere My Love

She lived in the only run-down house in the neighborhood: a two-story Victorian with a pepperbox turret and windows of leaded glass, a sagging roof with missing shingles, and a number of blackened brick chimneys. What little paint remained was no longer white but crusty gray, its walls barely seen through the dense cedar trees that surrounded the property. Weeds sprouted from the unkempt, split-rail fenced yard; and rather than a nice paved driveway like all the others in the neighborhood, she had only a short gravel apron for her car. The man of the house had died before I was born, leaving her alone in the old place for all those years. At night, nary a light ever shone in any of the windows.

And sometimes after dark, I could hear her voice echoing out of that old house, raised in songs that seemed to me unearthly.

Of course she was a witch.

Her name was Jeanne Weiler, and she was my music teacher when I was in elementary school.

Looking back now, I would have to say she was quite an attractive woman, though at the time, she presented such an imposing image that just being in the same room with her intimidated me to the edge of fright. She stood almost six feet (which, when I was just over four feet tall, seemed so very high indeed), had long, wavy black hair that she often wore stacked atop her head, and possessed the most piercing green eyes I think I've ever seen even to this day. She virtually always wore a severe, tight-fitting black outfit that showed off a fine figure unappreciated by my youthful eyes, but which spoke of no impropriety — only dignity.

And despite my fear of Mrs. Weiler, I loved her so. While I couldn't begin to have sexual thoughts about her in those days, I reacted physically to her presence by having chills and almost uncontrollable trembling. I recall many a time when, had she but asked it, I would have fallen to my knees and kissed her feet and been so excited by the prospect that I might have wet my drawers.

All the more reason to be assured that she was a witch, for this was power — the purest power ever exerted upon me, miles and leagues beyond any held by my parents, or any other teachers, or the minister at church, or any of my fellow fourth graders. I was afraid of her because she could make me do things. Anything.

But she always spoke kindly to me, treated me with the same respect with which she treated all the kids. All the parents liked her. I know she was aware of the effect she had on me because I would often catch her glancing at me with appraisal in her cool eyes, one hand curled beneath her chin as if she were contemplating things held in store for me that I could not imagine.

And oh, her voice! She would sing so many songs to us as she attempted to teach us music, and that sweet alto would weave its way through my mind down to my core, tugging at my soul with sorrow or joy — whatever emotion to which the song was tuned. I remember she would sing "A Time for Us," the theme to *Romeo and Juliet,* with such passion that the whole class would be in tears.

No one else could have ever done that to me, or to any of my friends.

Because *she* was a witch.

Some of the songs we had to learn were stupid, and she took great pleasure in watching us humiliate ourselves by singing them — badly, at that — and I loved her all the more for it. Things like "Morning Comes Bringing" and "Dreidel," and "Cherry Ripe" made my teeth grind, but because she desired it, we would sing our little hearts out, and she would smile in pure joy. She was our mistress and could not be refused. She would reward us sometimes with milk and cookies or even let us out five minutes before the bell rang in the afternoon, for hers was the last class of the day.

Late in the school year came the day that I learned what she'd had in store for me from the beginning. Not only for me, I might add, but for Johnny McCrickard and Tina Truman as well. The horror of it all nearly destroyed me, and I think the time she announced it was the first and only time I ever hyperventilated uncontrollably. Johnny and Tina didn't have such strong reactions, but the dread showed just as plainly in their eyes, and in their chalky faces. The rest of the class, of course, cheered and sang their praises to Mrs. Weiler, no doubt relieved that none of them had been similarly singled out.

Johnny, Tina and I were to sing. Solos. Not only in front of the class, but in front of the school. We had shown such superior achievement that Mrs. Weiler was certain we would shine, thus making her — and our parents, and everyone — just unbelievably proud.

Johnny would sing "The Impossible Dream." Tina would sing "Love is Blue." And I . . . I would sing "Somewhere My Love," Lara's theme from *Dr. Zhivago,* the big blockbuster of the day.

Mrs. Weiler looked pained and fearful when I began breathing and sobbing so hard — and came immediately to me and stroked my hand, and gazed at me with terrible sadness in her green eyes. And almost immediately the paroxysm passed. Kneeling before me, she looked truly beautiful, and I wanted to kiss her. But she said, "Warren, you can do it. I know you can. Won't you sing for us? Won't you please?"

And taking a deep breath, I said, "Yes," because I could not refuse her.

The big event would happen two weeks later, at a special assembly held in the evening so the parents could come. There was plenty of other programming: scholastic awards, athletic awards, a farewell presentation for Mrs. Clairmont, who would be retiring at the end of the term. The music event would not occur until almost the end of the assembly, which gave the three unlucky participants all the more time to sweat and fidget.

And through it all, Mrs. Weiler stayed by me, whispered

little encouragements in my ear, ran her fingers affectionately through my hair — making me melt as her power coursed through my body like an electrical current. She was kind enough to Johnny and Tina, but her attentions were focused on me; an attempt, I suppose, to cast a spell upon me like none she had ever conjured before. It must have worked, for by the time I was to sing my song, my heart was thumping and my knees were weak; yet I went out on stage after Tina and Johnny had done their numbers with only the desire to please Mrs. Weiler in my heart. The multitudes of eyes on me, and all those expectant faces, including my mom's and dad's, meant nothing. Only the green eyes behind the stage curtain gazing at me with such tenderness had any influence on me whatsoever.

Mr. Curwen, the pianist, began to play, and I kept my eyes on Mrs. Weiler, waiting for the nod that would give me the cue to begin. When it came, I stepped up to the microphone — and the voice that came out was no longer mine. It was a rich, hearty stranger's voice, entirely on-key and without a trace of quaver. "Somewhere my love, there will be songs to sing . . . although the snow covers the hope of spring," I sang, surprised and shocked by the entity that must have entered me for the sole purpose of releasing its voice via my mouth. I saw my teacher leave her place behind the curtain and make her way down the stage steps, coming slowly to stand at the edge of the platform before me. Her eyes flashed, and this thing of Mrs. Weiler's making, it seized my lungs and my vocal cords, and it had its way with me until the music ended, and I stood there, alone in a vacuum, without so much as a whisper of breath to break the silence.

Until I looked down at the green eyes and saw them smiling. And then a single pair of hands came together, cracking in the air like a gunshot, and a moment later, a thunder erupted in the auditorium, a monstrous peal of applause joined by the crying out of hundreds of voices. I nearly swooned, for it seemed that a cold wind swept over my body, threatening to topple me as my adrenaline high faded, leaving me unsteady and on the verge of hyperventilating again.

I was upheld by Mrs. Weiler's strong hands though, for in

an instant she was beside me, and I finally looked into my parents' eyes and saw them beaming with pride. I smiled, probably for the first time since the news of my "perform-ance" had been broken to me. And without looking at her, I knew Mrs. Weiler's eyes were focused on me, perhaps in attempt to take back the thing she had released to take possession of my body. Was it a kind thing? I wondered. A dangerous thing? A forever thing? All I knew was that for time it had been mine, and Mrs. Weiler had made it so.

Because she was a witch.

That night became something special in my memory. Afterward, I sang and I enjoyed the sound of my voice, but it was always *my* voice. The sounds I had let fall from my lips at that assembly surely had come from something apart from me, and try as I might, I could never regain it. Only Mrs. Weiler knew the secret.

And shortly after school ended for that summer, Mrs. Weiler died. I do not know how or why, only that I never saw her again. And I cried, harder than I cried when my grand-parents died, more bitterly than when my father passed away a couple of years later. My mother is still alive, and I love her dearly, yet I cannot imagine shedding tears more meaningful when her time comes than those I shed for Mrs. Weiler.

One day when I was eighteen, I went to the house where she had lived, for it still stood then, and indeed, remains today as something of a monument in this old town. On that day, though, remembering so well the effect she'd had on my life, I wandered around the place, overcome by a feeling of melancholy. I stepped up to the rickety front porch and tried the front door, not expecting it to be unlocked.

But it was. As if I were expected.

So I went inside and as soon as I stepped over the darkened threshold, the scent of her rushed into my nostrils, undiluted after nearly nine years. Dust-shrouded furniture remained in place, as if nothing had been touched since the day she had died. A grand piano occupied one corner of the large living room, and stepping up to it, I touched a key. A clear note rang out, and so I played a few chords, to my surprise finding each key in perfect tune. I had learned how to play piano over the course of several years, though never as well as I would have had Mrs. Weiler been there to guide my hand and attune my senses to the music.

But what came out in that dusty old chamber was a clear melody — "Somewhere my Love" — a song I had never played myself, now played as perfectly as I had sung it on that night in fourth grade. I felt the same current in my soul that I had the night she had released her power into me, and I would have sworn for a time that I heard her voice singing the words in accompaniment.

I suddenly stopped, and the notes echoed away into the darkened halls of that house . . . stirring something. Something that whispered my name and touched my cheek and brushed my lips with a sweet caress.

I left there knowing I would return. Soon.

And I did.

Once I had graduated college, I disavowed the ritual practiced by my friends and virtually all the rest of the town's youth: leaving home for greener pastures, never to return, or if so, only for brief family visits. Instead, I managed to place myself as music teacher in the local school system.

And I moved into the old Weiler place, which is where I still live. I often wish I had been able to know her as an adult, for I had come to understand her power and her love of music. I came to feel what she must have felt when a beautiful melody played and touched her heart. I still feel her and hear her and smell her in the halls of this house, and within these walls, I feel the magic she once gave to me on the stage of our little elementary school.

I take that magic with me every day, and when I encounter a little one who shares, however vaguely, the power that Mrs. Weiler bestowed upon me, I give to that child all I can spare, conjuring up that *thing* that once took me and that still lives within the walls of my old house. It doesn't like light, but favors the dark, so in the evenings, I walk with it and sing, or play the piano or the guitar, or whichever instrument that brings it pleasure. It prefers the old things, so I don't change the furniture, or otherwise renovate the place any more than necessary to keep it habitable. And I remember those times when I was a child and heard Mrs. Weiler's voice in the night but did not understand.

Of course I am older now and understand so much more. And though most of the children do not understand, there are those few who one day *will.* They are the ones upon whom I focus — to perpetuate the spirit that Mrs. Weiler passed on to me. I can do this; I have that power.

Because, of course, I am a witch.

Godspeed, my love, till you are mine again.

Orchestra

"And how shall we play without him?" Jacob Kravitz grumbled. "He's the only one who knows the music well enough to conduct!"

"Well," sighed Bert Hoffman, "we will *have* to find someone else. One does not cancel the Halloween program after all the work we've done!"

"By the way, what happened to him?"

"That's what I'm saying — he is just gone! No one has seen him since he left the auditorium last Friday. His car is gone, but they say everything in his house is still there. All his clothes. His valuables. Everything. Why can't you conduct?"

"Pah! I'm no conductor. I've never lifted a baton in my life."

"You could conduct in your sleep!"

"Get out. Besides, who would you put on first violin? Jennings?"

"He's as good as you."

"Never!"

The elderly pair fell silent, occasionally casting annoyed looks at one another. A shower of golden leaves wafted down on their heads as a draught of chilly Lake Michigan wind shook the trees in Lincoln Park. Across the sidewalk, an exceptionally broad man settled onto a bench, the wooden planks uttering an annoyed groan beneath him. A willowy 12-year old would have been hard-pressed to find space beside him.

"Oy," sighed Kravitz. "There are only two weeks to the

performance. Who would learn Vaughn-Williams, Hovhaness, and Sibelius and do what we must do with it? In two weeks? So, are the police suspecting foul play?"

"Police only suspect foul play when they have blood and a body. Weintraub is off with some young vixen."

"He is 74 years old! A vixen would kill him."

Across the way, the very large man chuckled at Kravitz's remark and lit a cigarette, which looked more like a lollipop stick in his massive fingers. Kravitz shuddered at the grotesque way the fat man sucked on the filter with his slick, pursed lips.

"So why not you?" pressed Hoffman. "You know the music better than anyone. You are the concertmaster!"

"I play the violin! I do not conduct! Plus, don't forget, I also man the organ in *Sinfonia Antarctica!* Who else could do *that?*"

"Pah!"

"Paaaah!"

Kravitz noticed the man across the sidewalk watching them with apparent amusement. "You know," he said in a much quieter voice, "Weintraub has a son in Philadelphia, and a daughter in Aurora. Has anyone thought to let them know their father has gone missing?"

"How would I know? The police, I'm sure, have contacted the family."

"You said the police think he's with a vixen."

"That doesn't mean he isn't dead."

"What *shtuss.*"

"It's cold and I'm going home. I think were going to have to draft someone from the ranks, its as simple as that. You're the senior man. The choice must be up to you."

"If it were my choice, I would cancel the Halloween program. I would cancel Halloween. It's a stupid holiday — as if it even qualifies to be a holiday," Kravitz sighed.

"Ah. You are capable of making an intelligent remark. However, the point remains unanswered."

The two men rose from their bench and started up the sidewalk toward the park entrance. Kravitz paused before the large man, who gave him an affable grin and took a long drag on his cigarette.

"Those things are going to kill you," Kravitz growled.

In a surprisingly light, silky voice, the heavy man replied, "The cigarettes will not kill me." And he drew back his slick lips in a wide smile, revealing a row of polished, white teeth.

Kravitz shook his head and turned away, pulling his coat tighter against the increasing gale. Hoffman sent him a knowing glance before bowing his head against the wind. *Damned old bastard.* Hoffman knew well enough that he refused to conduct because, as a violinist, he did not have to step into the spotlight; he only had to play in the company of his fellow musicians, where he could thoroughly disregard everything in that field of blackness beyond the stage lights.

Stage fright. Pure and simple. Standing at the forefront with a baton, he would choke. And he could not bear such failure in front of an audience.

He and Hoffman parted ways on Lincoln Avenue, each heading back to their respective homes, Kravitz to the north, Hoffman to the south. They had known each other for more years than either could remember, and both had known Weintraub, conductor *in absentia,* for the almost fifteen years they had been playing with the Chicago Cosmopolitan Symphony Orchestra — a grandiose title for an only slightly organized company of talented amateurs.

Terrible that such a fine man could vanish under such mysterious circumstances.

By the time Kravitz reached the door of his ancient apartment building on Belden, the streetlights had begun flickering on and the temperature had dropped from barely tolerable to insufferable. Even pulling open the heavy door hurt his joints, and when the blast of warm air from the foyer washed over him, it not only broke the chill, it stifled him.

Halloween performances . . . what a stupid tradition.

*A*t three-thirty the following afternoon, Jacob Kravitz found himself jarred from a light doze by the buzzing of his doorbell. *"Momzer,"* he muttered; he had not meant to fall asleep in his recliner. He planned to meet Hoffman for dinner — an almost nightly ritual — at five-thirty. But who would be at the door now?. Too early for Hoffman, too late for the mailman.

"Yes?" he barked into the intercom by the front door.

"Hello," came a silky voice, slightly distorted by static. "I have come to speak with you about the orchestra. I understand you are in need of a conductor. My name is John Hanger."

"The orchestra? Why have you come to me?"

"I spoke to a secretary at your office and she recommended I speak with you."

Kravitz chuckled. The symphony's only office was the den of cellist Luther Corcoran's house; the secretary would no doubt have been his wife. "Come up, third floor." He pressed the buzzer to admit his visitor through the front door.

After what seemed an inordinate amount of time, Kravitz heard a heavy creaking on the stairs outside his door. Never one to take chances, he peered curiously through the peephole and saw a familiar figure appear on the landing: the huge gentleman from the park bench yesterday. *Momzer* indeed. Shrugging off an inexplicable twinge of discomfort, he opened the door.

"Good afternoon," said John Hanger. The huge man held out a swollen hand, which Kravitz took hesitantly. He had expected a clammy grip, but the handshake was firm and dry.

"Come in," Kravitz said, motioning for the man to enter. John Hanger pulled off an overcoat the size of a parachute, which Kravitz took and hung on the coat rack behind the door. The big man looked to be in his early fifties, with very close-cropped, gray-flecked brown hair and wide — seemingly unblinking — blue eyes. "I recognize you from the park. I don't allow smoking in my apartment."

"That's quite all right, sir. Anyway, I'm led to understand you would be the gentleman to speak to about the position of conductor."

Kravitz motioned for Hanger to sit down on the couch. As the giant settled awkwardly into the plush upholstery, Kravitz sat back in his recliner. "I'm led to understand the same thing. It's my job by default, I suppose. I helped found the symphony many years ago and now they all see me as their grandfather. So what on earth brings you looking for a conducting job?"

"The playbills in the park for your upcoming performance caught my notice. And I couldn't help overhearing your conversation yesterday. As sad as it is for someone you obviously care about to go missing, it's also apparent that canceling a performance you've worked so hard on would be an equally terrible tragedy."

"Quite, quite," Kravitz said with a nod. "I take it you have conducting experience?"

"Music is one of my passions, Mr. Kravitz. I have worked with many orchestras in my time, though I confess it has been many, many years. I used to be friends with Dimitri Mitropoulos. I'm sure you are familiar with his work with the New York Philharmonic. I also understand you are to be performing *Tapiola*, by Sibelius. A most fitting 'fantasy' piece for Halloween, I might say. But I once had the honor of meeting Sibelius himself on a visit to Finland, just before his death, in the late fifties."

Studying his guest with an appraising eye, Kravitz said, "You must have been quite young at the time!"

Hanger chuckled. "I am no doubt older than you might think. But my appreciation for music began at a very young age. You might also find it interesting that I made the acquaintance of the composer Ralph Vaughn-Williams, in England, quite a number of years ago. His ballet, *Job*, is one of my favorites — as is *Sinfonia Antarctica*."

"You sound like a well-traveled man."

"I have spent time in almost every civilized nation on earth, and some not so civilized. I carry in here," he tapped his forehead, "the musical history of the entire world. As I said, music is my greatest passion. To be perfectly candid, I have been away from Chicago for a long time. To conduct an orchestra such as yours — and on Halloween, which I confess is a meaningful time to me — would be a great honor."

Kravitz groaned inwardly at the man's apparent reverence for the pagan "holiday." "I assume that you are willing and able to provide some references?"

"I can provide you with a full list of credentials. However, it is my hope that you will merely allow me to audition for you. At the next rehearsal of your symphony, I would like to have the honor of conducting. And, after you have had the opportunity to evaluate my performance, should you have any reservations whatsoever, I will understand and withdraw my application."

Kravitz clicked his tongue. "Sounds fair enough. We are supposed to have a rehearsal tomorrow night at the Park East. Mind you, since Mr. Weintraub disappeared, no one has yet made the decision whether or not to continue on schedule. And, you must understand, there is always the possibility that there has merely been some unfortunate miscommunication, and our regular conductor will be available to perform."

"That would be fortunate indeed."

"Very well, Mr. Hanger," Kravitz said, almost surprised at himself. "I will contact the members of the symphony to let them know that tomorrow's rehearsal is on. And you may have your audition."

The huge man's face split into an almost revoltingly wide grin, the lips shining wetly in the afternoon sunlight. "Thank you ever so much, Mr. Kravitz. I assure you . . . you will not be disappointed!"

*T*he very idea of such a huge man holding a baton and conducting nearly two-score musicians seemed almost absurd, but as John Hanger expertly drew the musical notes in the air with the simple tool, Jacob Kravitz marveled at the dexterity in those monstrous paws. The giant barely glanced at the sheets of music on the stand before him; most of the time he kept his eyes closed, as if reading the notes mentally. As Kravitz played the opening *détaché* notes of *Tapiola* on his ancient violin, which had been hand-made by his own grandfather, he could watch only Hanger's baton.

My God, this man was a better conductor than Weintraub could have ever dreamed of becoming!

Kravitz immediately felt a pang of regret at having thought derisively of his old friend. Yet his fellow musicians had instantly perceived the energy and passion the huge man positively radiated, and responded to him with unprecedented vigor. As the dark notes of the Sibelius tone poem rose in volume and intensity, punctuated by deep rolls of the kettle drum, Kravitz could see an infectious enthusiasm for the music glowing on the faces of the players.

The Park East was empty except for the orchestra and its new conductor. The stage belonged to them two nights a week until the performance — which was now less than two weeks away. Beyond the stage, the auditorium hid in darkness, and here in the island of light, Kravitz felt secure and in his own element. When the rows of plush chairs were filled (the Park East had the charm of a semiformal theater as opposed to a grand concert hall), he would hardly know the difference, for the stage lights created a comfortable dividing wall between the musicians and their audience.

Kravitz was able to give his fingers a few moments' respite as the woodwinds section, led by his capable friend Bert Hoffman, huffed and cavorted through the second passage of the Sibelius opus. Arthritis had begun working its painful effect on Kravitz's joints; as yet it had not affected his playing, but he could foresee the dreaded day when forming the notes on the fingerboard and even holding the bow could cause him considerable difficulty. But these grim thoughts were quickly dispelled by the zeal that the conductor spread through his charges. When Kravitz again lifted the bow and drew it across the strings, he was certain he had never heard such perfection emanating from his own instrument.

Hanger had already led them through a wonderful rendition of the third movement of Hovhaness's moody and mystical *Symphony of Light* — a piece that Kravitz could play blindfolded, since the orchestra played it every Halloween. The finale would be Movements 3, 4 and 5 of Vaughn-Williams *Sinfonia Antarctica*, a magnificent, if dark-toned tribute to the Scott expedition to the South Pole. Long and difficult, it would present Kravitz an opportunity to shine, for he had himself written the arrangement for the Chicago Cosmopolitan Symphony, adapting many of the traditional parts meant for brass and woodwinds to the strings, simply because the orchestra barely had enough of a horn section do to the piece justice. As *Tapiola* finally wound to its close, Hanger cast Kravitz a knowing look, as if to say, *I expect from you the very best you have ever delivered.*

And deliver he did. Following a brief break for refreshment, the orchestra began anew, and Kravitz's fingers moved as they had not since he was a young man in his prime. Accompanying the rich tones of the oboes, clarinets and French horns, Kravitz's string section played the most powerful, harmonious notes he had ever heard rushing forth from the instruments chests.

And as the music built to a crescendo, Kravitz simply turned in his chair to the electronic organ set up just behind him. And with visions in his head of the icy wilderness of the southernmost continent — from McMurdo Sound, over Victoria Land, past the monumental peaks of Mt. Markham and Mt. Kirkpatrick, across the Beardsmore Glacier to the South Pole itself — he fingered the keyboard of the organ to fashion chords, produced electronically, whose resonance seemed to rival the pipe organs of Europe's most splendid cathedrals. He simply could not believe the music that he and his fellow players were producing with their own hands.

And when it was all done, Kravitz slumped in his chair, thoroughly and utterly exhausted, yet exhilarated to his soul. At the front of the stage, John Hanger merely laid his baton on the stand before him, bowed curtly to his orchestra — yes, *his* — and said in his soft, silky voice, "I thank you all so much. I hope to have the opportunity to perform with you again."

Without so much as another look toward Kravitz, Hanger lumbered off stage left, wiping his hands briefly on the pants of his well-pressed, obviously personally tailored suit. With a renewed burst of energy, Kravitz sprang from his seat and followed after him, catching him on the stairs that led into the darkness beyond the stage.

"Mr. Hanger," he called, his voice seeming little more than a whisper. The giant turned slowly around, his gaping blue eyes reflecting the stage lights like cold lanterns. His pursed mouth again spread into an unbelievably wide grin.

"I would like to shake you by the hand, Mr. Hanger." Kravitz extended his, and it was clasped firmly but gently by other's great paw. "That was the finest performance I have ever attended, much less been a part of. Your skills are exceptional indeed. And I would like to offer you the part of conductor for our symphony."

"Why, Mr. Kravitz," Hanger beamed. "It would be my honor."

"Come to my house tomorrow afternoon and we can discuss whatever details may be necessary. You realize, of course, that we are amateurs, and we see very little, if any, financial remuneration."

"Of course, Mr. Kravitz. I was aware of this from the beginning. As you have probably realized, money is of little concern to me. I desire this opportunity strictly for personal satisfaction."

"Of course. Again, sir, you have my admiration for a wonderful, and need I say, successful audition."

John Hanger chuckled. "It did go well, didn't it. Until tomorrow, then, Mr. Kravitz." He once again clasped hands with Kravitz, and then, with surprising speed for one of such stature, disappeared into the darkness. A moment later, a rectangle of light appeared at the far end of the theatre, and the huge silhouette materialized there briefly as he exited. Then, the darkness was again complete.

As Kravitz stared after him, he clicked his tongue, thinking that tonight's rehearsal had indeed been an audition, not by John Hanger for the orchestra, but quite the other way around.

*T*he next two weeks passed uneventfully. If an investigation were being made into the disappearance of Stanislaus Weintraub, it was progressing either slowly or not at all. The orchestra rehearsed its two nights each week with John Hanger in confident command of the music and personnel. Indeed, for the first time in years, each session drew 100 percent attendance from the members. And finally, Halloween night arrived with Jacob Kravitz feeling exuberant and more confident than he could ever remember.

Yet, at the back of his mind, a strange, ambiguous cloud lingered, that he felt could somehow be traced to the very presence of John Hanger, the mysterious man who appeared only at rehearsals, never accompanying any of the more socially-active players who went to nosh afterwards. Hanger presented only the most dignified and courteous face to his new friends, as he insisted on calling the musicians; but those cold blue eyes gave Kravitz the idea that something possibly unwholesome lurked deep inside that massive skull.

"So, what *does* anyone know of this man's background, other than what he's told us?" he asked Bert Hoffman as they shared bagels and coffee in Kravitz's apartment on that afternoon of All Hallow's Eve. "He says Chicago is his home, and he's obviously traveled the world. Such an odd, solitary fellow. I'd say he's probably lonely, wouldn't you?"

"How the hell would I know?" muttered Hoffman. "You never asked him for any of his so-called credentials. It's a little late for that now, though, eh? Even you wouldn't be that rude."

"Of course not. I'm just curious, that's all."

Hoffman was thumbing through the pages of the Chicago Tribune and finally exclaimed, "Aha!" He handed the paper over to Kravitz with a smug little smile. Sandwiched between advertisements for a pair of local haunted houses — both of which lauded themselves as the world's largest — was a small display ad for the Chicago Cosmopolitan Orchestra's concert that evening. There had been a very brief notice about it in the Friday entertainment insert, proclaiming it as a landmark achievement for the amateur company. But that was about the extent of the advance publicity; advertising was an expensive proposition. Most of the orchestra's audience consisted of long-time aficionados and those who had heard word-of-mouth promotion by the company's friends, relatives, and the musicians themselves.

As Kravitz pushed the paper aside, his eye was drawn to a small headline that read, "Body of Missing Man Found on North Shore." A sudden cold chill swept over him as, for a moment, he thought he saw the name "Weintraub" amid the text. But upon scanning it further, he saw he was mistaken. The individual in question was named "Weinberg."

Almost morbidly curious, he began reading the article:

A body, identified by police as Isaac P. Weinberg, was discovered Friday A.M. by a boater in Belmont Harbor. Weinberg, 64, of Skokie, had been reported missing almost four months ago by neighbors when he failed to respond to numerous attempts to contact him. According to a police spokesman, the body was found floating the water in a badly decomposed condition, indicating it had been exposed to the elements for period of days or possibly weeks.

Friends of the victim maintain that Weinberg was a some-what reclusive, but a respectable gentleman with no known enemies. Investigators had been probing his disappearance, with few leads, since June.

There was more to the article, but Kravitz felt no compulsion to finish it. Certainly, in a city the size of Chicago, this kind of terrible thing must happen with uncomfortable frequency. But Belmont Harbor was not far away. Not far away at all.

"Bad story," Hoffman grumbled, seeing Kravitz's dismayed expression. "I'm sure *that* isn't what happened to Weintraub. He's out living his second childhood. That would be just like him, wouldn't it?"

"Yeah, sure," Kravitz said half-heartedly. "He's always had a childish streak in him."

"Worse than yours, even."

"I have only sophisticated streaks."

"Pah!"

"Paaah!"

The two ate their bagels and sipped coffee in silence for a time, and finally Kravitz noticed that it was going on four o' clock. The concert started at eight, and the musicians were to be at the Park East by six-thirty to set-up and make a final run-through of a few difficult passages. Never one to procrastinate, Kravitz began making overtures to rid himself of his guest.

"Look at the hour. Off with you. You're already running short of time to dress yourself."

"I can be ready in ten minutes."

"Nonsense. You're worse than an old woman. Go, already. Go. Go."

"All right, I'll go. You obviously need that much time for yourself. I should hate to be responsible for you coming to the concert looking like something the cat threw up."

"You're still here."

"You've lost your mind, old man. I'm long gone."

"See you tonight."

"Till then."

"Happy Halloween."

"Get out!"

*T*he tuxedo felt stiff and constricting, yet once he began playing he was able to lose himself in the music; even the heavy, uncomfortable jacket could not hamper his performance. The complex but eerily melodious notes of the Hovhanness symphony flowed from his violin as if by magic, with scarcely any effort on his part. His instrument, which had been played first by his grandfather, then his father before him, had become a mere amplifier, the physical device for producing the music in his soul.

At the forefront stood John Hanger, a behemoth in tux and tails, the sheer formality of his attire somehow ascribing dignity to his ungainly, massive form. As in rehearsal, he stood with eyes closed, his hands in constant, refined motion, his baton directing the musicians with precision and passion. Beyond, in the great field of darkness, Kravitz could sense the presence of the audience, unseen but for an occasional stirring of black within black: a non-threatening entity as long as the stage lights maintained the wall of separation.

The audience had been unbelievable, in the words of his friend Hoffman. "The house is almost full," he'd said just before the curtain opened. "We've never played before such a crowd!"

Indeed, as the strings wove their magical spell into the darkness, Kravitz could feel all those pairs of eyes watching him and his companions with a greater intensity than usual. But rather than intimidating him, those presences combined with Hanger's own, drawing out yet more feeling from his violin strings. When the Hovhaness movement drew to its close, the applause that rang from the darkness overwhelmed him. He had never heard such a clamor from an audience!

The Sibelius opus began to a hushed crowd, and as in rehearsal, the notes flowed from Kravitz's bow and strings with a kind of disembodied life. The knowledge that there were now other souls being touched by its dark, haunting beauty brought an almost physical pleasure, the music caressing him and loving him, responding ardently to the touch of his bow. He occasionally added a flourish by plucking the strings *pizzicato,* creating a whole new texture to the sound.

Hanger had called the music appropriate for holiday; but then, that was precisely why it had been selected for the event. Out there — in the audience — the listeners were awestruck. Perhaps there *was* a spirit in the season that complemented this music unlike any other, Kravitz thought. Any conscious resistance to that idea had by now melted away.

And finally came the huge, majestic Vaughn-Williams symphony. A crackling energy charged the concert hall, like the moments before a lightning strike. Kravitz could not recall ever experiencing anything similar during a performance; furthermore, he could read the same feeling in the faces of all the players around him. Next to him, the youthful but typically impassive face of Bryan Jennings beamed with uncustomary excitement, proving to Kravitz that this was indeed a phenomenon, catalyzed by the mesmerizing power of the giant at the front of the stage.

Now and again, John Hanger's eyes would open and focus on Kravitz's own, as if to convey some secret to him; that all of this, somehow, was meant for Jacob Kravitz and no other. *Ridiculous,* he thought, trying to dismiss such an egotistical notion. But as he played on, automatically now, Kravitz concentrated only on the movements of the conductor, watching his every gesture and glance.

John Hanger never once opened his eyes except to cast him that same look of confidence, as if he, at first violin, were the only player in the entire orchestra worth a moment of the maestro's notice.

As the crescendo rose, and Kravitz turned to play the organ keys that would send thunder through the hall, reflecting the splendor of the great ice peaks of the Antarctic wilderness, Hanger's eyes burned at him. And suddenly, all the magic of the moment dissolved into tremors of apprehension; a sense of underlying wrongness, a reinforcement of his first impression that, somewhere behind Hanger's cold blue eyes, an unknowable darkness lurked.

And then it was over. The music ended, and the unseemly feeling dissolved into dreamlike, hazy memory. The audience rose and the conductor bowed, and applause shook the walls of the auditorium until Kravitz thought his eardrums could take no more. The house lights came up and he could see them: all those bodies, all those hands beating together in a frenzied chorus of unconditional gratitude — surely out of proportion to the reality of the performance itself!

Now, his only remaining fear was that of being exposed to the audience; that peculiar sensation of stage fright that tortured him, yet lured him time and again to play to those who would come to witness.

Then, John Hanger was holding out his hand to him, beckoning him to take a bow. *But why?* He was just a violinist, an accomplished, yet undistinguished component of the orchestra as a whole. But next to him, young Bryan Jennings was clapping and smiling at him, and over in the brass section, Bert Hoffman's face positively glowed, his hands adding measurably to the thunderous applause. What had he done? He had only played the violin, as it was meant to be played. Nothing extraordinary there.

Yet the audience would not release him from his obligation. Finally, he bowed low, never understanding why, only realizing that this formality was required of him, and the hundreds of eyes in the hall would never release him until he had satisfied their expectations. He knew he should be pleased. Honored. Flattered. Yet he felt only bewilderment.

Finally it was over. The curtain closed, the lights dimmed, and the orchestra was sequestered behind its shield of heavy fabric.

"Jacob!" cried Bert Hoffman, rushing up to him. "I've never heard such magic coming from those strings before! What a show! What hands! You have surpassed yourself!"

"I . . . I just played," he managed, smiling broadly in spite of himself. "The entire orchestra was brilliant. No one can be singled out."

"Perhaps," Hoffman said. "Except for him." He pointed to the giant who still stood at the front of the stage with his head lowered, apparently gathering his breath.

Around them, the musicians had begun packing their instruments amid rounds of congratulations to one another. Kravitz placed his own violin carefully into its battered but sturdy case and shook hands with his friend. "I will meet you later," he said. "I must have a word with our illustrious conductor."

"Very well. We will *tsimis* tomorrow, no?"

"Sure, sure." Kravitz picked up his case and approached John Hanger rather tentatively, almost afraid of disturbing the great man in his reverie. But he finally cleared his throat and the cold blue eyes opened. The huge face split into one of those impossible grins.

"Mr. Kravitz," purred the silky voice. "You were magnificent. Magnificent! It is hard to believe you are playing with a group of local amateurs. Did you miss your calling by never joining a professional, touring symphony?"

"You're too kind," he replied softly. "But I have never seen anyone conduct with such intensity, such style. And you seem to have made a special effort to encourage me. *Only* me. Why would this be?"

"I merely wished to convey my appreciation, Mr. Kravitz. No one else here has exhibited such finesse, or such devotion to the music. You truly do love the strings."

"I can't deny that."

"Mr. Kravitz, I would be honored if you would come to my home to share a toast with me. I have wine, brandy . . . whatever you prefer."

"That's kind of you. I have never even inquired — do you live nearby? I don't have a car."

"I live very near here. An easy walk, and the night air will do us both good." He withdrew a handkerchief from his tuxedo jacket and wiped his brow — the most mundane of gestures, which, to Kravitz, seemed an almost reassuring affirmation of the giant's humanity. "The air seems very close here. I hope I didn't overexert myself."

"All these bodies generated some heat. I have never seen it so packed. You yourself made quite the impression on the audience, I'm sure."

Hanger nodded, a mere shade beneath arrogance. "I am always compelled to give my best. Now, will you accept my offer of a drink? I confess . . . I would appreciate the company."

Kravitz remembered his own assertion that Hanger must be a lonely man. No doubt he wished to share his success with someone. Who more natural than the one who had made the greatest contribution — at least in his own mind? "All right," he said with a little smile. "It would be my pleasure."

"One moment, and we shall be off."

Kravitz gave him a little bow and waited while the big man lumbered away, most likely to freshen himself. This was the opportunity, he thought; he could freely ask some questions about John Hanger's background without seeming to pry. He would merely be showing friendly curiosity about a professional colleague with whom he might be working on a regular basis.

A few moments later, Hanger returned and beckoned Kravitz to accompany him. As they left via the rear stage door, he noticed the big man's unblinking, blue eyes. They seemed alight with anticipation, and Kravitz once again felt a little twinge of uneasiness about this leviathan of a man. He could hardly change his mind now without appearing hopelessly ill-mannered. Besides, others in the orchestra knew who he was with. Surely, this uneasiness was as foolish as his stage fright.

He heard a few childish giggles somewhere nearby. Looking toward the sidewalk on Lincoln, he saw several youngsters dressed as devils, ghosts, and witches, all carrying bags of their evening's treats, laughing and making their way up the street.

It was after ten o'clock. Wasn't it too late to be out trick-or-treating?

Swallowing hard, he clicked his tongue, tucking his vague suspicions into the dark corners of his mind, telling himself that, after such a promising show as tonight, John Hanger's foremost consideration would be making sure his prized violinist would be around for many more performances to come.

*T*he first thing Kravitz saw as he entered the almost absurdly tiny basement apartment was a small Star of David etched above the door frame. The flat was merely an efficiency with a single bed (hardly large enough for such a man, he thought), a kitchenette littered by a few clean but haphazardly stacked dishes, a large reclining chair and a cloth-covered dining table. Tall bookshelves — filled to overflowing — made up one wall; the one window facing the street was barred and dingy, covered by a yellowing diaphanous drape. There was no television or stereo or any other modern electronic equipment that he might have expected from an audiophile.

The whole place seemed quite out of character for the man. Given the giant's cultured manner and expensive dress, Kravitz would have expected little less than opulence.

Hanger politely took Kravitz's coat and hung it from a peg on the wall next to the front door. "Would you care for a glass of wine? Or would you prefer a brandy?"

"A brandy, I think," Kravitz replied uncomfortably. The big man took a decanter from a shelf next to the refrigerator and poured a polite portion into two large snifters. "Are you Jewish, Mr. Hanger?" he asked at last.

"No, I am not a Jew, Mr. Kravitz. However, I have what you might call a certain history with the Children of Israel." Kravitz almost started at the epithet. "I have a unique appreciation for the antiquity of the culture, for the civilization whence the modern Jewish community sprang. You are not Orthodox, I take it."

Kravitz chuckled. "No, I fear I have not been so faithful over the course of my adult life. I suppose I have regrets in this regard. But then, who doesn't?"

"You came from the old country originally?"

"I was born in Milwaukee. To some, that is the old country."

Hanger laughed and sipped his brandy. Kravitz took a swallow of his own. It was sweet and delicious, the burn in his throat quick and numbing. The giant then struck a match, and Kravitz feared he was going to light one of his filthy cigarettes. But instead, Hanger turned to a small table next to his recliner and lit a short black candle that gave off the scent of cinnamon and honeysuckle.

"I suspect, Mr. Kravitz, that you are bewildered by my living quarters. I am sure you must have had different expectations."

Somewhat taken aback, Kravitz could only nod. "Well, I am not one to judge."

"No, of course not." Hanger drained his snifter and poured another. Without asking, he took Kravitz's and refilled it as well. "This is merely one of many places I use for shelter. I move about as my needs change. I shall no doubt be seeking a new abode in the near future."

"Your travels," Kravitz said with a weak nod. He had begun to feel lightheaded — moreso than he would have expected from a single snifter of brandy. "But surely, you plan to perform with the orchestra again, don't you?"

"There will be more performances."

At the distant reaches of his perception, Kravitz heard a dull roar building, like a train approaching through a long tunnel. He slid into one of the chairs at the dining table. "I'm sorry, Mr. Hanger. Suddenly I feel a bit discombobulated."

"Yes."

The cold blue eyes were now glaring at him, curiously, appraisingly. The whole room seemed to blur, with only the huge silhouette remaining in partial focus. "What . . . what's going on?"

"You are soon to have your shining moment, Mr. Kravitz. The performance of a lifetime. The performance that will be your legacy. *Jew.*"

A horrible chill passed down Kravitz's spine. But his limbs had frozen, and the thunder in his head increased with every beat of his heart. "Hanger . . . you have poisoned me!"

From the cavernous chest rose something between a laugh and a growl. "Poison? Oh, no, Mr. Kravitz. Merely an anesthetic to facilitate your conveyance to your new stage. In a few moments, you will feel nothing. Rest easy, my friend. The drug itself is quite harmless."

Kravitz's lungs struggled for air; the room began to spin and the roaring now drowned all other sound. As he tried to stop the mad reeling, he gazed at the tiny frame bed in the corner. It was too small for such a giant, and it was not bowed in the middle, as it should have been had John Hanger ever so much as lain there. Surely, that bed had never been used — not by this man.

He tried to speak Hanger's name, but nothing escaped his lips, not even a whisper. He saw blazing, golden eyes, and grotesque, pursed lips spreading into a grin that split the huge face from cheek to cheek, exposing a row of teeth that ended in razor sharp points.

A living, blazing jack-o'-lantern face moving steadily closer to his own. . . .

The last thing he remembered was the smooth, silky voice of the maestro breaking through the thunder and whispering in his ear, *"Shalom."*

*J*acob Kravitz slipped back into consciousness to the sound of muted, almost melodious moaning coming from somewhere nearby. His eyes fluttered open, but darkness replaced darkness, and he could feel only frigid air around him. As his nerves began to reactivate, he realized he was lying on his back on some cold, rough surface – *stone,* he thought. And the first moan hed heard was joined by another, then another. Low, masculine voices, weary and full of pain, those uttering them quite unseen and possibly as incognizant of their surroundings as he.

His throat felt dry and raw, but after gathering a lungful of air, he finally managed to utter, "Hello? Where am I?"

A moment later a weak voice replied, "Who is that?"

"Tell me where I am," he groaned.

"I don't know," came the low whisper. "Who are you?"

"I am Jacob Kravitz."

"Kravitz! My God, my God, it's me. Weintraub."

"Weintraub!" He could feel his energy beginning to return little by little. He tried to move his arms but found them pinioned by something cold and unyielding. *Steel.* "Stan, what is this place?"

A familiar, chilling, silky voice now rose out of the darkness. "My friends," it purred. "The Children of Israel. Welcome to your new stage."

"Hanger!"

"An adopted name, but feel free to use it. I have known many names. But the soul has only one name, and mine, both soul and name, have been preserved for eternities that you could not imagine. There are many of you here now . . . all collected by my own hand. Tonight, you shall make a joyful noise, as decreed by the very word of the Lord, your God. Tonight, on the very night that glorifies those who were once proclaimed false. This night, now so ironically termed 'hallowed.'" A low chuckle wafted through the darkness. "It *shall* be a hallowed evening."

"What kind of madness is this?" whispered Kravitz.

A pair of cold blue eyes appeared in the darkness, disembodied, gleaming. "The madness of so many centuries, Mr. Kravitz. I was a King in Moab, until my rightful place was usurped by the Children of Israel. And I was persecuted for the worship of false gods, and driven out of my homeland. And when I sought to reclaim what was mine, I enlisted the services of the sorcerer, Balaam, only to be betrayed when he himself became a servant of Israel's arrogant Father. And seeing this, my friends, those who *I* worship granted me the means to avenge myself upon our mutual enemy — through those such as yourself."

"Balak," hissed Kravitz. "You refer to the story of Balak."

"For an unorthodox man, you know your scripture, Jacob Kravitz. The name of this soul is indeed Balak . . . Jew. And this soul has passed through the ages, in many guises, allying itself to those who would smite Israel's children, and their Father Jehovah. Soon, my friends, you will learn the truth of that which was once called false."

From somewhere far away, the faintest flickering gleam, possibly from torches or candles, illuminated the walls of whatever chamber enclosed them, walls of rough-hewn stone that rose into pure darkness far above. They could only be underground, Kravitz thought — but *where? How?* Bound on a slab next to him, he saw the withered, naked form of his friend Weintraub, his head rolling slowly back and forth. Beyond the old conductor, he could see the pale shapes of countless other bodies, splayed on stones just as he was.

Before he could speak, a deep vibration passed through the slab beneath him, then another. A heavy booming . . . like great footsteps shuddering through the earth, reverberating through the chamber. And in his field of vision, far above, something began to take form; a tall, spindly shape, something inhuman but walking, with cold eyes of blue like those of John Hanger . . . but so much larger, burning icily high above.

More heavy vibrations followed, and a sulfurous, fetid odor washed over Kravitz as more of the half-seen silhouettes appeared in the darkness around him. The low voice of John

Hanger now chanted, "Ia, ia, gh'nagh ngai agkha nyem r'lyea . . . *selah!*"

As the terrible stench swirled through the air, infiltrating Kravitz's lungs, he heard Hanger say, "The breath of the Old Ones shall keep you alive and aware for countless days, much in the way it has preserved my own life. Our respective fates, however, shall be very different. In the days of Moab, there were special punishments meted out by the Children of Israel to worshippers of false gods. Now, in keeping with your faith, the *true* Gods shall mete out that same punishment to you."

In the flickering light, Kravitz saw John Hanger's huge silhouette appear above him, standing on a raised dais. The great arms rose as if to conduct, and a moment later Kravitz heard a familiar voice cry out nearby; Stan Weintraub. He turned his head to see a vague shadow swirl down from above and encircle his old friend's arms like the legs of a monstrous spider. A burst of flame erupted in the air above Weintraub's prone figure, and suddenly he loosed a scream of raw and pure agony. A long gash had opened in his chest, and thick stream of hot sparks fell from the fireball into the bloody wound. The spidery shadows quickly encircled the mutilated torso, closing the gash. The stench of charred flesh soon mixed with the sulfurous odor of demon's breath.

"The Children of Israel sewed burning coals into deep cuts in the bodies of my people, as punishment for their faith. And so it shall be for all of you — for time immeasurable. Now, my friends . . . let the orchestra play." The blue eyes of John Hanger — Balak — gazed deeply into Kravitz's. *"This,* my friend," he said softly, "is truly to be your finest perform-ance."

As a fireball suddenly burst into life above Kravitz's head, he saw a spidery shadow forming around it, slowly lowering itself toward him. He saw the maestro lift his arms and draw the first musical note in the air as, all through the darkness, the chorus of agonized screams began.

Jacob Kravitz's voice soon rose above the rest, in a virtuoso solo, while the cold blue eyes of the Moabite Gods gazed rapturously at him from high above. For the first time in all his years of performing, his fears of failing in front of his audience were quickly, wholly forgotten.

Petey in La-La-Land

Officer Villard had taken just about all he could take of the falsetto whining from the seat next to him. So they wouldn't have to talk, he had allowed Petey Sowyers, the snitch, to turn on an oldies station. To Villard's chagrin, the Sow, as he was affectionately called, turned out to be a compulsive singer, whistler, hummer, drummer, and general noisemaker, especially when anything by Diana Ross came on. Villard had already made whistling a capital crime; the nasal vocalizations were about to go the same way.

"Hey, Petey. Shut the hell up."

"I'm so sorry. I didn't realize it bothered you," Petey said with an effeminate lisp. "I'm tense."

"I know you are. Just look out the window and make no noises with your body."

Petey scratched his fastidiously brushed but dandruff-riddled beard, gave Villard one of his "I may be an asshole, but it's all natural" smirks, and focused on the dirty streets passing by just below them. "I don't like this neighborhood, Roy. It's diseased."

"Welcome to the world, chief."

Petey didn't use drugs, illicit or otherwise, and had a constant cold. Villard tried counting the seconds between sniffs, but never got past one-thousand-three. After having ridden in the squad car with him for nearly fifteen minutes, Villard had decided that Petey was absolutely the most annoying soul he had ever met. But what Central Command wanted, Central Command got, and that meant Petey rode in Villard's car.

Petey didn't like guns, either. "Look here," Villard said. "When we get there, you're going to use that weapon like you know what you're doing. I'm not out here to get killed because you're a fuck up. Got me?"

"That's not very nice, Roy. You don't like me, do you?"

"Bravo, asshole."

Petey scrunched his face up, dejected. He gazed at the nearly gutted buildings of Inglewood passing by just below, and when a Four Tops song came on the radio, he joined in, his voice abruptly diving an octave too low as the harmonies rose. Following the 4/4 beat, Villard reached across and gave Petey a sound slap to the face in sync with the crash of cymbals. "I mean it."

Petey sighed heavily and turned toward the window, pretending to take an interest in the graffiti scrawled over the neighborhood walls. According to the brains at HQ, Petey was the leading expert on local cults, having once been a member of the Bahai Jazz Residue: a short-lived bunch of good-health fanatics whose surviving members disbanded when they discovered that their favorite means of subsistence — a homemade, supposedly all-natural jello — gave them worms that devoured their insides. Pity the Sow hadn't succumbed, Villard thought; he'd probably whistled the little mutants right to death.

Villard swung the air car to the right, cruising down La Brea toward West Hollywood. A gaggle of blighters were gathered on the sidewalk around a guru, scarcely taking notice of the police vehicle bearing down on them. It looked like they might be dealing cock hash; this was the neighborhood for it. Villard slowed and came to hover a dozen or so meters above them. He tapped Petey on the shoulder.

"Are any of them Shriekers?"

Petey squinted at the group, some of whom had begun to meander away, ostensibly occupied with other, legitimate business. "That looks like Hirsch Petrasik," he said, pointing to a stubby figure next to the guru. "And the grayhair is Alvito Scarrus. He's one of John Hanger's dealers."

"Then we will talk," Villard said, and cut the cruiser lifters, lowering the car gently to the road. As the hydraulic doors hissed open, Villard activated the zone scanner, which would pinpoint anyone in line of sight who might bring a weapon to bear while the car's occupants were outside, then hit him with a lethal disrupter burst. The scanner had saved Villard's life at least twice.

Petey disembarked with a look of trepidation. The Shriekers were a relatively new cult who sought spiritual purity through sexual perversion and violence, hence their quaint nom de guerre. The Shriekers had recently begun dispatching missionaries into the field, converting few, but baptizing multitudes. Just two days ago, a pair of Shriek brothers had witnessed to a young socialite from Beverly Hills, sodomized her, and send her to the great beyond with a stick of dynamite lodged in her bowels. Central had given Villard the task of putting a stop to such unpleasantness.

A few of Petey's old brothers had joined the Shriek Church, possibly inspired by the worms in their systems to go out in style. Villard saw a look of relief cross the Sow's face when his scoping of the crowd failed to identify any of his familiars.

Villard slowly approached the guru and his number one. The stubby Petrasik whispered something to Scarrus, then waddled up to intercept Villard and his straggling partner.

"Good morning, Mr. Officer sir." Petrasik spoke with a thick Eastern European accent. "And to you, too, Mr. Man."

"What're you selling out here, Hirsch?" Villard asked. "It wouldn't be some of that hard-on stuff, would it?"

"Oh, but no. Coffee. We have coffee." He reached into the pocket of his jacket and withdrew a small brown bag. "See? Can't get coffee in this neighborhood, so Mr. Scarrus brings some from Pasadena."

Villard took the pack and sniffed it. It wasn't cock hash, a hallucinogenic the Shriekers favored because of its unique side-effect that gave men a rock-hard erection for a period of hours. Coffee indeed.

"Here you go, Petey," he said, tossing the pack to the Sow. "It's on me."

"Aren't you going to buy a cup of coffee, Mr. Officer?" Petrasik looked hurt. "It's a cold morning."

"Sorry, Hirsch," he said, giving the graybeard who sat on the sidewalk a quick once-over. "I want to talk to your man there."

"Mr. Scarrus doesn't talk to police. I talk instead, eh?" He stepped in front of Villard.

"Take a number, Hirsch. You're next in line." He gave the smaller man a gentle shove, just enough to set him off-balance. Petrasik stumbled awkwardly, then scurried back into Villard's path.

"Hey, are you the boss of the world? I already say Mr. Scarrus won't talk to you."

Villard smoothly drew his pistol from his side holster and aimed its snout at Petrasik's. "Hirsch. Move."

Behind him, Petey squeaked in fright. Petrasik eyed the barrel thoughtfully and with a sigh took one step sideways. He bowed curtly and lifted an arm towards Scarrus. "He will see you now."

Villard nodded his thanks and approached the seated man, lowering his gun but not reholstering it. A semicircle of bowls filled with packets of coffee and several paper cups surrounded Scarrus like battlements. An urn of hot water bubbled behind him. The graybeard must have been about sixty, his features hidden amid creased folds of withered skin. Shaggy brows hung low over his eyes, which burned brightly in their deep sockets.

"What have we got here, Mr. Scarrus? A little hash with our coffee?"

"G'wan, gi' fucked. Sella coffee only, no hash."

Villard reached for one of the bowls, picked it up and pulled out a packet, then dropped the bowl on the pavement. Its loud shatter drew a spiteful hiss from the old man's lips. Villard tore open the packet and emptied the powder into his palm. Amid the deep umber granules, a few dull brown lumps nestled like dried beetles.

"Must be Colombian, Alvito." He tossed the powder over his shoulder into Petey's face. Petey sneezed. Villard's gun barrel rose and settled itself on the bridge of Scarrus' nose. "Stand up."

"Sumshit," the old man growled, then painfully rose, wary of the gun staring so intently at his brain. He swayed slightly as he stood, and raised his arms to maintain his balance.

"Petey, come here. Open his coat up."

Reluctantly, Petey approached the guru, and with trembling hands, took hold of the shabby overcoat. He unfastened the sole button, and opened the coat. Scarrus wore a pair of loose-fitting canvas trousers, and from between his legs protruded a stiff divining rod. Petey gasped as if he'd been goosed.

"Guess what, Mr. Scarrus. You're busted."

"So wutzit to ya, Mr. Shithead. John Hanger gonna mow you ass down."

Villard pulled his cuffs from his belt and easily looped one end over Scarrus' outstretched right arm. The cuff beeped, and closed tightly around the wrist. The old man's eyes bulged as current buzzed through his body, paralyzing his limbs. If someone tried to remove the cuffs or take him away before another police unit came to deactivate them, a lethal electrical charge would take him out, as well as anyone in contact with his body.

"So, Alvito. Where is John Hanger?"

The glaring eyes nearly popped out of their sockets. Scarrus' lips twisted into a grimace. "Gi'thefuckouta my face, you. Hanger gonna burn you ass, you moo-fucker."

Petrasik stomped up to Villard's side. "You're not supposed to do this, Mr. Officer. You have no warrant."

"Hirsch, I don't need a warrant to bust a man dealing shit on the street. Guess what else. You're busted too."

Sudden fear blazed in Petrasik's bloodshot eyes. "Oh, no, I only sell coffee here. You got nothing on me."

"Hey, Petey," Villard called. "You want to open Hirsch's coat for me?"

"No, wait, wait," Petrasik grumbled. "Since what time of day is it a crime to be horny, eh?"

"I don't see any beautiful ladies lined up to give you a blow job, Hirsch. Or are you fantasizing about Petey here?"

"Roy!" wailed the Sow.

"Sorry. Now, Hirsch. Where's John Hanger? You know. John. Hanger."

"How would I know where is John Hanger? He's no personal friend of mine."

"Is that so, Petey?"

"Not . . . according to my sources," he stammered. "I

understand Mr. Petrasik sometimes . . . oh, dear . . . has some relations with him."

Villard raised an eyebrow. "You heard him, Hirsch. You going to call Petey a liar?"

"Well, I —" he broke off as the gun barrel scrutinized his nose. "So, I only see him once in a moonlight. I don't know where he is now."

"And when was the last moonlight you saw him?"

"Uh, maybe, uh, last night."

"Where?"

Petrasik tried to back away from the insistent pressing of the gun barrel, but found his retreat blocked by the rigid Mr. Scarrus. "Uh, I think it was at Broadway Cannon's. On Wilshire."

Villard looked at Petey. "You know the place?"

"It's one of the Shrieker temples. The Jazz used to meet there sometimes."

"Is Hanger there now?"

Petrasik's eyes radiated a seemingly inordinate amount of terror. He shook his head. "Wouldn't know."

"I'll take that for a 'yes.' Give me your arm."

"Hey, what for?"

Villard took hold of Petrasik's right wrist and handed Petey his pistol. "Aim it at his head. If he so much as flinches, enlighten him."

Petey looked at the weapon dubiously before taking it. "Is the scanner going to zap me?"

"Not unless you point it at me." Villard withdrew a small injector shaped like a ballpoint pen from his pocket, placed the tip against Petrasik's forearm and pressed the plunger. With a hiss, it released a radioactive compound into Petrasik's bloodstream that would allow the police to track him anywhere in the city.

"You're violating my constitution," Petrasik mumbled. "And all for coffee."

"That's pretty rude, considering I'm not taking you to jail. But you might want to watch who you party with. They find out you've been inked, they might get a little mad at you."

Villard took his gun from Petey and turned back toward the air car. As they started to climb aboard, a sharp whooshing sound roared from the roof of the car, followed by a high-pitched ringing. Villard spun around and saw Petrasik topple, a small handgun falling from his grip. As he struck the pavement, the top of his skull popped off like the cork of a wine bottle, loosing a frothy slush of blood and cranial fluid. Some pinkish flecks of brain splattered the Scarrus-statue's trousers.

"Damn fool," muttered Villard as he slid into his seat. "He should have had decaf."

The Sow stared at Villard incredulously. "Roy, that's cold."

*B*roadway Cannon's looked deserted when the cruiser pulled up to its front entrance. After dark, the old saloon attracted most of the neighborhood's vermin, but in daylight, it was shunned as if it housed a leper colony. The car's sensors, however, detected at least one occupant.

"He should have known," Petey whined. He hadn't shut up about Hirsch since they'd left Burbank. "He *had* to have known."

"Petey, when a man like that gets inked, his life on the street is forfeit. He knew that."

"You saw how scared he was. And not of you."

"It was his choice to be where he was in the first place." Villard punched his location into the computer tied to Central dispatch, requested backup. The computer replied that no backup would be available for at least an hour. "Shit." He opened his door and stepped out, leading with his gun. It was fully loaded and he carried a pair of hundred-round clips in his pocket. Once he went inside, the zone scanner would be useless. He pulled his bullet- and beam-proof assault vest from the back of the car and strapped it on, then grabbed his night-vu goggles, figuring they might be necessary inside. He gave Petey a Volte pistol with one clip. He didn't worry about Petey turning on him, because now that they had been seen together, Petey would need Villard for his own protection.

"Inside, you say nothing. You don't hum. You don't whistle. One wrong breath and I'll shoot you myself."

"I know, Roy, I know. Don't you want to wait for another unit?"

"Petey, I don't get paid to wait around for back-up. Let's go."

The Sow gulped, then fell in behind Villard, who crept quickly but silently toward the steel-plated doors. He tugged the handles, not unexpectedly finding them locked.

"Is there another way in?"

"The office door is around the side."

They proceeded down the alley on the right of the building, where Villard saw a small stairway leading down a few meters ahead. He went down on tiptoe, tried the door, and this time found an entrance. His instincts warned, *trap!* but he fought them back, knowing that retreating was not an option. He slipped into the dark interior, and waved the reluctant Sow in after him. A dank, sour odor assailed his nostrils. He pulled the night-vu goggles over his eyes and scanned the room. It was a small office, empty except for a few boxes piled in the corners. Tattered cobwebs hung from the overhead fluorescent fixtures. On the left-hand wall, a dark blotch formed a weird pattern, and taking a step closer, Villard saw that it was a stylized phallus, scrawled in what looked disturbingly like blood — the emblem of the Church of the Shriek.

They moved out of the room, into a dark, featureless hallway. A closed door lay at one end, a stairway leading down at the other. Petey pointed to the door and whispered. "That's the saloon — or the sanctuary, whichever it's being used for. It's probably empty now."

Villard nodded in agreement, and turned to the right, toward the stairway. He paused when he heard a low scuffling sound coming from somewhere below. When the noise did not repeat itself, he continued on his way. At the top of the stairs, he stopped and peered down. Nothing but more darkness, impenetrable even with his goggles.

Gun at the ready, he started down. His mind reviewed what he knew about John Hanger, the cult leader. A foreigner of indeterminate origin who'd come to the U.S. at the turn of the century, Hanger had shortly thereafter become known to the authorities as a drug runner and financier of numerous pornographic enterprises. He had never been arrested — he moved constantly and was suspected of having murdered any number of investigators who had attempted to nail him.

Now, six months after he had settled in L.A., his Church of the Shriek had become a real nuisance to the police department and an embarrassment to the mayor.

So they had put Villard on it. And they expected results.

That man now lurked somewhere in the dark corridors below. Broadway Cannon's didn't look very large from outside but, apparently, beneath it hid a labyrinth of passageways and chambers; on all sides, Villard could see more portals, all disappearing into dark distances. And decorating the walls, the ubiquitous Shriek symbol: a bloody reminder of who owned this territory.

John Hanger reputedly kept no bodyguards. That much seemed evident, but Villard would be surprised if he and Petey hadn't already been detected by any manner of electronics. His goggles would make any laser or photoelectric sensors visible to him, and the zone scanner would jam any sonic traps within a kilometer, but there were still ways his own defenses could be bested. He had to assume Hanger knew they were here.

"Roy," whispered Petey. He pointed down a corridor to the right. "A light."

Villard nodded, and turned toward the tiny light in the distance. It looked like an open door somewhere ahead. He listened for a moment, heard nothing, then proceeded. At fifty meters, they stopped; Villard had seen a shadow moving inside the illuminated doorway.

From that direction came a low, whispered moan. It gradually rose to a rhythmic chant. *"L'ai elai ima l'ai elai omat. . . ."*

"Prayer," whispered Petey.

Villard motioned for Petey to remain in place. He moved forward stealthily, gun barrel homing on the open door. A second before he reached it, the repetitive droning stopped. Villard leaped into the room, swinging his weapon in the direction he anticipated as the source of the chant.

No one was in the room.

The only furnishings were a small wooden desk covered by white linen, with two tall, burning candles atop it, and a weirdly-shaped ottoman in the center of the room, supported on four legs that looked like a lizard's, its cushions molded to resemble a human torso. The walls seemed to be a sculpted frieze of indistinguishable figures — tangled and twisted into an abstract mosaic — until Villard realized that the shapes were actually pieces of human anatomy, randomly pieced together. Arms, legs, hands, skulls, penises, even mummified internal organs — all nailed to the wall and wreathed in barbed wire.

No doubt the sacrificial remains of those John Hanger had failed to convert.

Villard swallowed the lump in his throat and studied every inch of the room. There was no other exit, at least that he could see. The ceiling and floor appeared solid, with no telltale lines or sectionals to indicate a hidden door.

He heard a sharp gasp behind him and whirled. Petey stood in the doorway, his eyes bulging as if they had been inflated with air. "Eeee!" he peeped.

Villard pushed him back. "Stay out of here." He looked both ways down the corridor, studying the darkness. His goggles revealed nothing.

Then, some indeterminate distance to the right, another light flickered on. And the low chant began again. *"L'ai elai ima l'ai elai omat. . . ."*

"Jesus," Villard whispered. He pulled a tiny shocker limpet from his belt pouch and activated its sensor beam with a punch of a small button. If anyone passed through the door while the shocker was activated, he would get a 3,000-volt thrill.

"Watch out behind us," he said. "Hanger may not be the only one here." Petey nodded shakily.

As they crept onward, the sing-song voice seemed to grow more urgent; but as it reached a crescendo, it suddenly fell silent. Villard found his fingers aching from gripping his pistol so tightly.

He suddenly froze in his tracks. A silhouette had materialized near the light ahead. It looked tiny — and it wasn't human. An animal of some kind, he thought.

The figure began to slowly move toward them, making no sound. As it approached, Villard swore it was increasing in size — not because it was moving closer, but because it was actually growing. In the dimness, Villard couldn't make out any details, but the thing also seemed to be changing shape.

It was twenty meters ahead now, and bore the form of a tall, broad-girthed man. Villard could hear slow, deliberate footfalls, but they seemed much too soft for the massive, oncoming figure. He looked left and right, saw an open doorway just ahead to right. He glanced inside, found it to be a small, empty chamber. He slipped into it, pulling Petey behind him. He crouched, leveled the gun, and called out, "Police! Freeze!"

Villard's warning rang like the blow of a hammer through the hallway. The huge silhouette ignored it, moving steadily closer with long, purposeful strides. Through his goggles, Villard saw a face beginning to form on the completely bald, football-shaped head — two gaping, pale eyes beneath bony, hairless brows, a crude, lumpy mound of a nose, and an incredibly wide, jagged opening of a mouth, leering as if it had been carved into the flesh with a dull knife.

"Three seconds, Hanger," Villard called, remembering the features he had seen from the one existing photograph of the man. The photo had conveyed nothing of the strangely *artificial* look the face wore, almost as if it belonged to a grotesque mannequin. Villard's finger tightened on the trigger. The shape continued to advance.

BOOM!

Villard had aimed at the ceiling above Hanger's head. A great shower of sparks rained down on the big man. Shards of tile and slivers of steel clattered to the floor, some striking the hulking shape, which finally stopped and shrugged its great shoulders to dislodge some of the debris that had fallen on him.

The head turned. Pale, dead-looking eyes regarded Villard incuriously. They gazed past him toward Petey. Villard felt his companion shrinking into himself.

The lower jaw fell open. "Hello, Officer," a soft voice said. The lips had not moved. "Hello, Petey. Have you come to join our Church too?"

Villard felt a cool chill creep across the back of his neck. He kept the gun aimed directly at Hanger's head, but for the first time in his career, his hand trembled. There would be no arresting this — *thing.*

Hanger took a heavy step toward them. Petey scrambled

backward, and Villard involuntarily drew back as if he faced a coiled cobra. The leader of the Church of the Shriek wore a black suit with a curious, noose-shaped collar. His clothes barely contained his tremendous bulk, and if his demeanor were less threatening, he might have looked laughable. But Villard wasn't smiling.

"You know, Petey," said the low, smooth voice. "You can still save yourself. Merely forsake the law, and you may leave here with me."

"You're in no position to make such an offer," Villard said, his throat dry. "Your church is now closed. You're under arrest for murder, among other charges."

"Look behind you, Officer."

"No chance."

"Petey, tell him what's in the room."

The Sow spun around as the room was illuminated, seemingly by magic. Villard heard a small gasp. "What is it, Petey?"

"The walls," he said. "The walls!"

Villard stole a quick glance back, and his stomach lurched. In that flash, he'd seen that, instead of being bare, as they had been only moments before, the walls were now spiked with long, jagged pitons at half-meter intervals, floor to ceiling. Gray and pink shreds hung from some of them, many looking disturbingly fresh. Great splotches of darkened crimson covered the floor like a map of the continents.

Hanger took another step toward them. Petey gave Villard a questioning look, and his face seemed to wither. He dropped to the floor, prostrating himself before Hanger. "Take me," he cried. "I'll go with you!"

Villard didn't hesitate. The gun found Hanger's gaping mouth, exploded in a thundering boom. The massive body didn't so much as waver. Villard pulled the trigger again . . . and again . . . three times, the successive reports blasting his eardrums unmercifully. A writhing cloud of smoke spread like a barrier between gun and target.

From the smoke, a monstrous hand lunged forward, grasping Villard's vest at the collar and forcing him back. The mammoth head of John Hanger burst forth and expanded in Villard's field of vision until the face was all that existed. The jaw dropped again. A growling voice erupted from the throat. "You will now die."

Villard was driven backwards as if he'd been hurled by a catapult. A sudden, piercing pain shocked his entire body, white-hot agony, and he screamed, seeking the release of a now inevitable death.

He was impaled on several of the long spikes, each one a stabbing, mortal wound. He screamed again, but consciousness remained, it remained. . . .

He saw the tip of a piton protruding from his right shoulder . . . one from his lower right abdomen — amazingly, the spike had penetrated his vest — punctured liver, probably his stomach . . . left thigh . . . right calf. Blood began to pour from the end of each spike as if it were tap, forming crimson pools beneath his feet, which dangled half a meter above the floor.

His right hand still clutched the gun, but the arm was immobile. He couldn't even move his fingers.

Through a haze of hot pain, he saw Petey kneeling before the feet of the black-suited giant. He again heard the chant, *"L'ai elai ima l'ai elai omat. . . ."*

Then:

"Do you, Petey Sowyers, join this Church freely, forsaking all else, to give your life and soul to the master of the Shriek, from now until forever?"

"Yes. . . ."

"Do you know the true name of your Savior, He whom you must follow, denying all others?"

"Yes. . . ."

"Speak that name."

"It is . . . Balak, the Beast of Moab. It is . . . your name."

"I claim you, Petey Sowyers. I baptize you."

Villard saw Hanger's hand reach for the fly of his trousers. It was unzipped, pulled wide. And Petey was bathed in a thick, golden shower that splattered over and around him with the sound of summer rain. But the thing that extended from between Hanger's legs was not. . . .

Villard gave a feeble push with his one free leg, but succeeded only in drawing another scream from his own lips. Blood gushed freely from his wounds. The room was beginning to grow dark.

Sorry, Mr. Mayor, he thought. I guess you're going to remain embarrassed.

He could still move his left hand. He forced it to crawl toward his right, toward the gun that still hung from lifeless fingers. Three times he came within an inch, only to be beaten back by the pain.

"You are one with the body of Balak," the voice rumbled through the thunder that had begun in Villard's ears. "I welcome you to the Church of the Shriek." An outstretched hand fed something to the kneeling Petey, who gobbled it greedily. Cock hash. Then, the black silhouette turned and approached him. He was now beyond any terror or revulsion. Only moments of life remained. The pain was beginning to diminish.

"And you," said the voice. "Welcome to Gehenna."

Hanger's maw opened and an immensely powerful, inhuman shriek erupted from the dark pit of the throat. Then, the master of the Church disappeared as if he had never existed. For a moment, the room grew clear in Villard's vision. Petey stood in front of him, dripping, regarding him with sour enmity.

"You could never have guessed," Petey said. "He's lived for centuries. He has the power of the Gods of Sumer and Babylon. Of Egypt and of Leng. You're no match for that. Sorry, Roy. It's for the best, you know."

Villard gave him a weak, pained smile. "I know," he gasped. "So is this."

His left forefinger found the trigger. The recoil sent the gun flying from his grip, but its job was done. Satisfied, Villard let the comforting fingers of death caress him, take him.

And the new Shrieker dropped to his knees as a geyser of blood spewed from between his legs. At long last, for the first and only time in his pitiful life, Petey Sowyers hit that high note.

Now I Lay Me Down to Dream

"Do you remember life?"

*"S*he was gone for so many years. I don't know how long. A hundred or more. Perhaps centuries. But she was here last night. I heard her."

"There are stories. People have heard her before. Long, long ago, though."

"Who is she?"

Suzette gazed out the window, down the long slope into the sea of morning mist that hid the river. "I don't know. She told me, I think. But I can't remember."

Arthur St. Georges, her husband, and Gordon Hatcher, her brother, sat to either side of her cushioned wicker armchair. She took a sip from her champagne and orange juice. This was the first time she had ever visited her brother's house; a beautiful place, one she had immediately fallen in love with. The drawing room picture window overlooked the hedges and gardens leading down to the banks of the Susquehanna, providing an intoxicating view of the ridge known as South Mountain when fog didn't enshroud the house.

"What about . . . the *other?*" Her brother's emerald green eyes beckoned hers. He was afraid.

"The one that screams."

"Yes."

"I have no idea. I did not encounter it in the dreaming."

Her brother had dreamed of a thing with black feathers and a white, featureless face, a thing that wailed horribly in the night, only vaguely glimpsed as it swept across a star-speckled sky. She had dreamed of the girl who wept and told her story: a story that had since dissipated like a mist into dark forgetfulness. That the two were related there could be no doubt; the one dream fragment Suzette could remember was the girl expressing an awful fear of the feathered thing. And Gordon had been dreaming of *it* for more than a week. Suzette had slept little on her first night here, and when she had, the sounds of bitter crying tormented her to her soul.

Her husband said to Gordon, "You've lived here, what, about a year now? Have you ever experienced unusual things in this house before?"

"Thirteen months. And no, I can't recall ever having dreams like these. I had read about the weeping girl in the library, but those stories tell only about those who've heard her. I can't find any account of who she actually is — or was." He visibly suppressed a shudder. "And certainly nothing of the *other.*"

Suzette knew her husband to be a skeptic in all matters not confined to hard facts and figures, but he had shown none of his usual cynicism when she had related her dream; and her brother, in turn, told them of his own prolonged series of nightmares. Quite the contrary, Arthur seemed strangely upset that the siblings should be so deeply affected by these interwoven dreams.

Whereas she would have expected him to scoff at the suggestion of preternatural phenomena — to blame stress or too much caffeine or poor diet — Arthur's first reaction was concern for her well-being. "I know it was a long trip, and I'd hate to disappoint Gordon, but if you think staying here will be upsetting to you, we can go back home. Just say the word. The decision is yours, of course."

She laughed lightly. "Don't be silly. I wouldn't cut our visit short because of a bad night's sleep. There is a mystery in this that I find fascinating."

Her brother nodded in agreement and gazed thoughtfully

around at the room; at its high ceilings, the crystal chandelier, the huge stone fireplace, and the cherrywood mantel above it. "I would hate for you to leave so soon," he said softly. "And yes, I would like to see this odd situation come to its climax. Immediately."

Gordon's eyes belied his light-hearted tone. Fear and lack of sleep had turned his face haggard, his complexion a shade paler than usual. Suzette's brother had always been sensitive and soft-spoken, but never timid or self-conscious. He was 36, three years younger than she. His black hair was graying rapidly.

Suzette finished her morning drink and set the glass aside, trying to focus on the few, ever-dimming images that lingered from the night. No good, though; she could remember only an overall impression of sadness and dread, sans specific details. Unlike her brother, she felt no actual fear, merely its shadow, cast upon her by the weeper in her dreams.

But out of the corner of her eye, she detected movement in the mist outside. Seeking its source, her eyes fell upon a dark blot in the white veil: something that was moving across the lawn down by the riverbank. Gordon and Arthur also noticed the shape and craned their necks to peer after it. Alas, it soon moved away, to be swallowed by the thick vapor.

Turning to her brother, Suzette found that his face had assumed the same pallor as the fog. He excused himself and left the room, and moments later, from the direction of the kitchen, came the clink of glasses and the gurgle of drink being poured from a bottle.

*T*hree years ago, Gordon had bought this house, after his wife of over ten years was killed in a tragic automobile accident. It seemed much too large a place for a single man, Suzette thought, but perhaps it indicated Gordon's hope that he might not be alone forever. A large, two-story Victorian, over a hundred years old but in immaculate repair, the house reminded her very much of the place where she and Gordon had grown up, not far away in Wilkes-Barre — no doubt the main reason Gordon had chosen to purchase it.

After receiving a Masters Degree in Psychology in the early

80s, Gordon had settled with his wife in nearby Eatonville, preferring the quiet, rural northeastern Pennsylvania setting to a more progressive urban environment where his considerable education might be put to better use. He had also studied philosophy, the arts, literature; by the time he graduated, he had already published a number of critical essays in some prestigious academic journals. Several of the leading universities in the country had expressed an interest in adding him to their faculties, but he declined the offers, deciding to engage himself in his own studies on his own terms. Financially, neither he nor his sister would ever need outside employment, for they had inherited enough from their late parents to live comfortably for the rest of their lives.

Gordon was still lonely, Suzette knew. She didn't know exactly what activities occupied her brother's days, except that he had told her in their correspondence that he continued to write philosophical and theological essays for various scholarly journals. And he had proudly shown her the little publications in which his work appeared, though she had never taken the time to read them, the subject matter being quite outside her range of interests. She preferred the more down-to-earth philosophy – and practice – of helping young abused children, both financially and with her time, at some of the shelters and clinics in her hometown of Harrisburg.

During the afternoon, she took a walk through the terraced gardens beneath a cool Spring sun. Gordon owned forty-some acres along the river, most of it wooded, and from the garden, she recalled him saying, a narrow path led into the trees that came out by the riverbanks at the northern edge of the property. She decided to follow it for a while and had just stepped into the shadows when she heard her brother's voice calling her name.

She turned to find him trotting through the garden toward her, a little abashed smile on his lips. "I saw you from the house. Mind if I walk with you?"

"Of course not."

"Arthur wanted me to tell you he was going into Eatonville to look at the shops. I think the seclusion here makes him restless."

"It does. But I know he enjoys seeing you as much as I do."

"He's a good man. I like him."

"How are you feeling this afternoon? You still look peaked."

He nodded. "A good night's sleep would do me right. Maybe tonight, eh?"

"I hope so, for your sake." She took his hand and gave it an affectionate squeeze. "Gordon, what do you think these dreams mean? With your background in psychology, in philosophy, surely you have some theory."

He shrugged. "Some people believe there are symbols in dreams that are common to all human beings. That these archetypal figures reside in the collective unconscious, sometimes coming forth as the result of conflicts in a person's life. Sometimes these symbols may even be tied to specific places. As the tales go, your weeping woman has been heard — though never seen — by other people who have lived in this very place . . . even before the current house was built."

"And what do you think about that?"

"Well, it's a manageable theory. I can accept it much more easily than I can certain other possibilities."

"Like what?"

"Some believe that events may be trapped in time, in an endless loop, like a tape recording. And the strange things that people occasionally experience — and call 'ghosts' — are merely distorted reflections of things that happened a long time ago."

"What about the thing you've dreamed of? How would you account for that?"

Gordon shook his head and said softly, "Of course, there is a particular Christian view that ghosts are not the spirits of the dead at all — but are demonic visitations. Any resemblance to people who once lived is merely a masquerade."

His voice had gone so low that Suzette could barely hear him. And his hands were now trembling.

"This idea frightens you?"

He did not answer her question. He was looking into the darkness beneath the tall oaks beside the path ahead. Striding ahead of her, he went to one of the trees and knelt at its base. To her surprise, he scooped up a thick black mass in his hands and held them out for her to see. He clutched a bundle of large black feathers, each nearly a foot long.

"There is no bird in this area with feathers like these," he said.

She stared at them, speechless. He was surely mistaken.

"And sometimes," he whispered, "according to those who believe, the demon wears no mask at all."

*T*hat evening, the St. Georges retired early, Suzette from genuine weariness, Arthur from boredom — though not that he would admit as much. They had all drank a fair share of Gordon's fine selection of clarets, which Suzette hoped would be conducive to a sound sleep, especially for her brother. His nightmares must be severe indeed, she thought, for even under the influence of the wine, Gordon appeared agitated by the idea of going to bed. He told them he planned to stay up reading or writing for a while.

Her dreams began as soon as her head hit the pillow. From far, far away, the soft sound of sobbing drifted slowly nearer, occasionally broken by indecipherable words. She could see nothing but a field of complete blackness that occasionally appeared to ripple, like a satin sheet being stirred by something behind it. Eventually, a silvery fleck of light appeared in the distance, growing larger as if it were rushing toward her through a long tunnel.

"Help me," the voice moaned. "Please help me."

Suzette found that she possessed an unusual alertness — and was aware that she was dreaming. Accepting this, she called to the light, "Who are you?"

The only response was a long, heart-wrenching sob. Then, a moment later: "Oh, it is coming for me. Help me get away from it. Please, I beg you."

"Tell me who you are."

"Oh — I am dead! Oh, no — I am dead!" As if shattered by this realization, the weeper sobbed even louder.

"Where did you come from? Please tell me."

"I remember life," came the soft moan.

"Do you have a name?"

Again, only bitter weeping answered her. The light in the field of darkness had grown much larger, but she could discern no features within it. It seemed to swirl or pulsate slowly, like something alive — like some kind of luminous invertebrate adrift in the black depths of the ocean. Suzette sensed an awareness, as if unseen eyes within the cloudy shape were watching her intently, assessing her intentions.

"Oh, no . . . it is coming," came the soft voice. "Bring me out. Please do not let it take me."

"What is it? What's coming?"

"The screaming thing. Please . . . save me."

Suzette felt the gaze upon her turning away, moving toward some unknown point in the endless darkness. A quavering sigh hissed in her ears.

"I can see it. So black, with feathers, and claws. It will take me if I am left here. Won't you help me? Please help me."

"What must I do? How can I help you?"

"Accept me."

"I don't understand."

"Oh please, it is here. Oh, no, it is here!"

And Suzette suddenly bolted upright at the sound of an awful scream that rang through the darkness — shrill, but of masculine origin. Beside her, Arthur sat up with a gasp, eyes wide, his thick hair askew. "What the hell?" he groaned.

A second scream followed, as if in answer to the first — from *outside* the house. Somewhere far away, obviously, but loud enough to be heard even through closed windows.

"Wait here!" Arthur commanded, rising from the bed and hurrying to the door without bothering to don his robe and slippers. But Suzette slid from beneath her covers, padding on bare feet to his side to listen expectantly at the door. He did not protest.

"That was Gordon," she said. "But what about the other?"

Arthur opened the door without hesitation and stepped into the long, darkened hall. Nothing appeared amiss; pale moonlight streamed through the tall window above the stairs to the right, while at the other end, thick shadows concealed Gordon's closed bedroom door.

"Downstairs," she said.

Arthur crept toward the stairwell, listening intently, with Suzette at his heels. When they heard nothing further, they rushed down the stairs, headed for the drawing room. There, they found Gordon seated in his wicker chair facing the picture window, his hands rigidly clasping his knees, his head cocked like a bird's in an attitude of listening. Suzette turned on a lamp — but even its golden glow couldn't warm the icy, bone-white sculpture his face had become.

His lips quivered and his voice came out as a stammer: "You heard it, didn't you? I know you heard it."

Suzette knelt at his side, taking his cold hand in hers. "I heard you. And something else, outside."

"Could it have been a bird?" Arthur asked, peering out the window at pure darkness. "A whippoorwill, maybe, or an owl?"

"No," Gordon said. "It was no bird. I saw it. God, it was so close. I saw its face. But . . . God . . . it had no face!"

"Another nightmare!"

"No. At the window."

Arthur peered through the glass at the pitch blackness beyond. Suzette caressed her brother's hands, hoping to warm them. So cold! How could they be so cold? She kissed the back of each.

"I wonder if we'll hear it again," Arthur said. "There *was* something out there. We both heard it."

"A bird. It had to have been a bird of some kind," Suzette insisted weakly.

Arthur turned away from the window, unable to see a thing with the lamp burning in the room. He seemed to register Gordon's shocking appearance for the first time. "This man needs sleep. He must go to bed."

Suzette nodded, tears pooling in her eyes. "Arthur, can you help him to bed, please? Please?"

"Of course." Together, they each took hold of one of Gordon's arms and helped him to his feet. He seemed to have no energy, no will to move. But he allowed them to guide him toward the stairs, where he finally waved them away.

"I'm all right. I'll go by myself."

And he did begin making his way up, slowly, with Arthur just behind him, holding firmly to the rail with one hand in case Gordon stumbled. Suzette remained at the foot of the stairs, watching with worry, waiting for her husband and brother to disappear in the darkness above.

And as they did, she turned and went to the front door, unlocking it and opening it to a chilling gust that whipped into the foyer, lifting her hair and fluttering her nightgown.

The night was clear, the sky lit by countless brilliant stars, a thin slit of a moon smiling wryly at her from high above. She stepped out, closing the door behind her, peering across the misty gray gardens toward the riverbank. She could hear a faint rush of water from the unseen Susquehanna. Her eyes flitted back and forth, from the distant black wall of trees to the nearby low hedges to the ivy-covered trellises at the ends of the house. Something lurked out here, something that screamed, something that her brother heard — and that the weeper in her dreams feared.

So cold out here. But she barely felt it. And while fear groped determinedly for her, its fingers would not close upon her. She would not allow it.

But there was something else. Sadness. Melancholy. It hung here like a cerement, blown on the whispering wind, wrapping itself around her like a clinging silk web.

Whoever the weeping girl was, this was *her* place, this benighted landscape beneath the glittering stars. Had she been someone who had lived here God knew how many years before? Perhaps she had died here and her remains lay directly beneath Suzette's bare feet. The frigid grass tickled her soles, and strangely, she found herself compelled to lie down, to prostrate herself beneath the grinning moon, to offer herself to whatever might choose to accept her as a sacrifice. But this mood passed within seconds and she shrugged to herself, wondering why she should be seized by such a notion.

And the cold began to set in, working its way into her flesh, through the blood and muscles toward the bone. In a moment, she would have to return indoors.

"So, feathered thing," she said aloud. "What are you? Why do you make her weep?"

Only the whispering breeze deigned reply. So with an almost haughty flourish, she turned her back on the night and stepped back onto the covered veranda, realizing her husband would by now be wondering what had become of her. She took the cold doorknob in hand, and as she pushed the door open, from behind rose a distant, shrill cry — so much like the one that had violently roused her from sleep.

So much like her brother's voice raised in terror.

She did not look back. Nor take notice of the low, sobbing voice that softly called her name from the darkness.

*T*he next day, Suzette's memory of her dream encounter this time remained clear; she could recall the voice, the sobbing, the strange light in a black abyss. Gordon, on the other hand, seemed to remember very little or else preferred to forget it. That he had actually seen something in the window that frightened him terribly she could not doubt.

"There is no bird in this area with feathers like these."

Late in the morning, Suzette and Gordon took another walk, this time along the river, leaving Arthur to spend some quality time alone with the daily newspaper. Though spring had only begun to chase away winter, the region had already seen heavy rainfall and the river climbed high up its banks.

"I'm worried about you, Gordon. Maybe you should go away for a while. You could come back with us. We would be happy to have you stay as long as you wanted."

Gordon shook his head. "How can I run away from dreams?"

"There's something more than that here."

"Why is this happening?" he said, staring at the rushing river. "Why now?"

"It began as soon as you became aware of the stories of the weeping woman, didn't it?"

"Yes."

"What about the others – the ones who have experienced this before? You don't have any clue about them?"

"As I've said, none of them have ever told of such a thing as I've seen. Only of the woman. But still, it seems familiar, somehow. As if I have encountered it somewhere long ago – perhaps among my studies. I will have to research some of my old books to see what I can find." Gordon paused. Then: "If it were not so frightening, this experience would be exhilarating."

"It had to have started somewhere, with someone. If only it were possible to learn that much." Suzette sighed. "Even *she* does not give us a clue."

"I'm so tired."

"I know. I want you to think about coming home with us. We can leave anytime. We don't have to stay here."

"It's my home. I still love this place, you know. I want to be happy here."

"I want you to be."

They stopped walking. Gordon lifted his head, gazed at the tops of the trees arcing over the water. "It's out here, somewhere. A dream made flesh."

"Or feathers."

He smiled humorlessly. "Yes. That."

*A*s the sun died in the west and dinner reached its end, Suzette found herself unusually alert, as if some primal, instinctive fear of the night had been activated. Even with the things happening around her, she had so far remained basically unaffected. Perhaps this was how the terror had begun for Gordon.

He appeared more nervous and agitated than ever. Even Arthur now told him that leaving might be a good idea.

"It's a three-hour drive home," he said. "But we could leave now, if you want. There's no point in staying if this is what comes of it."

Gordon adamantly refused. "I'm not leaving. I cannot stay away indefinitely. What if I come back and everything is exactly the same? Or what if it follows me?"

"There's no denying that possibility," Arthur said. "But maybe it won't. Wouldn't it be worth taking a chance?"

"Would it follow you, Gordon? Does this phenomenon center on a person — you — or on this place?"

"How would I know? And don't forget, Suzette. It has touched you as well."

"I have not forgotten," she said softly, looking out the window at the purple twilight. The temperature in the house seemed to be dropping along with the sun.

"I will compromise," Gordon said at last. "If tonight the dreams are bad, I'll go back to your house and stay as long as you will have me. Fair?"

"Fair," Arthur agreed with a smile. "I can't imagine anything healthier for you."

*S*he appeared.

Light in the darkness, like before. And the voice. Sobbing. Calling Suzette's name.

"You know me."

"Yes."

"What is your name?"

No reply. Merely a low whimper coming from the light.

"Where do you come from?"

"Out of the fire."

Suzette felt the eyes on her. Searching. Seeking — something. "How can I help you?"

"Accept me. Please. It will be here soon."

There was such sadness in the voice Suzette could not help being moved to pity. The voice was strangely beautiful. So thin and wistful.

She felt a tugging somewhere within. Curiosity.

"Touch me."

The unseen eyes enveloped her. The darkness grew cold. And in a roaring flood, a whole new existence opened before her, washed over her — the life of another.

She was a young girl, living in a tiny house in the forest with her mother. Her father and brother were dead. The days and nights were lonely and frightful, and oftentimes the sounds of gunshots rang through the forest.

One day they came: the British army. The ones who had killed her father and her dear brother. Soldiers took their house, ate their food, though they had so little. One of them forced himself upon her, made her share his bed — the bed that had been her own.

Darkness, nighttime.

They slept. And stealthily, taking a knife from the kitchen, she slew the man who had conquered her; she cut his throat as he dreamed. And not stopping there, she had gone to the others and spilled their blood. They paid. They had to pay. They had killed her men.

But armies leave sentries. As her knife penetrated the flesh of a sleeping soldier, strong, hot hands grabbed her and threw her to the floor.

And moments later, the agony. Hot fire piercing her chest, her throat, as bayonets tore through her flesh, spilled her blood.

"Oh, no, I am dead."

"God!" Suzette cried silently. "And you are in Hell. Oh, no, no. . . ."

"Accept me. Please . . . accept me."

In the rush of grief that swept through her, Suzette reached out.

When she opened her eyes, it was still night. Arthur was sleeping next to her, restlessly, for he kept shifting positions and his breathing seemed labored. Pale, silver moonlight glowed through the drawn satin drapes, and from far away shrilled the whistle of a lonely train. Suzette sat up, eyes searching the room, letting them grow accustomed to the darkness.

A draw of breath came from a darkened corner of the room. She and Arthur were not alone.

She faintly made out the silhouette of a figure seated in the upholstered chair in the corner. The breathing grew deep — so heavy that it seemed to come from a great animal. Surely, not from her brother!

Reaching toward the window, she pulled aside the curtains, allowing the moonlight to shine in the room. The silvery beams crawled across the floor to where her brother was sitting.

He was dressed in his bathrobe and slippers.

He had no face.

"You may not leave."

It was Gordon's voice — almost. Deeper and coarser, and slower than her brother's natural speech. And the sound terrified her. Something within her.

"Oh God, the injustice," Suzette whispered. "How could she have been condemned?"

"Release her, or I shall take you with me."

She felt herself rising from the bed, though she had not

willed it. Yes, there was someone else inside her: the poor, sweet girl. . . .

Suzette wanted to run, to fly away.

Gordon's body slowly stood, his joints creaking and popping as if rigor mortis had settled in them. The voice from the faceless thing said, "One who leaves must be returned. And there is no statute against taking another."

"She only defended herself. Have you no mercy?"

"There is no mercy in the spilling of blood."

"She was justified."

The moon shone on the pale oval atop Gordon's shoulders. For a long moment, as if the featureless face were a giant cyclopean eye, an alien gaze transfixed her, sending hot shivers through her every limb. The Gordon-thing's chest expanded, and a second later, the horrible scream she'd heard before in the night shattered the silence of the room, so full of fearsome power that she dropped to her knees, covered her ears, and squeezed her eyes shut.

"The judgment is not mine," came the voice, after the scream at last began to fade.

"Spare her," Suzette pleaded. "Allow her to escape her torment."

"I must not."

She looked back to Arthur, still asleep in the bed, unshaken by the horrible scream. But his features looked pained, his cheeks moist with tears. It was not a natural sleep.

"Leave this house," Suzette said, her voice driven by the spirit within her. "Leave us forever and do not return!"

But then, as if enraged, Gordon took a quick step forward and his hand encircled her wrist — burning her! God, his touch was like hot steel, and she smelled smoke — the organic smell of singed flesh.

"No!" she cried, in her own voice, trying to back away. The thing was far too strong. "Leave me alone, please!"

And another rush of images filled her vision, a chaotic montage of flames and blood, of tormented souls — and the sound of so many voices, raised in an endless chorus of inhuman suffering.

The soul inside her, the one she had brought forth from her dream, seemed to be *ripped* from Suzette's body, all the while begging her to hold on, to allow her to share the flesh so that she might not be condemned yet again, and for a moment, Suzette longed to submit to that will. . . .

. . . Until she realized what the thing that held her arm was itself transmitting to her.

"She has lied to you."

And when Suzette saw the truth, she screamed and pulled away from the iron grip, fell to her knees — alone, no longer possessed by the weeper's spirit.

The room spun around her, and a thunderous roar in her ears seemed to crush her entire body. For a moment, looking up at the thing that held her, she saw her brother's face gazing in terror at the moonlit window.

And a veritable explosion of black feathers came down upon them, swirling and fluttering in the air — all as hot as fire.

The room — the house — shook with the sound of the demonic scream, this time in harmony with another: a feminine, agonized voice that Suzette knew would never be heard again by anyone in this life.

"**S**he is gone."

Moments after the thing had departed, Arthur awakened, a frightened cry on his own lips, as if his sleep had been wracked by nightmares he couldn't possibly understand. He gazed at Suzette and Gordon in bewilderment, running a hand through his mussed hair.

"I heard it," he whispered. "But I could not move. I was being held down — like I was underwater. Drowning."

"You could not have been allowed to interfere."

Gordon sat back down in the chair where Suzette had first seen him. "I hurt."

"So do I," Suzette said, trying to assess the aches and pains that shook her entire body. Her wrist where the thing had touched her burned fiery red, and blisters were beginning to form in a pattern shaped by Gordon's fingers. "I need something to drink."

Arthur touched her shoulder and hurried off to get glasses of water for both her and her brother. She sat on the edge of the bed, gazing at Gordon with both concern and relief. He looked an inch away from death, his face chalky white, his eyes weak and red. But she knew that he would not be troubled by the feathered thing ever again.

"God," she groaned. "The horror of them."

"He was once a man," he said softly. "But he had become . . . demonic."

"Yes. She wanted to escape so badly. One could almost feel sorry for her."

"He was her brother."

"Yes." Suzette smiled weakly at him. "It is because of our own relationship that they were able to come so far. She has been trying to escape for so many years. But it was not until our own lives, entwined as they are, gave them something to grab hold to."

Arthur returned in a moment with the water, and both Gordon and Suzette drank greedily, welcoming its cold relief in their parched throats.

"Why did she want you?" Arthur asked, sitting next to Suzette.

"Only by escaping into the living could she be made free from her torment. But it is against nature. He came to take her back. In a way, he showed us kindness."

Gordon gazed at the moon. "To think what could wait in store for *us*. My God."

Suzette slid from the bed and knelt at Gordon's feet, taking his hands in hers. "That fate will never be ours."

Arthur came to her side as well, and touched Gordon's shoulder. "Do not fear it."

Suzette looked back in her memory, saw what the thing had revealed to her. "She killed them. Her brother, and her father. She murdered them."

"Why?" Arthur asked.

"She was loyal to the King. A Tory. They were not. It was not the British soldiers she killed."

"But her own family!"

"Her heart was cold. At least it had been — in life. No longer. Now she truly regrets."

"That," said Gordon, staring into the night, "is surely the greatest tragedy of all."

Quiet and calm, Suzette lay in the bed next to her husband. Only an hour remained before dawn. They were exhausted, and still in pain, but no longer subject to any physical danger. She had put burn cream on her wrist, knowing the pain would be worse later in the morning, as the shock began to wear off. But she could sleep now, knowing that nothing else would invade her dreams.

She and Arthur had seen Gordon to bed after he had washed himself with soap and cold water. He was still so weak he could barely walk, but tomorrow, hopefully, his strength would return. When Gordon had settled beneath the covers of his bed, Suzette leaned down and kissed him tenderly on the cheek, and he had pulled her to him in shaky but firm arms.

"I love you, Suzette," he said. "You did the right thing."

"I love you, too. Sleep well now."

"I will."

Now, with her husband at her side, she felt safe and secure, protected by her bedclothes from the cold night. She had left the curtains open so the moon's crescent eye could send its silver light into the room, dispelling the shadows in which the horror had earlier thrived.

Still, she found her hands shaking.

That poor, poor girl.

Somewhere, perhaps only in her memory, a shrill cry rose in the darkness — but so far away it was barely audible.

"Now I lay me down," Suzette said aloud. "Now I lay me down to dream."

And then she was asleep.

Silhouette

*I*t's true; I swore that I would never go back to that house. But of course I went back. How could I not? Being sent to Chicago on business wasn't something I could have foreseen when I'd beat such a hasty retreat from that city almost ten years before. Certainly, when my company informed me that in order to research a major software vendor up north I would have to spend a week on the Gold Coast, my first impulse was to demur. But then, anyone who works for *Microworld* magazine knows better than to demur when the boss hands out an assignment.

And rationalization came easy; even easier when my cab from O'Hare embarked down the Kennedy on its way toward the Loop. After ten years, here I was thinking how much I'd really loved living in the city (except at rush hour) and how familiar everything seemed, though lots of new buildings had sprouted along the skyline and daytime traffic, even at off-hours, had gotten heavier. No, it wasn't a return to Chicago itself that I had forsworn; merely a return to a particular house.

But from my hotel I could reach the place in a matter of minutes by taxi — or if I gave myself a little more time, by walking. And that is what I ended up doing, on this May evening after I'd concluded my business for the day. The allure was too strong to resist, for in ten years fear subsides. Wounds heal. The intellect rationalizes.

On my walk beneath the streetlamps that were now firing to life amid the twilight, I didn't know what to expect, or what I would do once I reached my destination. For all I knew, the house could have been torn down years ago. But suddenly, there it was, standing agelessly behind the short, black iron-rung fence that surrounded the narrow grassy lot. It was a typical brownstone set among dozens of similarly designed dwellings, camouflaged in normality to anyone not searching specifically for ghosts. Hiding on a relatively quiet residential street between Lincoln and Clark beneath a canopy of brooding maple trees, it might have escaped my own notice but for the broad front porch and circular stained glass window just above it; little features that distinguished the house to perhaps no one other than myself, and those who'd shared at least a few of my experiences here.

And then I saw it. *The head!* In the small, warmly glowing window next to the porch, that unnaturally elongated silhouette, the shape of something inhuman. It was still there.

I shivered. Behind the window, I knew, stood a two foot tall crucifix, the body of Christ backlit by a small lamp, casting its shadow upon the translucent window shade to give the impression of a weirdly distorted figure looking out upon the night. I had been similarly struck by its suggestion of the grotesque when, at age 21, I glimpsed it for the first time, and I had certainly never forgotten about its effect.

That the effect persisted almost certainly meant that my friends still lived in this house, a fact I confirmed by stepping up to the front porch and finding the name "Breheim" still adorning the rusty black mailbox beside the door. Surely I must have considered this possibility on my journey here, but at the moment, my mind seemed fogged; I lingered on the porch for several minutes, foolishly intimidated by the prospect of knocking.

Finally, I lifted my hand and rapped soundly on the door, half-hoping I'd hear no stirring inside, no boards groaning to signal the approach of the building's inhabitant. But those noises came shortly: a soft, tentative creaking, a momentary scrabbling at the lock. And the door swung open to reveal a dim figure, who shortly reached to flip on the porch light. And when we gazed at each other, she sighed and nodded slightly, her suspicion that I would one day break my vow now fulfilled.

"There have been changes made since you stayed here," she said softly.

She turned away and I followed her inside, drinking in the smell of the place, which remained exactly as I remembered it: a slightly musty, sweet scent mingled with the not unpleasant whiff of mothballs that seems to pervade old houses. The furniture was different, though. No longer the old antiques, these were relatively new pieces of expensive design. The walls, once papered with a mildew-tinged flower pattern, were now bare, painted pale beige, with ivory molding. Above, a dim chandelier conjured a comfortably warm atmosphere in the living room, its light barely spilling into the dining area through an archway at the room's far end.

Nina wore a tasteful suit of black and tan, her auburn hair impeccable as always, her fingers decorated with many glittering rings. Still very attractive after ten years, I thought; yet she looked . . . old. Weather-beaten. The creases at the corners of her eyes were deep. Her walk, once so deliberate and assured, seemed unsteady, almost faltering. She was over 40 years old now; but she bore a weariness laid upon her by more than just time.

"Walter is in the den," she said, her voice low and edged with the roughness of a heavy smoker. "He will be happy you've come."

"I see your financial situation is no longer grim," I said with a chuckle. When I'd lived in the upstairs apartment, Walter and Nina Breheim were barely surviving week to week. My monthly rent payment essentially kept them afloat. But over time, I'd become more than just a tenant. We were quite close, then.

She led me back to the small parlor that had always been Walter's sanctuary. I knew I'd find him in front of his music machines: in the old days a tower built of amplifiers, receivers, cassette decks, turntables and speakers twice as powerful as the building's plaster — or the neighbors — could bear. Now, his modernized system was just as powerful but occupied only a fraction of the space, with speakers only a few inches high. The shelves of record albums still reached the ceiling, though, and had been joined on all sides by almost as many compact discs. And in his same old battered rocking chair, headphones covering his ears, Walter sat with his back to me, seemingly unaware he had a visitor. His hair, once jet black and moppish, was now close-cropped and iron gray.

"Walter," Nina said softly, touching his shoulder, and he turned. His cool green eyes had grown even colder, and peered out from sockets that seemed to have been drilled much deeper since I'd last seen him. But those eyes flashed with surprise and something like pleasure, and I found myself smiling like a fool, ridiculously pleased I'd seen fit to bury my old pledge.

"David!" he cried and stood up so fast that his headphones slipped off and clattered to the floor. He ignored them. "David Isley! I don't believe it!" He grasped my outstretched hand, his grip still painfully firm, firmer than I could match. Like Nina, he seemed to have aged more than I would have expected in ten years. He was probably 45. He looked 60.

"You need a drink," Nina said. "Still gin and tonic?"

"Tanqueray."

She smiled. "Sit down. Back in a moment."

I took a seat on the dusty rose loveseat that occupied the corner adjacent to the sound system. The parlor, at least, though updated, was the same place it used to be.

"What on earth brings you back here?" Walter asked.

I gave him a brief rundown of my assignment, cited the proximity of my hotel as the reason for my visit. Nina returned momentarily with drinks for all of us and sat down across from me, studying me intently with her deep violet eyes. She lit a cigarette and I noticed the slightest trembling of her fingers.

"So you couldn't resist coming to see us," Walter said. "I always thought you might. I'm glad you were able to overcome your, uh, objections."

At that, we all fell quiet for several moments. Walter gazed pensively at me.

"So," I said at last. "Is it truly gone?"

"Yes," Walter said. "It is gone."

Nina nodded in agreement. "Since that night, we've slept well."

It was to their credit that my friends had been able to remain in this house after everything that happened, after what we'd discovered. And I believed them, that the house was clean; certainly it must be, since here they sat, sharing drinks with me. Still, I knew that Walter and Nina had been fundamentally changed. The house might no longer be haunted, but these people were.

By their memories.

"Let me take you upstairs," Nina said. "We no longer rent the apartment. It's strictly for guests. We would love to have you stay with us rather than at the hotel."

I shrugged. "I'll have to think about that."

Nina and Walter both rose and ushered me back through the living room to the entry foyer and the steep stairwell to the upstairs apartment. I must admit to feeling a little apprehensive at the idea of returning to the very rooms where I had once lived, where so many of the things that prompted me to flee the city had taken place.

"You won't recognize the rooms," Walter said. "We have made changes."

I stopped then, just as I was about to set foot on the stairs. I was facing the alcove whose window overlooked the sidewalk. A short lamp with a crystal base provided warm, golden light, and a large, ornately framed mirror hung upon the wall.

The crucifix wasn't there. No body of Christ casting its shadow on the translucent window shade. But I had *seen. . . !*

With a hoarse gasp, I slipped into the past.

*N*ina Breheim had inherited the crucifix from her parents, and seemed to find it attractive in its place. I didn't care for it, not after seeing the way it looked at night, silhouetted eerily against the window like some twisted denizen of the grave who, if indeed risen, had come forth with purely evil intent. But I was always polite in my remarks about it, even once we got to know each other well. Nina and Walter had befriended me so readily that I could never bring myself to offend either of them over anything so trivial.

But in all other matters there was honesty between us. I settled in with them shortly after arriving in Chicago fresh out of Beckham College, hoping to pursue a career in journalism. They offered the upstairs apartment for relatively low rent, and having virtually no savings to draw upon, I could hardly be particular in my choice of lodging. But it was a fine place for a young single man to live, with one bedroom, a bath, kitchen and small living area. The Breheims had just bought the house at quite a reasonable price, but had still exhausted most of their money in the process. They needed a good tenant.

They cheerfully helped me move my few belongings into the apartment, and invited me to share any and all meals with them, as long as I chipped in on the food. They were a few years older than me, but as they apparently had few friends in the area, they seemed to desire my companionship as much as my money.

Our first dinner together became a drunken party.

"Back in Nova Scotia, my Grandad was a judge, you know," Walter told me, tossing back what must have been his fifth gin. "In those days, in Breton Cove, there weren't but two judges. And hardly anybody had cars back then, but both of them did. Now wouldn't you know that the two of them ended up getting the first two speeding tickets in Breton Cove! Of course, since they were the town's only judges, they had to sentence each other. Well, Grandad figures that he'll show due professional consideration, and fines the other judge a dollar. Then they switch robes, and our other judge says, 'Now that we have cars in this town, it's up to us to set a good example. But two tickets in one day? Suddenly speeding has become a trend!' So he fines Grandad 25 dollars."

Nina and I laughed, though I knew she must have heard that story countless times. I later learned, in fact, that Walter always told that story when he first got to know someone. She'd heard it on their first date. And sure enough it worked; he'd hooked her.

I lived in the house for over a month without experiencing the first hint of any disturbance, thinking I'd be happy to stay as long as the Breheims would have me. I found work in the circulation department of The Sun Times, an admittedly lowly job, but lucrative enough to keep me in my rooms and with plenty of food and drink. I even went out to nightclubs most weekends, sometimes accompanied by Walter and Nina, though they had grown staid enough to prefer their own living room most evenings.

It began on a cool September night, the kind I most enjoyed: just right for sleeping with the windows open and bundling up in the covers. Traffic after midnight was generally light, and the trees and houses muffled the noises from nearby Clark Street. When I awoke, it was just past 2:00 a.m.; I thought some of the neighbors must have taken their baby out and it wasn't happy to be roused at such an hour. The crying started low and weak, but escalated steadily into a mournful wail. I first felt pity for the child, then anger at the parents for allowing it to continue for so long. Then I began to wonder if perhaps the child had been left out in the street.

I rose from bed and went to the window, only to find that the sound did not come from the street after all. The wailing seemed to echo from the hall beyond my closed bedroom door. None of the other windows were open that I knew of, and surely, neither Nina nor Walter would have admitted company with a child at this hour! Opening the door slowly, I looked out into the hall, dark but for a circle of multi-colored light cast from the stained glass window.

The sound definitely from below; perhaps one of the downstairs windows was open and the crying was echoing through a nearby alley. But I didn't intend to go exploring, and, muttering something one shouldn't mutter about children, I turned to go back to bed. But then the door to the stairwell opened and Walter appeared, silhouetted against the light from the foyer.

"Oh, you're up," he said quietly. "You hear that crying?"

"God, yes."

"It seems to be inside the house."

"What?"

"Yes. Come down."

I joined him in the living room, where the crying grew louder.

"I've checked everywhere. It sounds like it's coming from the basement."

He led me to the kitchen and the door that opened to the unfinished basement that they used only for storage. Yes — now the sound seemed very close at hand. But then, even as we stood there, the crying began to trail away, falling completely silent when Walter opened the door. Flipping on the light, he took a few tentative steps down, shaking his head as if realizing this was a futile quest. He turned back before reaching the bottom.

"Had to have come from the alley outside," he said. "To-morrow I'll see if there are any windows open or broken. The furnace is in the basement; maybe somehow the sound was echoing through the conduits."

We agreed to leave further suppositions till morning, then bid each other a second goodnight and returned to our respective bedrooms. As I headed up the stairs, I found myself stepping gingerly, furtively, almost as if my softest footfall intruded too loudly upon the darkness. I realized then that I was quite nervous, far moreso than one should expect after hearing something so basically frivolous as an unidentified crying. Before slipping back into bed, I closed the hall door and locked it, as well as my window, feeling that open portals left me somehow exposed. And sleep eluded me for a long time after I'd turned out all the lights, for every little sound I heard startled me into canny wakefulness.

The next morning, the sun was a welcome arrival, despite my intense fatigue from such a poor night's sleep.

Walter, it turned out, ended up having to work that day, a Saturday. He was a pharmacist's assistant at a nearby drug store, on-call almost around the clock. So we did not see each other that morning at all; in fact, he did not return home until after dark. Nina, however, had breakfast with me, and told me that she too had heard the crying but hadn't bothered getting out of bed. For some reason, the noise had not affected her the way it had Walter and myself.

"He was like you," she said. "Seemed nervous and restless when he came back to bed. I can't imagine why you were so upset by the crying of a baby."

"It's not so much the crying itself," I told her, "it's just that the conditions seem so strange."

"True," she said, sipping her morning coffee. "This is a very old house, though, and the other houses nearby, the alleys, they trap noises. When I was a little girl, we lived down on the south side of the city in an old place not much different than this one. Sometimes at night I could clearly hear people talking from way down the block. The wind would echo through the nearby alleys and through our chimney, creating a weird harmony, almost like something alive. Yet it was a comforting sound to me."

"Interesting," I said. "I suppose it takes a while to get used to the noises when you move into a place."

"Exactly," she said. "Well, maybe we should check to make sure we don't have any open or broken windows. A lot worse than stray sounds might end up getting inside."

I agreed, and once we finished our coffee, we went down into the basement: a dim, murky place even with the light on. Many boxes and pieces of old furniture had been stacked haphazardly, making it difficult to forge a path. But all the windows were locked, and none were so much as cracked.

We returned to the relative brightness of the kitchen and each had another cup of coffee. She had errands to run, and I intended to call some of my friends from work so we could make plans for another night on the town. Yes, I drank too much in those days, but my drinking was happy, almost carefree. Drinking in the years thereafter had less innocent implications.

I did go out that night, and came home to a good night's sleep. Indeed, by then I'd virtually forgotten the uncomfortable incident of the night before. Walter and I never discussed it again even when he made his own thorough check of the basement to make sure he could find nothing amiss.

But the following night, I found myself again feeling unaccountably nervous. At first I could not even trace this uneasiness back to the sound of the baby crying. I knew only that my body felt tense and my mind would not succumb to the allure of sleep. At one a.m., I was still awake and fidgeting.

Nothing happened, though. Not one unusual noise, not a single unidentifiable movement. Eventually, fatigue overcame my anxiety, but when it did, the dreams that flooded my unconscious made me later wish I'd remained awake after all.

I was in the Breheim's house, but it seemed to be another period in time. The furniture was all different, even older than the second-hand pieces that now occupied the rooms. Two people sat in chairs in the living room: grotesquely old, *twisted*-looking people, I thought. A man and a woman, hair thin and completely white, faces withered and wrinkled so that the features themselves were almost unidentifiable. I seemed to be peeking into the room from a concealed place, perhaps the dining area, in hopes of avoiding their notice. For reasons I did not understand, I did not want them to see me.

Then, the sounds! Beginning softly, then rising: a chorus of insane, gibbering voices, forming meaningless syllables that overlapped and harmonized, argued discordantly. When I looked at the old woman, her eyes were closed, her mouth open, her face raised to the ceiling as if all her attention was directed to the sounds. The man seemed to listen just as intently, but his eyes were open, now focused on the front door.

The Breheims' crucifix was there, in the alcove — an incongruity that somehow upset me even more than the noises and the strange couple that occupied the dream room.

Then the wailing began: the same child's mournful crying I had heard the night before while I was wide awake — that Walter and Nina had heard as clearly as I.

And finally came the thumping. Rhythmic, hollow; like giant footsteps approaching from a distance. It grew louder, providing a cadence for the ethereal voices. It came from behind me, from the direction of the kitchen.

From beyond the door to the basement stairs.

As the thumping drew nearer, the two ancient faces turned towards my hiding place. And two pairs of eyes fell upon me, instantly widening as my presence registered in their unfathomable brains. A symphony of wistful musical notes rose into a shrill, warbling cacophony, and a deep baritone suddenly spoke in the empty air, enunciating syllables I could not completely understand but that sounded like, "I see you. . . ."

The old woman stood up, and I saw that she wore a

shapeless, dust-colored smock that fell over what must have been an emaciated body. The man rose as well, clad identically to her. And two pairs of bare feet left the floor, and their bodies hovered in mid-air before me, their eyes now radiating an awful heat that seemed to sweep over and through me.

A childish giggle came out of the air.

And behind me, the door to the basement crashed open.

I sat up in my bed with a cry, bathed in cold sweat. The window was open.

But it had been closed when I went to bed! I had not opened it again since the night I'd heard the crying.

I got up and lowered the sash, only to freeze in my place as a deep drumbeat echoed from downstairs. My heart raced into overdrive, and I held my breath, anticipating a repetition of the noise.

It came again seconds later: a heavy *thump* somewhere below — very likely from the basement stairs, I thought, just like that from my dream. And then came another sound that surprised me as much as the other had terrified me.

It sounded like madrigal music; delicate vocal harmonies drifting softly up the stairwell, and I thought Walter must be playing music in his parlor. Perhaps, I considered with some relief, the thumping had just been something on a record.

But I realized I was mistaken when moments later I recognized the voices as belonging to Walter and Nina. They were intoning "Holy, holy . . . holy," in lovely harmony, their voices muted into chamber music by the depths of the house. I could only listen, hypnotized.

After a time, they fell silent. And I realized that the thumping had also subsided some time earlier. Their familiar voices had actually been soothing after the intense terror born in my nightmare.

At last I was able to go back to bed and drift to sleep, despite being troubled by so many disturbing questions — not the least of which was the extent to which the Breheims were involved in something that now seemed not just inexplicable — but strangely sinister.

"**N**o, I don't recall being awake at all," Nina said, sitting across from me at the breakfast table. I never heard anything. Did you, Walter?"

He looked uneasy. "I — I remember having bad dreams. But nothing else."

Nina looked at me so curiously I could not believe she was telling me anything but the truth. And Walter obviously appeared fatigued, as if he hadn't slept any better than I.

"What were your dreams?" I asked. "Can you remember?"

He shook his head. "Not distinctly. I think I remember music."

"Music, yes," I said. "There was very strange music, if it could actually be called that. Haunting."

Nina's eyes took on a far away look. "Wait. I seem to recall dreaming of . . . sounds, if not music. Heavy sounds. Like a heartbeat."

"It wasn't a heartbeat," I said. "I think it was footsteps."

"Something was coming," Walter said softly. "Yes. Something terrible."

"Then I heard you," I said. "I heard you both. Singing. Or chanting, really. 'Holy, holy . . . holy.' Quite lovely — yet frightening in context."

Nina smiled weakly. "I don't think either of us are known for our vocal prowess."

"Don't be modest, Nina," Walter said. "We both sang in the church choir, David. But that was years ago."

"I see," I replied, nodding. "So is it possible the both of you were singing in your sleep?"

Walter chuckled. "I don't see how. We haven't even practiced."

At that, I had to laugh. But now, even our nonchalant Nina seemed to fall into quiet contemplation, a dark shadow settling upon her face. "I would be lying," she said, "if I told you this didn't sort of freak me out."

"Likewise," Walter said. "David, you say your window was open but you did not open it. And I can assure you, neither of us has been to your rooms and no one else has been in the house — at least no one invited. Most likely you opened it in your sleep. Have you ever sleepwalked?"

"No, not that I know of. No more than the two of you perform concerts for somnambulants."

Nina's face brightened and Walter chuckled aloud. "Touche, monsieur," he said. "If it were past noon I'd buy you a drink. As it is, you'll have to settle for another cup of coffee."

I smiled and handed him my cup. He poured, and we finished our breakfast mostly in silence, each of us puzzled — but worse, for the first time since we'd met, uncomfortable with each other. I don't think any of us were prepared for that, or willing to allow it to continue.

*T*he question was, what did one do about unexplained sounds and unsettling dreams? Especially when there seemed to be no pattern to them. . . .

Oftentimes, we could go days, occasionally weeks without a single restless night. Other times — especially when any of us was alone in the house — the sound of a baby's crying would begin soft and low, always beginning in the basement, only to become a whirlwind of miserable wailing that seemed to echo from *behind* the walls. But as soon as the basement door was opened, the crying would quickly fade away.

One evening I came home late from work to be greeted by the sound of bitter weeping. This was no mystifying child's cry, but a mature, adult voice, wracked with heavy sobs.

It was Nina. She knelt on the living room floor, leaning against the sofa, her face buried in her hands, chest heaving as she cried. At first she didn't see me come in, but when I went to her side, she looked up with tear-jeweled eyes.

"They killed it," she whispered. "It was just a baby, and my God they killed it."

I knew immediately that something must have happened in the house. She was not referring to some outside event. "What was it, Nina?"

"I had fallen asleep on the couch," she said, struggling to catch her breath. "I heard it begin to cry. And those voices started. Christ, David, there's something in this house. I could see things — vaguely, like shadows. They were beating it, two old people. They beat it and threw it down the stairs. Then they went after it. Oh God, the voices. You should have heard the voices."

"Did you dream this?"

"I — I did, but I didn't. I mean, I was lying here, asleep. Then I woke up, *I woke up!* But the room was different. Everything was old."

I touched her hand; it was icy. "Everything's all right now," I said, though I felt my own heart quailing. "Nothing's changed here."

"I know," she said, wiping her eyes. "It all seems to be fading. Almost like a dream. But David, I didn't dream it. I was awake. I swear to you, I was awake."

"I believe you," I said, truthfully. "Let's get you a drink."

She accepted my hand and I helped her to her feet, where she managed to stand shakily on her own. She slowly headed toward the kitchen, and I followed a couple of steps behind. "Where's Walter?" I asked.

"He called and said he had to work late."

It was now almost nine. I made a gin and tonic for Nina, and as an afterthought made one for myself. As she sipped it, her nerves slowly settled. But I could feel something in the house. An atmosphere of tension; of expectation.

"I won't leave this house," she said firmly, as if anticipating my suggestion. "This is ours, we bought it." She even worked up a little smile and said, "No squalling shadows pay the mortgage here. We do."

I smiled too, but suddenly a movement from the direction of the dimly lit living room caught my eye. A shadow seemed to be creeping across the floor, a movement so subtle I wasn't sure I was really seeing it — such as may happen when one looks at a partially open door in the darkness and swears that it's slowly opening, when in reality it's motionless.

I didn't say anything, for fear of upsetting Nina further. But as I watched, the shadow took on the distinct form of a very small person, shuffling slowly forward — stopping just short of the open door.

Ever so slowly, a pale globe slid into view around the side of the door, like the face of a featureless moon. It stopped before fully revealing itself, as if an eavesdropping child had carelessly stepped a hair too far into the open.

I felt goosebumps on the back of my neck. But unwilling

to give in to fear, I instead dashed through the dining room into the living room, ready to confront whatever apparition dared invoke my wrath.

Of course, there was nothing and no one in the living room. We were alone in the house.

"David," called Nina. "David, what is it? Did you see something?"

I sheepishly returned to the kitchen and laid my hands on Nina's shoulders. "I thought I did. Just a trick of the eye, I guess. Maybe the lights from a passing car. Now you've gotten my nerves on edge. That's very naughty, you know."

She reached up and squeezed my hand, and all my fear dissipated beneath a rush of affection for her — no, nothing adulterous — and my previous suspicion that the Breheims could be somehow responsible for the things happening here vanished completely.

But regardless of the complete innocence of my feelings for her, when Walter opened the front door a minute later, I drew my hand away quickly and felt myself blushing. Fortunately, Nina was quickly up to greet him and by the time he came in to say hello to me I was completely back to normal, such as it was.

O n my way up to bed that night, I could feel an uncustomary chill in the stairwell, and what seemed like an electrical charge building in the air, like the tangible atmospheric ionization before a thunderstorm. Still, there's something inside the rational man that leads us to carry on with our normal routines, regardless of the evidence of our senses, as if the clinging to familiar dogma is an amulet to counter any unknown.

I went through my nightly ablutions, prepared for bed as always, picked up a book, and settled beneath the covers — leaving not only the bedside lamp on, but the lights in the living room and bathroom. It was Thursday night, and I had to go to work as usual in the morning. I very much wanted to get a good night's sleep, and strange as it seems, even after the episode with Nina and the apparition I *thought* I'd seen, I managed to relax somewhat.

Not only that, after reading until my eyelids couldn't prop themselves open any longer, I drifted into an uneasy, but undisturbed sleep.

At least until I heard a heavy thump sometime much later in the night.

I woke up surrounded by darkness. All the lights had been extinguished. The digital clock read just past 3:00 a.m. And the baby was crying.

"Oh God," I muttered aloud, sitting up and rubbing my eyes, having reached the point where I was more angered than frightened by the unwelcome disruption. But when another thump sounded from beyond my door, a little shiver passed up my spine, for it was louder and heavier — and seemingly closer — than any I had heard previously. This seemed to be coming from the stairwell right outside my apartment door. And it was drawing nearer. A jarring *thump . . . thump. . . .* that clearly meant something was on the steps, moving closer with each repetition.

I have never had a victim's mentality; I was not prepared to wait placidly for a potentially dangerous visitation. So, turning on all the lights, I hurried straight to the kitchen and grabbed the biggest butcher knife from the cutlery drawer. And with only the briefest hesitation to half-heartedly pray for my own deliverance from evil, I stalked straight to the stairwell door, stopped and grabbed for the handle.

Thump. It was close. Whatever *it* was.

Drawing in a steadying breath, bracing myself for the sight of something I might not completely comprehend, I pulled the door open.

But even this mental preparation could not prevent me from gasping in shock when I realized what I was seeing. Illuminated only by the hall light shining down through my open door, a rigid figure was *bouncing* up the stairs on one blunt end: the crucifix from the downstairs window, Christ's head thrown back and mouth gaping in unutterable agony. The wooden eyes, lit with the unmistakable fire of *life,* glared at me in terror, as if the force animating it was powerful enough to dethrone God himself. In the background, the baby's screaming rose higher and higher, finally drowning even the thumping on the stairs.

When this travesty was one step from the top, I slammed the door shut and pressed myself against it, wondering if I would then feel the thing begin to beat ferociously against the panel at my back. I could not think clearly enough to wonder what it might do to me if it did break through. Even if it didn't do *anything,* its very presence threatened to shatter my remaining sanity. In retrospect, I've sometimes wondered if that was not the intent of its motivating force all along.

But nothing came. In fact, moments later, the crying, the pounding on the stairs, all had fallen silent — except the frantic pounding of my heart. But no! Far below, something began clanging sharply, like iron against stone. Over and over again, stronger, more determinedly, and I knew in my soul that this was something different, something of human design. It was in the basement.

I opened the door and — of course — found the stairway clear. I hustled down, made my way through the dark living room to the kitchen, where a light now burned and the basement door gaped darkly at me, emitting the sharp, furious clanging.

Indeed, I now saw that the single bulb below was lit, and I could hear a deep gasping for breath between the iron pounding. Bolstered by this sign of human activity, I rushed down to find Walter with a pick axe in hand, drawn back to strike at the brick wall at the far northern corner of the house. He saw me, but did not pause. Only after he'd swung several more times, shattering brick and spraying red dust into his face, did he speak to me.

"It's here, David. By God, I followed it and I found where it comes from. Here. Back here."

I leaned close and saw that he'd knocked out a portion of wall roughly a foot in diameter — and beyond lay a chamber of darkness of unknown depth. Barely giving me time to move away, Walter drew back and smashed away another section of bricks with the pick, this time tugging a few of the fragments toward him. And from this chasm now spilled the single most appalling sight ever beheld by these eyes:

A pile of old bones, gray and brittle with age, coated with red brick dust, some obviously broken by Walter's pick axe.

A skull rolled from the opening. Just a small thing, about

the size of the half-seen moonface that had peered around the door the afternoon before.

I barely glanced up when a moment later I heard Nina's footsteps on the stairs, followed momentarily by a succession of short, hysterical screams.

*T*he much older-looking Walter now stared at me with an expression of concern. Nina looked on with an air of trepidation, as if all the fears of the past might somehow intrude upon the peace they had known for better than a decade.

"Are you all right?" she asked.

I just shrugged. "I don't know. Sometimes it doesn't seem like I've ever been away, that it could ever really be over. I mean, how do we *know* it's over? After what we saw?"

Walter nodded thoughtfully. "I know, my friend. I still have dreams. Not like before. But of course I'm still bothered. *It* had to come from somewhere, right? That's what haunts us. Where it came from."

"But by staying here, we've managed to achieve some kind of closure," Nina said. "There's never been any evidence that it could ever happen again."

I wanted so badly to tell them about what I'd seen in the window on my approach, but I knew it would only upset them uselessly. They had learned to live with their memories. I had not. I didn't want to undermine the foundation they'd built by revealing what could still conceivably be written off as a delusion on my part.

Not that I believed that, of course. If anything, I was sure now that some residue of that ancient force remained in this house, and my own presence had perhaps momentarily catalyzed it. But only for that moment, I told myself.

"Well," Walter said. "Let's go upstairs."

I followed them up, remembering the horror of that thing bouncing on its end up the stairs, the face of the crucified, wooden savior reflecting such hellish agony. Maybe my coming back was not a good idea after all.

But no. The joy of seeing my friends again could not be overpowered even by the reminders of that old terror.

Sure enough, the upstairs apartment was very different

than during my stay. Once gloomy with age, it now seemed bright and new, with fresh wallpapering and paint, contemporary furnishings, new light fixtures and lamps — so great a change, in fact, that I could not picture anything ominous or menacing daring to trespass here.

"It's lovely," I said. "You made a wise decision."

"Would you like to stay? We certainly would love to have you, David."

I had to shake my head. "I appreciate that. But . . . I can't. I just can't."

"I understand," Nina said. "I can't blame you. But promise us this. If you come to town again, do not hesitate to come again. Please?"

"I will," I promised. "I will come again."

We returned downstairs and I had one more drink before I had to start back to my hotel. As we stood facing each other by the front door, I said to Walter, "You know, on that night when I heard you singing. Do you really have no memory of that?"

"None," he said. "But Nina and I spoke of it at great length. You know, there was something very powerful in this house. Something we don't have all the answers to, and never will. But I think somehow our souls were affected by this thing. Even though we were not aware of it at the time, I believe our own spirits were reacting. And counteracting. I think perhaps they preserved our bodies independent of our will. Think about that, David."

"Indeed," I said. "Well. You have no idea how good it was to see you."

Both of them came forward to embrace me. Yes, our companionship, I knew, had been sealed by our experiences here in the same way that soldiers become brothers on the battlefield. Our battle had been on a different plane.

I left the house with a brief look back, noting that the window where the crucifix had been was now properly empty; but I couldn't suppress the chill from knowing that, for the briefest moment, on this very night, *something* from the past had paid us an unwelcome visit.

And then I heard it. Behind me, rising lightly in the night, barely discernible. Softened by the distance, mingled with a low breeze, the lovely, haunting harmony drifted to me, and my quick glance back revealed two silhouettes on the porch, standing rigidly side by side, a faint luminescence in their eyes — a reflection from streetlights, I told myself. Merely a reflection.

"Holy, holy . . . holy. . . ."

I ran. I ran until I reached Clark and on and on, chased by the music long after it should have been smothered by the sounds of traffic and jets and el trains and nearby pedestrians. But it rang in my ears and my skin felt cold, for the air around me still held a charge like the one I'd felt in the stairwell on that final night. I knew that coming back had activated it, but I prayed it was only temporary and that by tomorrow morning, all would have returned to normal.

No, it wasn't just that the bones were small, and that so obviously a baby had been beaten in that house and bricked up while still alive. Murder is a human act, and however atrocious, nothing a human being can conceive or do is shocking. Nothing. Only something inhuman, something beyond our comprehension, something that serves to remind us of just what our place is in this world can shock the soul the way the Breheims and I were shocked.

Those bones — I'll never forget the weird angles of those bones, the single gaping eye socket in the little, horn-studded skull. That the thing was ever born, that it once lived and was killed in a house in which I spent months of my life — *that* is a fact that haunts and shocks me, and Walter and Nina Breheim.

That, and my own inevitable conjectures of the thing's unknown, unspeakable lineage.

The Forgiven

"Say it!"

Dyer's eyes were two smoking pistols, black and deep. His right hand, raised above his head, gripped the handle of a gleaming straight razor; his left clutched a straw-like tuft of his victim's hair, pulling the head back so the jaw hung slackly open. The man, eyes bulging in terror, could barely force air in and out of his lungs, much less comply with his captor's command.

"Say it!" Dyer cried again, tensing his right bicep in preparation to strike with his razor. "Go on."

Webber tried to speak, but managed only a weak gurgle deep in his throat. A thin stream of saliva ran from his lower lip.

"I know you can do it," Dyer said, voice now soft, controlled. His tensed muscles relaxed slightly. "Say, 'I love you. I forgive you.'"

At last, Webber found his voice. Weak, and raspy. "I . . . can't."

Dyer shook his head in disgust. His victim was tied securely to a wooden armchair in the bedroom of the rented house; the man's face blazed with reflected white light from the bare bulb atop a shadeless pole lamp next to the chair. Webber's sweat had formed a pool around the legs of the chair, and several thin tributaries of blood added a crimson tint to the fluid. The hemp rope that bound his wrists to the armrests had chafed his flesh, which now burned bright red and glistened with stinging perspiration.

"What . . . do you want from me?"

Dyer laughed softly, lowering the razor for a moment. "I want you to forgive me. It's your Christian duty."

"Why are you doing this?"

"It is *my* duty."

The tense fingers released Webber's hair, and his head drooped heavily forward. Dyer leaned down to look directly into his victim's bloodshot eyes. "I want to know . . . how do you feel?"

Webber glared back for a moment, disbelieving, then his will faltered under the penetrating stare. "I'm . . . scared."

"You should be. Do you want to die?"

"No . . . of course not."

"Do you want to go to hell?"

"No."

"Then forgive me!" Dyer spat at him and slapped him resoundingly across the cheek. "Say it!"

Webber's cheek went crimson from the blow. His eyes dulled briefly in shock. Dyer's blood cooled again and he leaned down.

"Say it into the machine." He pointed to the cassette recorder on the bed, its spindles revolving with a soft whir. "I want your family and friends to know how bravely you died. You're not a hypocrite, are you? You have faith?"

Webber stared at the younger, wild-eyed figure, voice again stolen by terror. A harsh sigh clawed its way up from his lungs.

Dyer had randomly selected Webber as his quarry, watched him for weeks, determined that he was just the right man: a family man, middle-forties, with a wife, two daughters — aged thirteen and nine — middle class. Church-going.

"You suffer the sin of pride," Dyer said. "Open yourself to the Lord and turn the other cheek. Isn't that his commandment? You are a God-fearing man. I know this, for I've seen you go to church and I've seen you pray." He wiped his own forehead, pulling back a strand of damp, sandy hair with the hand that held the razor. "Do you think you're not going to die?"

Webber gawked at him, his brown eyes drawn to Dyer's opaque gray lenses, his features twisted with every possible facet of fear. "Why?" he gasped. "What do you want?"

"What do you think I want? Tell me."

"I don't know what you want."

"All my life I've wanted know . . . to see . . . how powerful is our Lord Jesus Christ. I must see His will overcome what would seem to be insurmountable odds. That's all. I *must* see."

Webber shook his head slightly.

"Do you think I'm a madman? A psychotic murderer? Is this what you think?"

"No, but I. . . ."

"Liar!" Dyer's hand smacked Webber's face again with a loud *thwack*. "I *am* psychotic, you fucking fool. I'm as loonie as a fucking goonie bird. And I am going to kill you. But I want you to forgive me. You say to me, 'Richard, I love you and I forgive you.' A man of God would be able to do that. You are a hypocritical, lying man. Me . . . I'm as honest as a saint. I don't lie. I speak truth, Tim. Can you do that? Speak the truth?"

"If you're looking for a man of God, why don't you talk to a minister?"

"The Lord Jesus ate with sinners and common men. Men just like you. Thieves, liars, cheaters. I know you lie to your wife, you know. What's your secretary's name . . . Jean?"

"No!" Webber cried, straining vainly at his bonds. "You don't know anything about her! Or my wife!"

"I know about *you*, Tim. I know how much it would tear you apart if I took your daughters. What if I were to bring them here, right here in front of you? I could tie them up. Slice off their little panties. And with this. . . ." He flashed the razor. "Go inside of them."

"Shut up! Shut up! You bastard! You. . . ."

"Forgive me, Tim, and I'll make it quick. Show me that the power of God is great. I know you're angry and scared. I understand that, believe me. But the Lord said, 'the things that are impossible with men are possible with God.' Surely you believe that. I saw you in church."

Webber could only groan. "Shut up. You *are* a liar. You bastard."

"Would you like to kill me?"

Webber's eyes grew bright. "I would. God forgive me, I would love to kill you."

"How do you expect to be forgiven if you don't forgive me? You don't love me, Tim, that's the problem here. You are commanded, 'Love thy neighbor as thyself.' My Lord, Tim, we're neighbors. I've practically been living with you for two months, and you never even knew it." Dyer's rented house lay only two blocks from his victim's. He had staked out the house and appraised its resident family with intimate precision.

Webber grunted, anger and adrenaline bolstering his spirit. "You're nothing but trash. Walking garbage."

"I don't like that kind of talk, Tim," Dyer said softly. He lifted his razor and Webber's face suddenly turned to chalk. "We grow by suffering. By the time we're finished here — and that time is entirely up to you — I expect you will have grown quite a lot. I sincerely believe I'm going to see the power of God show through in you. I have high hopes for you, Tim." Dyer then gently placed the gleaming blade of the razor over the little finger of Webber's right hand. The older man tried to curl the finger under his palm, but the binding rope prevented him lifting the hand more than a centimeter. His fingers could only helplessly grip the end of the chair arm, vitally exposed.

"Please," he whimpered. "Don't. I'm . . . sorry."

"Sorry?" Dyer cried, his composure spontaneously withering. "I'll show you sorry!" He brought his other hand up and placed it heavily atop the blade, then brought his weight down fully. The blade sliced cleanly through muscle and bone at the knuckle, and the pink digit shot three feet into the air, followed by a thin geyser of crimson.

Webber screamed shrilly, the cords in his neck nearly bursting through his flesh.

"Forgive me, Tim," Dyer said softly. He picked up a towel from the pile he had placed on the bed specifically for this purpose and gently wound it around the bleeding hand. Webber gasped brokenly, and his head slumped forward. His eyes had gone dull and vacant.

"No, no," Dyer said tenderly, taking a glass of water from the nightstand. "Here." He splashed it into Webber's face; his victim sputtered and gurgled and moaned in agony.

Dyer retrieved the severed finger and held it up for Webber

to see. The older man seemed to wilt with a shuddering moan. Dyer tossed the finger into a corner. "Look, Tim, I'm sorry. I told you I'm going to kill you, right? It can be easy or it can be hard. You still think you can get out of this, but you can't. Even if you could, you'd be damned, Tim. You'd go to Hell. Sayeth the Lord, 'Whosoever will save his life shall lose it; but whosoever will lose his life for my sake, the same shall save it.' Really, Tim, your best bet is to profess your faith, admit you are a sinner, and forgive me. Come on. Admit you've been a hypocrite all this time. It'll do you good."

Webber could only sob softly; his body convulsed.

"Please . . . forgive me."

No response.

"SAY IT!"

Blood now mingled with the pool of sweat beneath the chair. The 100-watt star atop the pole lamp burned ambivalently as, outside the shaded window, the sun began to drop slowly toward the horizon. Dyer heaved a deep sigh.

"We could be here until midnight at this rate." He *harumpfed* disgustedly. "Let's start again." He rose, glanced at the cassette deck to check his tape. "Halfway through side two. That means we've been here over an hour. Your family will have a lot to endure when they hear this, don't you think? I hope you'll show them that you're really a fine husband and father and that you're no longer a hypocrite. Hey . . . would you like to say something to them?" He picked up the microphone and held it in front of Webber's face. "Tell them hello. Say, 'Hi, Nancy. How are you? It's me, Tim.' Come on, say it."

Webber weakly gazed back at him, feeling the warmth of blood dribbling down his chin from a bitten lip. Dyer suddenly thrust the razor behind his right ear, applying just enough pressure to bring a grimace of pain to Webber's face.

"Say it or lose the ear. Right now."

Taking a slow breath, Webber whispered, "Hi . . . Nancy."

"See!" Dyer exclaimed exuberantly. "Now we're getting somewhere. Say 'how are you?' Come on."

"How . . . are . . . you."

"Say, 'It's me, Tim.'"

"It's . . . me . . . Tim," he repeated, dropping his head in shame.

"Say, 'I love you, Nancy.'"

Webber tried not to speak. The pressure behind his ear grew sharper. "I love you," he blurted. "Nancy."

"Now say, 'I love you, Richard. I forgive you.' Say it."

The razor pressed hard.

"I . . . I. . . . no."

The razor swept forward. The lobe and lower half of the ear fell away, accompanied by a deluge of rich blood. Webber screamed again, his voice high as a tortured sow, his back arching almost to the point of breaking.

Dyer stood up and paced. "Dammit, Tim, you're prideful. You're so certain you can persevere and somehow get out of this. But you're alienating yourself from the love of Christ. With an ego like that, you'll never get past St. Peter. 'How hardly shall he that has riches enter into the Kingdom of God,' sayeth the Lord. Jesus wasn't referring only to money, my man, no sir. You are rich in pride, Tim. It's a tough obstacle. But don't you see I'm here to help you?"

"You're twisting the truth into lies," Webber cried amid his pained breathing. "It's you that's the liar!"

"I forgive you for that," Dyer said. "You're hurt and angry, and I'm sure you're confused. But if a self-professed lunatic can do it, then surely a Christian man like you, a normal, *sane* man, can humble himself before God and do the right thing." He sighed and paced again. "Well, I don't have a lot of pride, like you. But I like to think of myself as a creative man. And now, I think I'd like to go fetch your daughter. I'll start with Ellen — she's the older one, right? I'll fuck her here in front of you, then I'll slaughter her like a little pig. Then it'll be Jenny, the younger one."

"No!" Webber screamed. "Don't you dare touch them! Fuck you, you son of a bitch! Damn you to hell! Damn you!"

Dyer sighed patiently, raised his razor easily and drew a slow, deep gash down his victim's cheek. Webber's voice rose an octave.

"You . . . son . . . of . . . a . . . bitch."

Dyer checked the tape, found it almost at the end of the side. "Gotta change the tape," he said, shutting it off and popping the eject button. He removed the full cassette, replaced it in its case, then took a new one from the stack on his shelf. He inserted the blank cassette into the machine and began recording again. "Maybe we can get through this before the end of side one this time. Personally, I'm getting hungry and would like to get this over with so I can have some dinner. But of course, if staying here all night is what it takes, I'm willing to make that sacrifice.

"But Tim . . . I *am* going to kill you," he said loudly, for the benefit of the recorder. "And before you die, you *are* going to forgive me."

*T*im Webber had lasted one more hour. He had finally admitted he was a sinner and forgiven Dyer, just as his torturer had decided he would get nowhere without Webber's daughter Ellen. As Dyer was putting on his jacket to leave the house, Webber had broken down, pleading for him not to harm the girl.

Satisfied at last, Dyer had slowly cut Webber's throat, leaning close to watch the life leave his victim's eyes. Webber choked on his own blood, his face contorted with his final agony. But he had died with an expression of rage that dampened Dyer's hope for him. The man had lied again. He had not accepted the Lord and forgiven his tormenter. He had died a liar and a coward.

Thinking back on that now, Dyer realized that his failure with Webber had been his ultimate undoing. Despite his best efforts, he had been unable to reach the man with God's Word. And those men prior to him had been no better. In fact, they had all died violently, full of hatred, so uncontrollable that he'd had to kill them prematurely.

The straps now around his own wrists immobilized his hands. The cold metal beneath them was slippery with his sweat. He hated to admit it to himself, but he was afraid.

"The Court of the State, having duly and rightly acted in accordance with the Law, has found Richard Dean Dyer guilty on three counts of murder in the first degree, and as such has sentenced the guilty party to death by electrocution. Sentence to be hereby carried out." The bailiff gave Dyer a penetrating stare. Behind him stood a priest and two armed officers, each eyeing him coldly, but with faces pale. The bailiff said, "Do you have any final remarks for the record before execution?"

Dyer looked sorrowfully at the priest. "I think this is a mistake. I'm psychotic, I told you that. There must be a new trial. They disregarded my insanity plea. It's not right."

Two officers checked the straps around his wrists and ankles, tightened them a final time. Then one of them lifted a roll of gauze tape and pulled off a length to be fitted around his eyes. The second held a black hood at the ready.

Frantically Dyer shook his head, glaring at the priest. "Dammit, Father, I did it for the likes of you. I tried to help those people. I was closer than you've ever been to saving those souls! Are you listening, Father?"

The priest sadly closed his eyes, cleared his throat, and opened them again. "Please . . . no more, my son. It is too late. I suggest you pray with me. There isn't much time left."

(Do you think you're going to get out of this?)

Dyer gaped at his assassins, who stood ready to prep him for death. He heard the rattle of the metal bowl over his head as it was lowered.

(Do you think I'm not going to kill you?)

"You're all wrong," Dyer whispered. "So wrong."

The bailiff looked to the priest and shook his head. "It's time, Father. I suggest you give him his last Rites."

The priest genuflected, and softly began to mouth the words of Absolution. "My son, are you sorry for having offended God with all the sins of your past life?"

Dyer shut his ears. He was going to die. He would forgive them. He *had* to forgive them. He nodded.

"Ego te absolvo. . . ."

Gauze tape covered his eyes and was pulled taut. The black hood fell over his face and the metal helmet lowered with a final clang. He felt hot leather straps being pulled around his chin, and a rubber mouthpiece being thrust roughly between his teeth. And then he could not even squirm. The chair embraced him with rigid finality. He felt water dripping over his hands, improving the contact.

In a muffled voice, he managed, "I forgive you . . . I forgive you . . . I forgive. . . ."

His words were cut short as his lips drew back in a fierce rictus. The first charge of 1,500 volts caught him like a fist. He felt his eyes bulge and his muscles convulse. His back felt blistered by a gust of fiery wind.

The next charge, 3,000 volts, enlarged his heart by half its size. Smoke curled from beneath his fingers. Every hair on his body stood rigidly at attention.

"Forgive. . . ." trailed away in his blackened brain.

*D*yer felt as if he had been clubbed as he opened his eyes. What on earth had he been doing when he went to sleep? Then he remembered. . . .

An uncomfortable chair. One that. . . .

Oh, God!

He felt a great weight in his hand, which he nearly dropped in surprise. When his vision at last cleared, the tableau before him was familiar, yet somehow *wrong.*

He wasn't supposed to be doing this.

He firmed his grip on the heavy mallet in his hand, lifted it and brought it down upon the head of the nail. A grunt of pain accompanied the striking of metal upon metal.

Dyer wore a plate of armor on his chest. Feet shod in leather thongs. A helmet atop his head sprouting bright red plumage. The uniform of Pilate's centurions.

Pain-reddened but remarkably clear eyes gazed into his own. As he brought the mallet down again, driving the nail through flesh and bone into the wooden crossbar, the man's eyes closed, yet the face — the most beautiful face he could ever envision — remained tranquil.

"No," Dyer said. "This cannot be me. I never betrayed you."

Clouds gathered in the bright sky over Golgotha. From somewhere in the distance, a roll of thunder echoed faintly.

Two other crosses had already been erected, each bearing the writhing form of a suffering criminal. Around the hill, curious spectators watched in fascination, while the voices of distraught women rose in a discordant howl.

"This cannot be me, don't you understand? I cannot be doing this," Dyer said, voice pleading. "I did it for you. I tried to save them."

As the guide ropes began to lift the cross from the ground, the eyes of the crucified man opened again and gazed at him steadily. In a soft voice: "It's not how I would have done it."

Dyer looked down at his garb, realizing what it meant. "No . . . I didn't mean do it to you! Not to you!"

The eyes of the Savior closed and gazed upon him no more.

"Please! Forgive me," Dyer cried. "Please . . . say you will forgive me . . . say it. . . . SAY IT. . . . SAY IT. . . ."

Bloodlight

*E*lizabeth moaned softly as Grant thrust the last of himself into her and withdrew slowly, teasing her by giving a final half-pump before his erection withered. He buried his face in the silky blond hair gathered at her throat, breathing a sigh into her ear that told her he was satisfied. Which he was . . . but only partly. He let one hand slide tenderly over one soft breast, down her abdomen to her hips. She turned her head so she could look into his eyes. He closed his.

"You're wonderful," she said.

"So are you," he whispered, not insincere.

"What's wrong?"

"Nothing."

Elizabeth sat up, forcing him to shift position. "I wish you'd talk to me. I thought we could share things, Kevin. You do this with me and then shut me out. I saw it coming. Damn it."

"I'm sorry." She tried to find his eyes again; he hid them. "It's not you. Please believe that."

"I'm not sure I can." Elizabeth squeezed his shoulder, then kissed his cheek before sliding off the bed. "Call me later. Okay?"

"You're leaving, then."

"I must."

He nodded. "I'll call."

She disappeared into the bathroom, turned on the water. A few minutes later she emerged, dressed. Picked up her pocketbook. Leaned down to kiss him once, then slipped out the door without a word.

Grant hadn't moved. Sweating, but numb from top to bottom. He didn't want to hurt her. She loved him, he sometimes loved her. As if he *could* love. . . .

So many women. Done everything there was to do with them. He thought Elizabeth would be the one to tame him; she almost had. Her sex was the sweetest he'd ever known. But after so many, what thrill was left? His was an obsession, a drive that gave him no peace. How many had he hurt without qualm? Did they even care, these women? He'd tried it with men, seeking that crucial new sensation. Pleasure, for a short time, then. . . .

Numbness.

Perpetually wending its way through his body and soul, snuffing every fire he managed to kindle. Turning the finest wine sour. It was killing him.

Absently, he rose and went to the bathroom, relieved himself. Glanced in the mirror. A dark shadow around his jaw, heavy pouches under his eyes. Creases in his forehead, and a wisp of gray that wasn't there yesterday marring sienna temples.

He soaked his face with steaming hot water, savoring the heat until it dissipated, like the thrill of making love to Elizabeth. She should have been the one. He wanted her to be the one. His heart thumped hard once in his chest before settling into a slow, steady rhythm.

Lifting his razor, he swiped at the whiskers, roughly, without cream. A tingle, and then a spot of red. He let it pool and run slowly down his cheek, where it spread among the bristles of his night-grown beard.

He wished for pain. Anything. Anything but the numbness.

*P*lain, double-edged razor blades weren't so easy to find any more. Everything was disposable, bendable, pivotable or teflon-coated. But he found a pack of Wilkinson blades and carried them home with senses suddenly keened: the same anticipation he felt before he went to bed with a woman for the first time. In his bedroom, he stripped off his clothes and stood before the mirror, studied his firm, well-toned pectoral muscles, the finely-angled bones of his cheeks and jaw, the well-defined network of veins in his slim forearms. His biceps were not large, but hard. He cared for this body, pushed it to its limit often. No scars except for a thin white line in the crook of his right elbow where he'd been cut by glass when he was twelve — a baseball from the game next door, exploding through the picture window of his parents' living room where he sat.

He lay down on his bed, eyeing the silver blade clenched between thumb and forefinger. Pain glinted in its keen edge, waited eagerly for him. He didn't want to damage this body; only to feel. To see the blood. To *taste* the blood.

Ever so gently, he touched the blade to his right palm, pressed one steel corner into the flesh. A tiny crimson stain appeared on the metal. A minute flash of fire in his palm, stinging his nerves all the way to his wrist. He winced, wondering now if he were doing the right thing. Was this not madness? Dementia?

No, it was the killer of numbness. The murder of creeping death.

He drew the blade slowly across the heel of his hand, barely biting into the skin. Didn't want to cut too deep. Not to damage, only to feel.

There. A stream of watery blood, running down his palm to his wrist. An almost sexual delight, yes. And pain. A small, insignificant pain, but it was alive and true. A method to feed the flames and banish the sensual darkness within him?

Dementia?

He sighed, watched the blood run a little farther, then gathered his nerve and lowered his hand to his mouth. He tasted salt and spice, in a sticky but satisfying draught. He realized then that his penis was throbbing, struggling against his jeans. With a shudder of excitement and disgust, he unzipped his fly and began to stroke his hardening cock with his bloody hand. He watched the red drip from his palm and run down his swollen member to his groin. It hurt, just a little. But the color of blood: so rich, so pretty. He felt its warmth, all the way to his heart.

By God, he *felt* it.

He climaxed so hard he almost feared he'd ruptured something inside. And when he drew his hand away, his penis was awash with bright blood, and his palm still leaked the crimson water of life. His racing heart kept going, going, didn't want to slow down.

The thrill. . . .

"*D*inner at my place tonight?" Elizabeth asked. "I'll cook. You bring wine. Red."

"Yeah, sure," Grant said into the receiver. "Sounds nice."

"Seven?"

"I'll come."

"Good." A long pause. "I love you, Kevin."

"You're sweet. I'll see you tonight." He hung up, exhaled deeply. He'd bandaged his hand, and it no longer hurt. He was glad, though, because a little fire still smoldered inside, and he didn't want to have to hurt constantly to keep the numbness at bay. It was nearly five o'clock, and the sun had crept behind the trees on its way to the horizon. He went to the window to stare at the golden beams cutting through the pine boughs that surrounded his house. His thoughts were of Elizabeth, of her delicate beauty, her soft, radiant hair the color of those beams. *Something* had touched him inside, something he hadn't felt for so long he'd forgotten what it meant. But it was beautiful. An almost romantic dreaminess. A treasure.

Brought by the blood.

What if, before he went to her, he drew a little more? Would it heighten the pleasure when they went to bed, as they inevitably must? What if. . . .

The idea chilled him, sent streamers of cold fire through his veins. But with that seed now planted in his brain, it could only bear fruit; if he denied it, he would not be able to function with her, not with an unfulfilled fantasy draped over him like a veil.

He went for the blade.

Again, he lay naked on his bed, holding the razor's edge against his palm. Drew it slowly along the old cut, opening it to a new pain that jangled through his nerves. The beautiful blood came, and this time he cut just a little deeper, knowing it was the wrong thing to do, but driven — as he was sometimes driven to masturbate until his cock was raw and stinging. The blood was a deeper color now, ruby-red, catching the sunbeams and sparkling like priceless jewels as it ran unchecked down his wrist.

He then lowered the blade to his erect penis; stared at the potentially deadly instrument with horrible fascination. He could still stop. He remained in control. He could prevent himself from succumbing to dementia.

But all it would take was the slightest touch.

He pressed the corner of the blade softly into the spongy dorsal surface of his penis. Hot agony flared there — from such a tiny wound! Just a nick . . . and that was as far as he dared go. A crimson dot grew where he'd cut himself, pooled and ran into his thick pubic hairs. Now — how would it feel when he entered Elizabeth, the tension of his erection reopening the little cut? Would pain cross the threshold into divine pleasure?

He lay there for a long time, until the sun's last rays disappeared and the room became a ghostly cavity filled only with shadow. His naked body stood out pale against the dark bedspread. The blood that had coagulated at his groin burned black.

Something tinkled outside, so he thought; a little tuneless windchime that barely pricked his consciousness. Turning his head, he saw the nearest trees slightly illuminated by moonlight, or so he thought until he realized the glow was tinted orange-pink. And it wavered amid the foliage, as if someone were approaching through the woods carrying a blood-colored lantern. He put away the little pain in his groin and sat up, wondering what the hell this might be. There was a path through the woods that led toward his nearest neighbor's house, half a mile up the Beckham Road, but who would be using it now, and for what purpose?

The tinkling sound became more pronounced, but it seemed to have no source — as if it echoed only through the chambers of his own skull. The light brightened as it drew nearer; then he saw the little pinpoint of ruby fire, floating through the darkness toward his window. Like a crimson firefly, the point of light came to rest directly beyond the glass pane, holding him hypnotized by its gentle swaying. And a moment later, the light began to fade.

No, not fade. *Transform.*

Something pale took shape against the black backdrop; a floating white wisp of smoke, perhaps, or a diaphanous sheet suspended in the air. Then, the strangest thing. . . .

He saw features. A face peering in at him. Something so thin, so bone-white. Inhuman. A tremor of terror seized him, but he could not move from his place. The eyes were black, hollow; like looking into a pair of bottomless pits gouged in chalky stone. White silk fluttered behind it as the wraith floated outside the glass, watching him, beckoning him with empty eyes.

"What the hell are you?" he whispered, unsure if he could even trust his senses.

No response. Only the dead, empty stare that burned all the way to his soul. Grant wasn't sure if he had actually willed it, but he lifted a bloody hand and waved at the thing — inviting it to enter.

A moment later, as if no glass separated the bedroom from the spaces beyond, the thing appeared in the air over the bed, hovering as silently as the breath of the dead. The air grew cold around him, and while he knew dread, his heart thrilled at the sight of this apparition. There was no numbness within him. Only piping hot blood, carrying fire to all his extremities — to his once again erect penis, an arrow of flesh pointing obscenely at the floating shape.

A thin, bone-white arm emerged from the fluttering white raiments and reached for his wrist. Frigid, skeletal fingers closed gently on his lacerated hand, lifting it up to the deep-set eyes. The touch of the thing — like ice — counteracted the fire in his veins, in such a stirring mix that Grant gasped in shock, exhaling a lungful of air into the ivory face shimmering just above his. He saw a thin black slit widen slightly, and within the opening, he glimpsed silvery sharpness, quickly hidden as the thing swallowed his breath. It raised his injured hand to that slit, and a moment later, he felt the chill of its thin lips on his skin; the gentle pressure as it drew blood from the razor cut. A quick gleam somewhere in the twin pits in the skull. And then, slowly, a seething, feathery mass tumbled down around its head, a soft mane of pure white hair that tickled his uplifted arm.

The shape drifted toward the foot of the bed. And Grant saw the narrow skull lower toward his bleeding penis. He trembled in anticipation, then felt the cold touch of its lips. He closed his eyes and, willingly, let the thing take from him. The sensation horrified him, but held him in thrall, and most importantly, drove any remaining vestiges of numbness from his body. Surely, this was insanity. But such beautiful madness! He felt himself coming to orgasm, and still the coldness gripped him, tugging at him, harder, stronger. Every muscle in his body constricted as he prepared to eject his seed to the maw of the thing that was stealing his life.

His entire body exploded, so fiercely that he screamed. A wave of coldness overtook his consciousness, and for several moments, everything went completely dark. He lost his grip on himself and slipped into a place that he had never seen or felt: a place that existed somewhere between night and day; a land where one might venture only in dreams. And here he lay until the morning sun peeked above the trees and warmed the autumn air to the temperature of blood.

*H*e woke to a pounding at the door; frantic, relentless. Groggily, he sat up, noted with little care that he was still naked and that crusted blood smeared the bedspread beneath him. It hurt to walk, but he managed to grab his bathrobe, stagger down the hall through the living room to the front door. Leaning against it, he called weakly, "Who is it?"

"Kevin? It's Elizabeth. Let me in."

"Wait a minute," he said, fumbling at the lock. When he pulled the door open, brilliant sunbeams fired into his eyes and burned him. He turned his head, holding up a hand as if to ward away the evil spirit of daylight.

"My God, what's wrong with you?" Elizabeth asked, rushing inside. "What happened to you last night?"

He stared vacantly at her, shook his head. "Nothing. Nothing happened. I fell asleep. I'm sorry."

"Like hell," she snapped, standing before him with eyes of

contempt — that a moment later turned to worry. "Look at you. Kevin, there's blood on your face."

"It's okay. I'm okay."

He let her lead him to the bathroom, where she stood him in front of the full-length mirror. He almost gasped at the sight of himself. His face had gone the color of ash, and his eyes peered from deep, dark-ringed sockets. A long smear of dark blood decorated one cheek. And when he looked at his right hand, he saw the jagged gash, now caked with clotted blood. He felt no pain. Only numbness. Numbness, everywhere.

"Did someone hurt you?"

"No. I just felt bad. Went to sleep. Must have cut myself somehow."

Elizabeth opened his robe, confirmed he was wearing nothing underneath. But then she noticed his groin and recoiled with a sharp cry. "Jesus Christ, what's happened to you?"

He looked down. Saw his blood-coated, shriveled member, the tangle of pubic hairs matted against chalk-white flesh. "I don't remember," he muttered. "I don't know what happened."

Not quite true.

He remembered a crimson light at the window. The white wraith floating above him. The touch of freezing lips against his skin. The pressure of his blood being drained.

Black, hollow eyes, glaring into his.

"Come lie down. You need a doctor."

"No. No doctor."

But he did not resist as she led him to the bed and helped him lie back. She cringed at the sight of the blood on the bedspread, but said nothing more. Instead, she went back to the bathroom, returning moments later with a wet washcloth. She wiped away the dried blood as much as possible, and set about cleaning the cut in his hand. He felt nothing.

After she had washed him up, she sat down on the edge of the bed, leaning over him with tears in her eyes. "Please talk to me. Tell me what's going on here."

He turned away from her. His eyes then fell upon the bloodied razor blade on the nightstand next to the bed. She saw it at the same time. Her eyes went to the stain on the bedspread.

"You did this, Kevin. You did, didn't you? Oh, God . . . you must be sick. You're sick." She broke down and wept then, her tears pouring through clenched fingers.

He lifted his good hand and touched her hair. So soft and lustrous. But she withdrew, and when she looked at him, her eyes were red with anger and revulsion. "Don't touch me. Goddamn it! I loved you. How could you do this?"

"I didn't. . . ."

His voice failed him; only because his brain could not find the words.

"You need help, Kevin. I'll call a doctor if you want. But I'm getting out of here. Stay away. Please, just stay away from me."

He nodded, closing his eyes against the daylight outside the window. He heard her footsteps retreating down the hall, then the front door slammed. A long silence afterward.

Sometime later, when he opened his eyes again, some of his strength had returned. He sat up, examined himself, felt a new disgust at what he had done to himself — and what he had allowed to be done. Still, he felt no fear of the thing that had visited him. No; more a fascination, a curiosity that overcame all other emotions. He rose, went to the shower and washed himself thoroughly, scrubbing himself so hard he opened the cut in his hand again. This time he felt it, but the pain was dull and distant, and only served to remind him that the numbness was returning, and that he really didn't care whether Elizabeth came again or stayed away for good.

"No," he groaned. "That's not right."

She had to come back. He loved her.

He knew how to love. He could never forget that.

*T*he phone had rung three times, but he didn't answer it. He spent the rest of the afternoon staring out the window, wondering why the daylight bothered his eyes so, but determined to face it. It seemed the answers lay up there, in that golden ball making its way across the sky. He remembered some far-off place he had visited during the night, a place of blood and dreams. In that place, there had been no sunlight.

There was color, but always muted by darkness. *Why?* he asked the sun. *Why weren't you there?*

Sometime late in the afternoon, he realized it was Sunday. Tomorrow he'd have to go back to work. The idea sickened him; long days of mindlessly producing campaigns designed to sell other companies' products. A nightmarish place, it seemed now, full of false, fluorescent sunlight and one tedious assignment after another. Sometimes he wondered if the numbness had not been born there, where everything but heart existed in the work he created.

And as the day waned, he began to feel a subtle heat rushing through his bloodstream. Anticipation. A growing intensity of sensation, like that which he'd felt last night. God, he wanted Elizabeth so. Wanted her body. To touch her, kiss her, enter her. To come inside her. To share his blood with her.

"You see, I *can* love you, Elizabeth."

Spoken to the dusk settling around the house. An owl called back to him. And the crickets began to sing.

Once the stars began to sparkle overhead, Grant went to his nightstand and took his razor blade, staring at its cold edge with the thrill of rapture. And it was no longer just Elizabeth he thought of. Somewhere, out there in the darkness, *something* waited, perhaps even watching him as he stood framed in the window.

He pressed the sharp edge of the blade into the flesh of his bare chest. Cut deeply. And pain exploded through his body; pain so severe he almost fell. But by strength of will he dragged the blade down the length of his sternum, mesmerized at the sight of his lifeblood pouring freely from the cut. It ran down his stomach to his crotch, again puddling in his curly pubic hairs. He gasped hoarsely as a new jolt of pain shook him and he dropped the blade from his trembling fingers. God, it hurt. It hurt *bad.*

He stepped forward and pressed himself against the window, staring deeply into the pitch black canopy of trees. His heart raced in anticipation. And, thank God, his wait was not a long one.

The little fire appeared in the distance, weaving slowly between the shadowed pillars of the woods. It made its way steadily toward him, casting its bloodlight upon the tall trunks along its path. He heard the tinkling of chimes in his head: a lyrical, inhuman voice singing to him, he thought. And the pinpoint of light drifted to a point just outside the window, where it hovered motionlessly for a moment before it began to dim, as it had the night before.

Then, the thing floated in front of him, just beyond the windowpane. The incredibly narrow, smooth white skull with gaping eye sockets, its flowing, feather-like shroud fluttering in the breeze. Its hair fell around its face, waving slowly as if with a life of its own. When Grant backed away, beckoning it to follow, a smear of blood remained on the glass.

The thing reappeared just in front of him, advancing slowly, forcing him to retreat — willingly — to the bed. He lay back as the wraith smothered him with its icy chill, consuming his every exhalation through the slit beneath the tiny knob of its nose. The pair of empty sockets burned at him, and he lifted his arms to invite it down upon him.

The skull-face lowered to his bleeding chest, and he felt the familiar pressure once again — this time with such force that he momentarily felt dread wash through his body. But it didn't last long; no, he surrendered himself to his visitor, realizing the consequences, but no longer caring. This was indeed the ultimate thrill, was it not? A purity of sensation, the pinnacle of his every desire. Truly, the experience of a lifetime: *death.*

The thing gazed at him, as if seeking permission to continue. Peering back at it, without fear, he nodded.

"Take me all the way."

*S*ensation began to return slowly. He opened his eyes and saw the featureless ceiling, the midnight blue beyond the window. The blood that remained on his chest was cold, black against his milky skin. He lifted one arm, effortlessly, for it seemed as light as a feather. And bone-thin, as if the very tissue within had been drained away. Lifting his head, he saw that his entire frame had withered. What remained was skeletal — frail. Yet power seemed to burn throughout his body, and, even greater, the desire for sensation ached in the pit of his stomach.

He rose. Drifted above the bed, as light as a smoke, his naked body gleaming in the moonlight that seeped through the window. He floated in front of the mirror, yet there was nothing there. Nothing at all! Only the reflection of his vacant room. The blood, now cold and dead, lingering on the bedspread.

Power! He could feel it coursing through him. One quick thrust of his mind sent him floating toward the window — and then through it, as if the solid panes were no more than clear mist. He rose into the night, his eyes black pools beneath the brilliant moon. His house, the woods around it, all shrank into the darkness as he ascended and drifted purposefully toward the town in the distance, where he would find Elizabeth and sate his burning hunger. She would know him, he thought; know his longing and submit to his will. He would have her blood, savor her essence as he'd so desired in life.

He felt his way to her — smelled her, tasted the air where she'd passed. He appeared at her window, saw her sleeping in the darkness, her gold hair spilling over her pillow. The hunger was almost maddening now.

He willed her to awaken. She stirred restlessly, and moments later opened her eyes. For a time, she seemed not to register his presence, but when her eyes at last regarded him, she drew back with a gasp. He raised his cut hand, which no longer dripped blood, and waved at her. She shook her head, her face taut with fear. But he soothed her, transmitting reassurance to her with his all-seeing eyes.

At last, she nodded to him.

He passed through the window, floated toward her — and nearly cried out as the sharpest pain he'd ever known flared in his gut. He must have her. Now! Now!

Her blood tasted wonderful . . . like honey and cinnamon, so sweet he wanted to weep. He drank deeply from her throat, ignoring the tears in her eyes that begged him not to kill her. Holding the power of her life and death in his hands, he felt compelled to laugh. To sing out in joy, to exclaim that, finally, he felt everything he had ever wanted to feel in his daylight years. At last, he pulled away from her, and she sank to the pillow, still alive, breathing shallowly. He had no desire to destroy her.

But now, his thirst momentarily quenched, something stung him — like the prick of a needle injecting novacaine into his still-living bloodstream.

"No," he whispered, realizing what was happening to him. "No, please."

Just as when he'd had sex with her, the satisfaction of his feeding slowly drained away, leaving him totally unfulfilled. An empty shell.

Numb.

This, the ultimate numbness of life beyond death. An eternity of craving awaited him, he now knew; endless eons of searching for satisfaction, only to be cheated at each scarlet fountain from which he drank. Horrified, he stared at Elizabeth, at the blood pouring from her beautiful neck. With his skeletal fingers, he touched her warm skin.

His had once been so warm.

If only he could have been satisfied then.

Elizabeth stirred and opened her eyes, looked at him without comprehending what she saw. He retreated now, floated through her window and away into the sky, a captive of the silvery moon above. Even his fantastic power of motivation meant nothing now — less than nothing. Every sensation, every nerve . . . dead.

In desperation, he searched the night for the thing that had visited him, the thing drawn by his need and the shedding of his blood. He called to it, peered into the woods for some sign of its telltale bloodlight.

But it was gone, its purpose served.

*E*lizabeth hovered between sleep and wakefulness, dimly registering a pain at her throat. But its meaning eluded her, for she could not remember what had happened in the night.

All she could recall was the sound of weeping. A familiar, bitter weeping, fading away into the distance.

Angels of the Mist

On nights when the mist wends its way through the streets and alleys of the kingdom, when the moonlight is diffused and describes soft, purple shadows beneath the eaves of sleeping houses, this is when the angels will appear. Silently they come: pale, slender things floating on cushions of billowy vapor, like the luminous, semisolid aquatic things that roll in on the tides of the ocean at night. And their voices, they whisper and sigh in the loveliest harmonies, like the sirens who sought to draw Odysseus to the rocks.

And not unlike the sirens they are, for I have watched the angels as they drift toward the earth, always singing and seeking. Whereas long ago tales were told about them, no one had ever seen them; no one alive, that is, and the songs they sing are heard only in legends. My minstrels sometimes composed their canticles around these legends and made them quite beautiful. But never was any manmade music so beautiful as the sounds that one night not long ago began to peal beneath the moonlight. Sounds that drew me from my bed to my window, where I looked out upon my kingdom and wondered at the source. It was a misty night then; a night like tonight, the kind they favor, a night that remains in my memory like the aftertaste of a sweet wine that has turned bitter.

I loved my subjects and they loved me, and I had been their king since I was just a lad, a lad with a face unmarred by these creases and chasms, and whose hair shone gold beneath a midday sun; not the king of now, whose wilding mane reflects silver moonlight like the mist that lifts its arms toward this embattled tower of mine. I sometimes wondered if I alone could hear the voices in the night, for never to my knowledge had a single subject so much as whispered of them. Often, I felt compelled to shout to my people, "Do you have ears, have you not listened?" and yet a strange reluctance would befall me, as if a will from outside could dominate my own. Not an evil will, but one that could not be resisted by the likes of a mere, mortal king.

Came a time that I awoke, and the voices, I found, were directed no longer at the ambiguous night, but solely at me, as if these seekers had finally found a special soul — for a purpose that only they knew, but which came in hints with every muted melody to reach my ears.

"Come to us," they said, with passion sweet. "We need you, we want you." This collective voice beckoned, and I found it delightful, for I knew it meant that I alone was party to these legendary whispers, that no one but I could share their secrets. And the underlying mourning, so hopeless, so melancholy, moved me to tears and I wanted to see the makers of this wistful music.

So they came. Ghosts I thought them, for seemingly without substance they drifted through the night, their countenances hidden beneath veils of willowy silk. Never too close, like frightened children, always remaining at a distance so that I could not view them clearly; yet distinct presences they were — no mirages or delusions, these. And somehow I began to sense a threat in their music that, before, my ears had either never detected or had willfully suppressed. Something about these angels chilled my blood, for theirs was a terrible beauty and the mournful sighs they breathed nevermore seemed so sincere. The visions of Heaven they had conjured faltered and collapsed.

"We will have you now," they called, and I became truly afraid. From beneath their veils shone embers of red, and I could only stare aghast as scores of them drifted in on an airborne tide. "We desire you. We will have you."

"I don't understand," I cried. "What do you want of me?"

"Your body to appease us. Your soul and your heart will sustain us if offered to us willingly. And you will be rewarded."

"No!" I cried, sensing a lurking untruth. "Why have you come to me?"

"Because you are king," they said. "And there is no more potent life than the life of a king. Come to us."

I knew there could be no denying them if they came to me. I realized they could take me by force if they so chose, but this was not their wish. "Leave me," I begged them. "Leave me and return no more. I regret ever hearing your music and casting my wishes upon it, for you are not what I thought I desired."

"We will not leave you," echoed their call. "Never will we leave you. We want you."

And the pain began. So much pain, conveyed by their voices — ringing in my head like the pealing of countless, monstrous bells, so loud and so insistent I thought my skull would crack. I think I became mad then, for I pleaded with them, cursed them, and finally, I offered to bargain with them. With this, the pain ceased, and before me, these wraiths floated above the mist with eagerness in their haunting, burning eyes.

"This, then, is what you will do," they whispered, and I was horrified.

But to stop the pain, I made my pact with them.

*I*n the daylight, when the angels hid from the world, I became more myself and went to seek guidance from my most trusted counselors. But I found I could not speak of the visitation, for my tongue froze — whether from witchery or mere human terror I cannot judge. All I know is that I, the king, must certainly have looked the fool calling the good men of my court together only to stumble over my own words and occasionally laugh nervously, all too disturbingly like the poor madmen rotting away in the darkness beneath my keep.

And that night — oh, that night — I myself went to the daughter of my highest court advisor, secretly, so that even her father would never know. She was so young — a beauty of only 17 years, but fully a woman in every way perceivable to the male sense. I lavished upon her my affections, and she

was flattered and perhaps overwhelmed, yet never losing a
moment's composure. So sweet and trusting she was, knowing that I, the king, was regarded by her father as the most
honorable man who had ever lived.

I took her to the tower, to the window where I had overlooked my kingdom and seen the silky raiments of those pale,
singing angels above the mist. And there, as she regarded the
night, a long, withered stalk, like a gnarled tree limb bleached
white as bone, but possessed of a claw-like, clutching hand,
reached through the window and grasped the poor girl
around her waist, in an instant pulling her through the portal
into the darkness; only the meekest of frightened chirps
escaping her lips before she was gone. I leaned forward,
shocked at what had happened, though I must have known
full well the preordained fate of this poor, lovely creature. I
cried after her, certain my voice would waken those subjects
sleeping in their nearby homes. Yet the mist stole even my
cries, for the guards in the hall, the timekeeper, the exotic
women of the streets who sold themselves to wealthy barons,
none heard so much as a moan from my agonized lips, or
the brief, parting scream from the doomed young woman.

Unparalleled misery prevailed the following day, for sun-
rise revealed the bloodless corpse of my previous evening's
guest in the castle courtyard, and her father, my trusted friend
and advisor, lost himself in grief more heartfelt than any I
have witnessed in all my years. Now, in front of all, I attempted to come forth and relate my part in the obscene
death of an innocent, knowing that it would mean the end
of my reign, of my wealth — of everything in my life I held
dear, if not my life itself. Again, I know not if it were some
spell cast by the angels or a heretofore unthinkable cowardice
betraying my will; as it was, I remained silent and clumsily
offered my condolences to my friend, swearing — falsely —
that I would break my back to see justice done. I could not
and can not explain or defend the complete and utter loss of
my honor, my whole being. I retreated to my quarters, knowing I was no king, but lower than the rats that scurried among
the garbage outside the court kitchens. Yet no tears deigned
stain my eyes, and what shame I felt paled beneath the pure
hatred that burned for those terrible wraiths that drifted

through the night singing their demands to a weak, pitiable monster of a man.

But the memory of that awful pain spurred me on. They would not have *me.*

That night it was a baby I offered them, stolen from the crib of a nursery for the militia men's wives. I knew not to whom the child belonged, believing that its anonymity might temper the sheer horror I felt at my actions. Yet when that ghastly, inhuman appendage reached through the window to pluck the baby from my arms, I screamed from the darkest pit of despair, flinging myself after it, stopping just short of falling to my own death from the towering precipice. This time, I heard the baby screaming as it was lifted toward the stars, its tiny voice full of terror and longing for the protection of a mother it would never again see. And as my own wailing replaced the child's crying in the night, the darkness was lit by countless eyes peering at me from the gathering mist, radiating their approval, assuring me that I had damned myself as surely as if I had willingly given myself to them and accepted their "gift."

In one instant, I saw the face of the girl they had only so recently taken, her soul now one with them, her body reanimated and greedy for the blood of the innocent.

Or of a guilty king.

My madness then must have been complete, for I swore at the darkness, drawing up from my black heart the warrior's will that had driven me in battle all those years ago; the will that had conquered lands and made peace, that killed where necessary and spared life at every possibility. *I* was the master in those days, and *I* would be again. *I* would never succumb to the manipulations of the inhuman spirits who wanted my body and soul.

And their voices replied, "We grieve, O King, for we take the blood of innocents only because you deny us your own. And you deny yourself the reward of eternity we offer. . . ."

Never had my kingdom hosted such bedlam as came with morning. With the discovery of the missing baby, which I learned belonged to one of the Captains of the Royal Guard, the people demanded action. Rumors of demons arose, not in hushed whispers, but in shouts, for some of the old men and women, those even older than I, could remember a day when the same brand of evil had stalked the land — evil romanticized by the songs of the minstrels so that until now it seemed only distant and legendary.

I think those closest to me quickly came aware that some cruel weight bore down upon me, yet even in their most bizarre dreams they never could have guessed the truth. Not even my most disloyal servant, if one could be found, might ever imagine that the ruler of the land from horizon to horizon had turned from regal monarch to slinking butcher.

And of course, the angels returned again that night — taunting me with promises of eternity in the mist, occasionally stinging my brain with songs that brought ringing agony.

Yet deluded, I raged at them. Despite their hold over me, I uplifted myself in my own eyes. "I am a warrior! The son of my father, who slew hordes of infidels to bring justice to this earth; and of his father before him, who brought his people across vast wastelands to this verdant kingdom so that all might know the gifts of this earth. You are vile things, so repulsive and horrible, you worms! I defy you! You may drag my kingdom and my body through Hell itself, but you shall not have me!"

An angel floated just outside my window, nodding its shrouded skull, lifting its arms unto me as if to embrace.

"Witness, then, what you have wrought."

I turned my back on the thing, then. Turned my back while rage and heartache grappled within my twisted shell. I did not at first hear the screams from below, so consumed was I with myself. When I realized the reality of the sounds, I hurried back to peer down at the streets, and what did I see but blood — blood! — coursing through the alleys, and pouring from windows. Bodies lifted into the air and carried into darkness, young and old alike, writhing and screaming in agony and disbelief. Pale things swooped and sang, wailing dirges so beautiful the spectacle became dream: a tableau of crimson rivers and grey mist.

Once I heard my name — my given name — shouted from below, and gazing down, I saw the father of the girl whom I had to delivered to these spirits, waving frantically at me with eyes as red as his attackers. For a moment, something hot burned in my eyes until I rememembered fury and thrust away grief. I wiped my eyes clear, only to see my friend's arms clutched by groping talons, whereupon his body was torn asunder and the misty murderers knelt to bathe themselves and drink the essence of what had once been good life.

On and on it went, and whence these angels came I could never guess, for there seemed to be as many as the stars. Perhaps it was the stars that bore them, though now and again, I caught sight of once-familiar faces, withered and pale, possessed of blazing eyes beneath raiments of silk, and I knew then that perhaps not so long ago, there might only have been one; a single angel of death whose gift was bestowed from one to another and then another.

After a time, I turned away, for the uproar in the streets had begun to diminish. Occasionally, a distant scream wafted on a breeze, to be stifled moments later, sometimes by sounds that made my stomach quiver. And even later, I found that all was silent, the only sign of life in the world the soft pounding in my ears from the black, pulsing thing buried in my chest.

A soft rustle drew me around, and there stood a thing of beauty, or rather, of former beauty, though still it were majestic. It was she, the one whom I had offered to them so recently, her thin-lipped mouth awash with fresh blood, but with eyes still red and unsated.

"No man could ever stand alone while those he loved were taken from him one after another. No man could listen to the sounds that have torn apart this night, remaining steadfast as this one has. No man could offer up the lives of his people when they were not his to offer and shed no tear. Yet you stand here still. Accept their gift and be done with it. See you not the horror of your 'will'?"

The words of this creature, though clear, seemed as lies when I looked upon its deathly pallor. I could not remember remorse. Nor guilt. Nor sorrow.

Only anger at the affront.

"You will not have me. Begone!"

And so she went, joining her drifting brothers and sisters of the mist, spreading the words I had spoken to them; spreading disbelief even among the dead.

"No one shall master me!" I shouted. "Not you for whom death is king. Not you for whom I bargained in blood, mistakenly."

The mist swirled outside my window, and my own blood boiled. Truly, they had wanted me from the beginning and I denied them. Even with their evil machinations, meant to prey upon my humanity, I defied them. I am a warrior still.

I am king, for this is my castle. I am king, even king of death, for there is no one living in the courts below. I am king, and I have won my battle against them, for I stand alone. I stand here, victorious, while outside, like furious banshees the angels do howl.

Vita Terra

"Hello, Reverend? Reverend Greene?"

Martin Greene looked up from his dimly lit desk, pushing away the page of his half-written sermon. "Yes?"

Wilson Carlyle, the church's sexton, stood in the doorway, holding a thick stack of file folders. "These are the ones you wanted?"

"Yes, thank you," he said wearily. "Just put them there." He motioned to the file cabinet next to the door. "It's late. Are you going home?"

Carlyle hesitated, then nodded. "I'm all finished here."

"Then I'll see you tomorrow."

"Yes, goodnight." The younger man turned but tarried at the door a moment longer.

"Is there something else, Wil?"

"No. I mean, I just wanted to tell you . . . I'm glad you've come back."

Greene turned from his desk and gave the other a warm smile. "It's good to be back. Ten years sometimes passes in the blink of an eye. Other times, it seems most of a lifetime." He gazed at the familiar walls of the office, at Rubens' crucified Christ hanging above the desk. He shook his head with an air of regret. "It's like coming back to an old friend who hasn't aged, while your own face bears the scars of many battles."

"I know it must have been hard for you," Carlyle said, feeling slightly more at ease having engaged the pastor in conversation. "What was it like in Indonesia? If you don't mind my asking."

Greene attempted to chuckle, but it hung in the dryness of his throat. Clearing it, he said, "Colorful to say the least. Trying, most of the time."

Faint apprehension shadowed Carlyle's face. "Is it true you were made to leave Bali?"

"Yes."

"Forgive me, I didn't mean to pry."

"No, no, it's quite all right. In the end, it was for the best. I'm here now."

"Yes, you are. I'm glad," Carlyle said with a genuine smile.

"So am I. Now, if you'd excuse me, I have a sermon to finish."

"Of course. Goodnight, Rev. Greene."

"Goodnight, Wil."

Carlyle stepped out and softly closed the door. As the light from the hall faded, leaving only the weak desk lamp to dispel the darkness, Greene shivered.

*T*he clock struck 1:00 a.m., and Greene had not written a word since Carlyle's leaving two hours earlier. He dropped his useless pen and rubbed his eyes, stifling a yawn. Attempting to work seemed futile, but he was ill-prepared for his first sermon at his home church in over ten years. He considered using of the lessons he'd written as a missionary in Bali but then decided against it. His congregation — the people of the Church of the Seven Stars — deserved to know of his work; of his experiences; of his faith. Most of them were people he had known far longer than those years he'd been gone. Anything less than his best would be cheating them.

Where are you? he silently intoned, imploring the ceiling. *Why won't you guide my hand?*

Where the Holy Spirit had burned, only ash remained. The emptiness hurt like a gaping wound. His pen and his voice, both silent. He had begged Christ to return to him, only to be rebuffed. *You have no right,* his soul cried. He had committed no sin. He did not deserve to be forsaken.

Shame immediately seized him, and he averted his eyes from the figure on Rubens' cross, unable to meet that agonized gaze. "I'm sorry," he said aloud. "When the time is right, you will return to me. I still have faith."

He bowed his head, but as he did, his eyes caught a brief glimpse of the visage gazing in through the office window. Terror gripped him, and a scream froze in his throat.

Rudra stared at him, laughing. *You have no faith.*

Greene felt the eyes of the congregation on him as he stood at the pulpit, the multitude of eyes eager for the wisdom he would share with them. The anthem had just ended, and the ringing echoes of the powerful pipe organ were slow to fade in the cavernous sanctuary. Every seat was filled this morning, most of the church's members having come to welcome him home.

"My friends," he began, his voice booming in the vast hall, startlingly loud. He lowered his voice. "Good morning. This is quite a change from speaking on a hillside to a small group of natives." His flock responded with bright, approving smiles. "It's nice to see familiar faces — as well as all the new ones. I've missed you, believe me. A lot has happened since I last stood here. A lot has changed. I've had the opportunity to minister in a part of the world that, by our modern standards, is very primitive and isolated. As most of you know, I have just returned from Bali, a small island country in the south Pacific, just east of Java. I'd like to take some time to tell you about this land of 3 million people.

"When you hear of the island of Bali, most of you think of an exotic, tropical land, like Hawaii or Tahiti. Of course, there are modern towns there, an airport, hotels. To the tourist, it seems as westernized as Hong Kong or Manila, at least superficially. But as one begins to look deeper, he'll find a whole different culture — an old culture, one that has remained virtually unchanged for thousands of years. Once you go beyond the capital city of Denpasar, you'll see the primitive villages, the natives, the tropical jungles of the storybooks. It is to this Bali that I set forth to minister.

"Increasingly over the last few years, there has developed a trend against what we would call 'progress.' The people of Bali are disturbed by westernization. They seek a return to their old ways. Whereas tourists were once invited to witness their rituals of worship, they are now strictly forbidden. While visitors are generally in no danger from these people, they will find themselves unwelcome, and they are not treated with the respect to which they might be accustomed.

"Sometimes, I will admit, God has seemed very distant during my term. The religion of Bali is an old one – pagan, by our standards. For example, their old ways teach that the island rests atop a gigantic turtle, known as *Begawang*. They have literally hundreds of deities to which they pay homage, in a strange blend of Hinduism, Buddhism, and animism. During their most sacred festival, known as *Eka Dasa Rudra*, which is performed in times of crisis, hundreds of animals are sacrificed in the holy village of Besakih. This ceremony, known as the *Taur*, has always been closed to everyone except the natives. But as a missionary, I was allowed to witness this event last year."

Greene had captivated his audience. The faces in the congregation had turned solemn, their eyes hungry for more details. He paused a few moments for effect.

"Though they are what we would call superstitious, the people of Bali are highly moral. Their lives are spent in hard work and religious devotion. They firmly believe in the balance of good and evil, and these *Taur* rites are performed to appease the gods – to persuade them to restore balance when evil is on the rise. Such was the case last year, when the volcano Gunung Agung, which has claimed thousands of Balinese lives over the years, threatened to erupt. Following their festival, the volcano fell silent, so very naturally, the natives offered thanks to their god Rudra.

"Rudra is the Balinese's chief deity – a fearsome, monstrous being, capable of both good or evil." Greene's voice lowered, not for impact, but because apprehension had begun to creep up his spine. "He comes in fire and darkness. He comes at the calling of blood, and will protect his people if they appease his desires. It was against this strong belief that I pitted the Word of the Lord.

"To the Balinese, my mission represented change. Now, they are not ignorant of Christianity. Missionaries have traveled there for almost three centuries. But the natives have never embraced our faith, and only in Denpasar will you find a few Christian churches. In my entire term, my congregation never amounted to more than a handful. And those who gathered with me were often ostracized for betraying the faith of their people."

Then, to his dismay, Greene's memory began to slip back to the island, to that day when his Lord had failed him. With the inevitability of nightfall, the unwanted recollection dimmed his vision of the congregation.

"My friends," he managed at last, "I have to pose to you a question. All of you here are faithful. Most of you live as devoted Christians. You know that the Christian's duty is to spread the Word throughout the world. In his own way, each of you is a missionary. But tell me. Does each and every one of you have the faith to go amid the followers of a very different, very powerful belief system and tell them that they are . . . wrong?"

Greene's voice rose as he struggled to keep the gathering storm out of his mind. "I tell you now, the most horrendous test of my faith came on this island. In this land of morality, in this land where every man and woman merely seeks harmony for himself and all life, I went to preach the Gospel. To turn these people away from the rituals that our Lord finds offensive.

"To them, I was a bringer of discord. I upset their balance. Challenged them with new ways. I insulted their morals. I asked them to believe that everything they considered beautiful was a lie, fabricated by Satan to deny them the blessing of our Lord God."

Now, Greene could no longer see his congregation — only the vegetation-laced mane and spiked bamboo teeth of the *barong*, the Balinese's sculpted representation of their beastly savior. He squeezed his eyes shut, trying to deny the ghastly vision. In fury, he shouted, "I went there armed with the saber of Christ's love! I did no wrong, yet I was expelled. Was I right? Is the Word of God right? I ask you. I beseech you. *Was I right?*"

His voice rang through the sanctuary like a howl. Shocked eyes stared at him; mouths gaped in surprise. For a moment, he could see them through the fang-studded maw of the *barong.* A long silence followed, broken by the thunderous beating of his heart. Finally, a voice called weakly, "Amen." A soft chorus of "Amens" followed.

Greene felt his skin tingling with fear and humiliation. What was happening to him? Disorientation — dislocation — gripped him, and the memory washed over him full force, allowing him no quarter. He froze at the pulpit, his eyes focused on the distant land of his most recent past.

The blurred images swimming before his eyes crystallized, and he saw the almond-shaped eyes of the high priest staring ruefully at him, holding Greene's small gold cross.

"No!" he cried, and, for a moment, he could see the sanctuary again. "Maybe one of you . . .," he stammered. His voice began to rise again. "I had no right to do what I did. Don't you understand? I had no right!"

Then, his vision cleared, and he stood in shamed silence before the stunned eyes of his disbelieving flock.

*G*reene let the afternoon sun bathe him as he knelt among the rows of his small vegetable garden. He had planted it years ago in the backyard of the parsonage behind the church, and his successors had tended it well so that for all these years it had flourished. Working in it soothed him in times of trouble, and never had trouble fallen so heavily upon him as it had today. His service had been a disaster, saved only by the intervention of his associate, Tom Hanes. After his unexpected outburst, he had excused himself quietly, embarrassed, undeserving of the sympathetic gazes of his congregation. He had shut himself in his office, fuming at himself, trying to keep from cursing God.

Not until late afternoon did he release himself from the confines of his office. He had prayed, intently, sincerely, and still he could find no solace. "My God, why hast thou forsaken me?" he cried to the sky.

With no answer forthcoming, he turned to his gardening. The little plot nestled within a grove of thick maple trees, encircled by a low wooden fence. The church stood on a hill at the edge of the deep woods, two miles from the small town of Aiken Mill, Virginia. From the western end of the garden, he could see the rooftops of town through a curtain of thick branches. This was Greene's home, the land that truly meant the world to him. If not for the hollowness of his heart, he could almost make himself believe that he had never left.

With his watering can, he drenched his sprouting beans, his lettuce, his carrots, and his tomatoes, refilling the can from the spigot whenever it went dry. The activity relaxed him until, after a time, he found that — to his dismay — the meager confines of his garden had been transformed into tall, verdant papaya, banana, and breadfruit trunks. Thick greenery swirled around his ankles, brushing him tentatively like the touches of curious children.

The high priest stood before him, studying the movements of his hands, the sweat that beaded his pink forehead. Greene felt intimidated, for the man's wizened features seemed to possess knowledge deeper than any he could ever hope for. Each wrinkle in the coppery skin had been etched by a life that was both a fierce competition and symbiotic harmony with nature. He held up a small, glittering object, and fear touched Greene's neck with icy fingers. The small cross fell from the priest's fingers, dripping like molten gold into the lush vegetation below.

"That's mine," Greene murmured, gazing curiously into the appraising eyes.

"Take it," the priest said in thickly accented English. "Pick up your cross."

Greene bent to retrieve it, only to pause as his fingers brushed the hair of a ropelike vine. It lurched as if alive, and he jerked back in bewilderment.

"What the hell?"

The scenery around him changed, and once again he stood in the backyard of the parsonage amid his little plot of vegetables. Off in the distance, a low wind rumbled through the pines and beeches like the deep voice of Gunung Agung. A cloud passed over the sun, and Greene suddenly wished to be indoors, away from the sights, scents, and sounds of the Earth and its life. Disgustedly, he turned toward the parsonage, only to find himself standing face to face with Wil Carlyle and Tom Hanes.

Hanes smiled at him. "We came to see how your garden

grows. It still means a lot to you, doesn't it?"

"It did," Greene said softly. "I don't know any more."

Carlyle held out a glass of iced tea. "For you."

Greene accepted it gratefully and took a long swallow. "Thank you," he said, then eyed his companions with an ounce of suspicion. "Have you been here long?"

"No," Hanes replied. "I'm a little worried about you, Martin. Want to talk?"

Greene shook his head. "I don't know if I can."

"What's that supposed to mean?"

He gave Hanes a look of sincere affection, then shrugged. "I'm confused, Tom. Bali was a hard place. I'm a country preacher. Ten years ago, you couldn't have convinced me that I'd be traveling around the world or working on tropical islands. The experience was wonderful, but I'm not sure I did the right thing." He sat down in his wicker rocking chair on the parsonage's back porch, motioning for the others to join him. "Ever feel like that?"

"I suppose so," Hanes said, sitting down next to him. "I guess we all do from time to time."

Greene shook his head. "Not like this. You know, during the service, when I said I had no right to be ministering, I meant it. I didn't mean for it to come out like that. But it was the truth."

Hanes nodded thoughtfully. "You have problems with your faith."

Greene repressed a sardonic laugh. "That is the understatement of the year."

Carlyle looked on in puzzlement. "Isn't there something we can do to help?"

"No," Greene said. "Suffice it to say that I've been put out of my league." He again envisioned the high priest, the clear eyes in the weathered face, the cross dangling from his dark fingers. "It used to be simple, Wil. There was God and there was Satan. It's easy to wield the cross and combat evil. But that's not the way things really are. Not like that at all."

"I don't understand."

"Listen, then," Greene said, staring past the garden, toward the woods that marched away to the distant Virginia mountains. "Look out there and listen."

As he fell silent, he sat back and closed his eyes, straining, yet fearful of hearing the sounds of nature beyond the fenced yard. They sat quietly for several moments, two of them doing so merely out of respect for the other. Greene recognized their deafness, painfully accepting that they could not hear what he heard.

"The wind," Carlyle said in a whisper. "Just the wind in the trees."

"No," Greene said. "In the trees . . . farther out. It's something you feel. I've felt it ever since I returned."

"And what do you think it is?" Hanes asked.

"It's what the Balinese revere. It's life in harmony with itself. Perhaps it's the earth talking to God." He sighed deeply. "Tom, you know I've always had the deepest faith in Christ. I wanted more than all the world to carry his message to as many people as I could. I've done that, willingly, joyfully. But He's left me, Tom. The moment I saw . . . and believed."

"Believed what?"

Greene rose silently and walked to the edge of his garden. The lush foliage seemed thicker and more full of life than it had only minutes earlier. From his pocket, he withdrew his small cross and held it up to the sun's waning rays.

Hanes and Carlyle came to stand on either side of him. Curiously they watched as he closed his eyes and concentrated on the low rumble far out among the trees. In his memory, the high priest spoke the words, *"Byong mi baung . . . eka dasa Rudra."*

Softly, he repeated, "Eka dasa Rudra."

Then he gently tossed the cross into the dense stalks of his tomato plants. It disappeared into the tangle of greenery.

"Why did you do that?" Carlyle asked, giving Hanes a concerned glance.

Ignoring the younger man, Greene turned to Hanes. "I want you to pick it up. Pick up the cross."

"Really, Martin," Hanes said. "I don't understand."

"Please," he insisted. "Indulge me. Take the cross."

Hanes studied him with eyes full of doubt, but, after a moment, he conceded. "Okay, sure. Why not?"

Greene tensed as Hanes stepped into the garden. In the distant woods, the rumble of the wind increased. In the periphery of his vision, something moved, but turning to look, he saw nothing.

Hanes knelt, reaching with one hand into the thickly entwined vines. Amid the leaves, Greene could see a glitter of gold. "Pick it up, Tom."

Something in the plants rustled, like a small animal scuttling through. A number of leaves shook violently. For a second, a gray shape protruded from the roots of a tomato plant, then whipped back into protective darkness.

"What the . . .," began Carlyle. "Is that a snake in there?"

Hanes looked back dubiously. *"Was* that a snake?"

"No," Greene said. Motioning toward the plants again, he said, "Bear with me, please."

Hanes started to reach for the cross again when, from all around him, the vegetation began rustling. The leaves and vines shook as if with a heavy wind, and a rough scraping sound rose from the thicket of tomato plants.

Carlyle looked fearfully at Greene, then at Hanes. "There must be snakes in there. Come on out, Tom." Hanes shrugged, as if uncertain about his strange challenge. But, turning with a sudden surge of confidence, he reached into the thick tangle of plants.

"Don't!" Carlyle cried, seeing a quick movement to Hanes's right. "For God's sake, don't touch it!"

Scuttling sounds now came from all over the garden. But Hanes withdrew his hand, holding Greene's cross. He stood and walked stiffly back to the porch, lifting the small object. Greene weakly accepted it in a trembling hand.

With a heavy sigh, he said, "You did what I could not."

"What is going on, Martin?" Hanes asked with a look of frustration. "Please. I want to understand." He cast a wary eye at the garden. "I don't care much for snakes, if that's what's in there."

Greene shook his head. "Perhaps if you'd been where I've been, you would have failed too."

"You look haunted, Martin. Tell me what you're so afraid of. Is it something evil?"

"I *wish* it were evil!" he said sharply. "I can understand evil." He looked out at the forest, listening to the song from its distant heart. "What I confronted was elemental, Tom.

Maybe it's just a natural part of God's creation. But it overwhelmed me. My faith crumbled. Listen to it, Tom, Wil. I tried to make them believe me. I taught them the Gospel. Then, the priest came to me. My faith could not stand up to his. He showed me the power of Rudra."

"What is that? A spirit? Something living?"

"It's what's inside those people. And it's real. It isn't evil, Tom. It's not some trick of the devil, meant to deceive. It's just power. The life of the earth."

Greene bowed his head, and Hanes laid a hand on his shoulder. "You're home now. You can put the past behind you and carry on."

"No," Greene said. "I challenged it . . . and then I ran away. But *it* remembers."

"Martin, whatever it is, I guess it's up to you to sort it out. If you're unwilling to let us help you, you'll just have to trust in God. I'll pray for you, my friend. Maybe you need some time. Maybe it's too soon for you to start working again."

Greene looked up and nodded, grateful for his friend's compassion. But he remained silent, which Hanes understood to mean that their conversation had ended.

Hanes gave his shoulder a final squeeze; then he and Carlyle turned to leave through the parsonage's side gate. Greene felt like weeping as he saw the expressions on his friends' faces — expressions that blatantly indicated neither of them believed that his tortured mind would be healed merely by taking a short time off.

*I*n one respect, Greene thought, they were quite right. Running away would only compound his problems. Now was the time for resolution. He had been blaming God for his own failure. He had always thought his faith was strong enough to weather any conflict; but when faced with this power, so utterly vast and beyond his comprehension, his most basic foundations had cracked as if made of delicate crystal.

He had not been "made" to leave Bali; that was simply his excuse for having been afraid to remain there.

But guilt and Rudra had followed him home.

He now sat in his wicker chair facing the dark forest that

stormed up to the parsonage's walls. Off to the west, a few lights from town flickered through the black towers, while, overhead, a spattered array of stars glimmered against an onyx canopy. The low, steady roaring in the woods drifted to him from the distance, at once ominous and melancholy; majestic and fearsome. With all the parsonage lights turned off, he felt as if he were once again suffocating in the shadow of Gunung Agung.

From the blackness at the garden's edge, something rustled. He felt the cold touch of dread, yet he could only wait silently in his chair, praying for strength he did not believe would come. At length, he heard the whispering voice of the high priest: "Pick it up. Take your cross."

Greene rose from his chair and slowly, deliberately walked into the midst of the garden. A low scuttling sound came from the tomato patch.

Something far out in the forest moved: a low thunder, buried in the roar of the nonexistent wind. The thunder began to advance slowly toward him, its power vibrating through the soles of his feet to his very bones. He heard a deep boom, followed by another, then another.

It was coming now. And there was nothing he could do to prevent it . . . or even slow it.

Along with the sound of monstrous thumping, Greene could hear the sound of trees cracking and toppling. Still, as yet, he could see nothing moving in the endless darkness. His nerves screamed, aching to launch him into a panicked sprint, but something other than terror rooted him to his spot. He forced himself to believe that it was faith. The vague, dark shapes of the trees began to sway as if with an onrushing wind, yet the air remained solemnly still. Limbs rustled like the crackling of old bones, and a nearer scuttling sound prompted him to look down. At his feet, a tangle of vines began to shift and writhe of its own accord.

Around him, the garden came to life. He could hear the scratching sounds of leaves and limbs twisting and twining; the groan of *something* struggling up through reluctantly yielding earth. Then, beyond the garden, the nearest trees creaked and then crashed down as the monstrous force behind them pushed its way through. Above him, something blacker than the night blocked his view of the stars, and he dropped to his knees as his muscles turned to slag.

"Almighty Father," he whispered, "I humble myself in your sight. I confess all my sins, my sin of disbelief, the weakness of my faith, the breaking of your sacred trust. I beg thee, Father, take me into thy kingdom."

The roaring from the forest swirled around him, ruffling his hair, ripping at his clothes. The Balinese's deity loomed above him, as black as the void of outer space. Rudra had answered Greene's challenge; but his defense — his very foundation — was built not on stone but on sand. As he stared, he began to perceive the true shape of the thing that towered 200 feet overhead. It was a massive trunk with multitudes of appendages composed of wiry vines and bracken. It bore a huge, mushroom-shaped head — a thick mass of rock, earth, and foliage. From that mass, a pair of luminous green disks gleamed eerily, searching for his own terror-glossed eyes.

Hypnotised, Greene barely felt the prickle of vegetation encircling his legs. He raised his arms to his sides in an attitude of crucifixion, as if the gesture might save him. From deep within the earth, a deep ringing sound reached his ears, soon becoming an articulate but inhuman voice; a voice whose words held no distinct meaning but that burned with accusation. A cold swatch of darkness smothered him, and, at last, realizing that the moment of reconciliation was at hand, he cried, "Unto my God I commit my spirit!"

As the echoes of his voice drifted away on the breeze, the night fell still, and once again the solitary stars peered down on a tiny, pitiful, motionless figure.

"**M**y God, what happened?" Carlyle whispered as he and Hanes burst through the gate to the garden. "Martin, where are you?"

Early morning sunshine bathed the vine-entangled garden, turning the greenery to brilliant, waxy amber.

Hanes absorbed the sight of the tropical jungle that had overrun the garden. Thick vines wound around the wooden fence. Huge green leaves of what appeared to be papaya waved in the light breeze.

In the center of the garden, a bracken-entwined crucifix wavered slightly, as if nudged by a breath of wind. Realizing what it was, Hanes rushed into the weirdly choked plot.

"Martin," he groaned, tearing at the vines clinging steadfastly to Greene's rigid body. "Martin, can you hear me?"

Carlyle gazed at the monstrously altered garden, jaw agape. Suddenly, he froze and pointed to a huge mass of tangled plants near the overgrown fence. "Tom!" he whispered.

Hanes turned and sucked in a shocked breath. Where Carlyle pointed, the plants had been woven into a *barong* — a maned, beastly head with thorn-spiked jaws spread wide. A pair of hollow, black eyes stared at them fiercely.

"He did this, didn't he?" Carlyle asked. "He arranged all this, didn't he?"

"Of course he did," Hanes breathed, shaken by the sentient quality of the organic sculpture. Turning back to Greene, he pulled away the snakelike vines that hung from his outstretched arms. "Martin . . . talk to me."

Greene's eyes fluttered open, and his lips parted as if to speak. But only shallow, hoarse rasps of breath passed his lips, and Hanes stared futilely into fixed and dilated pupils. Then, without warning, the vines began to crumble, and the body toppled straight into Hanes's arms. The alien vegetation almost immediately began to wither, the leaves graying and turning to ash before the two men's disbelieving eyes. Hanes gently lowered Greene to the ground, trying to rub warmth into a cold hand. The eyes remained dead and sightless, though the heart continued to softly pump life into the body.

"What in God's name happened?" Carlyle asked in a tremulous voice, hovering nervously over the two men.

Hanes shook his head. "He faced his demon."

"Is he alive?"

Hanes looked up for a moment, shook his head, then peered back into the glassy eyes. "The body lives. But there is no one inside."

A gust of wind shrilled through the forest, sweeping away the rapidly decaying tropical flora. Within minutes, garden had reverted to the modest crop of vegetables that Martin Greene had loved — tiny, meager, but healthy. As the wind passed, Hanes heard the rumbling farther out: a melancholy, lonely sound like distant summer thunder.

For a moment, he thought he understood the message in that far-off roar, and he shivered. Then it was gone. He started to rise and carry Greene back to the parsonage, but he paused when a glint of gold in the tomato patch caught his eye.

He reached for Greene's tiny cross, but, as he did, a fierce scuttling sound erupted all around him. He saw an indistinct gray form behind the dense leaves begin to crawl clumsily toward him.

For a moment, stark terror overcame him. But then, with firm resolve, he reached in and pulled the cross from the foliage. He held it up, blessed the power of the Lord, and then dropped his friend's most personal keepsake into his own pocket.

Carlyle helped him lift the pastor and carry him into the waiting house. Behind them, something scuttled angrily through the garden, then fell forever silent.

The Children of Burma

The Manuscript of Colonel Kenjiro Terusawa,
Imperial Japanese Army

*I*n January, 1942, I was appointed commanding officer of the 212 Engineering Corps, a unit of the XV Army in Burma, under the direct command of Lieutenant General Shojiro Iida. For over a year I had been the Corps' executive officer; as commandant, I was charged with the responsibility of renovating a captured British airfield near the village of Myatauki, a tiny settlement of Burmese natives on the border of Thailand, about 200 miles southeast of Rangoon. In the opening days of the new year, the army had begun its invasion of Burma, both to secure its valuable oilfields and to erect a bulwark against an advance by the British from India. Gen. Iida's most immediate goal, however, was to sever and seize the Burma Road, the only means the Chinese had to supply their few strategic bases in the Yunnan Province, several hundred miles to the north. Achieving this objective would require close air support. The 212 was ordered to be on site by the morning of 21 January, and was allotted 48 hours to complete its assignment; the invasion timetable called for an Army Air Force fighter squadron to be operating from the field by 23 January, and for the airstrip to be able to support heavy bombers as needed.

For a week, escorted by the 213 Infantry Regiment, 33 Division, my unit had traveled at high speed up the Kra peninsula from southwestern Thailand on the Tenasserim

Road, occasionally skirmishing with scattered regiments of
the Burma Rifles, all of which were summarily defeated. Our
march took us through dense jungle and low-lying farmland
along the Andaman coast, but at Ye, we turned eastward,
separated from our escort, and began a long climb into the
Bilauktaung highlands on a narrow, treacherous path the
British had carved through the trees and underbrush.

Our ascent took us through some of the darkest and most
humid jungle we had yet experienced, but my unit's bulldozers efficiently cleared our passage whenever necessary. Along
the route, we encountered a wrecked tractor and a large pile
of crushed rock, indicating that the British had intended to
upgrade the road prior to their departure. By midmorning of
the 21st, we finally saw a thinning of the green canopy far
above and ahead, guiding us toward the plateau where the
airfield lay. As the bulldozers and supply trucks rolled out of
the jungle, the grating rumble of their engines, no longer
smothered by the thick vegetation, echoed across the field
like the exultant roars of lions suddenly freed from captivity.

The runway was a long, rutted swath of blood-red earth
that stretched into the distance. I judged it to be no more
than 300 meters in length; too short to accommodate any
plane larger than a Ki-43 Hayabusa fighter. The only struc-
tures I could see were an open-ended Quonset hut and a larger
metal framework building that had never been completed —
apparently a hangar. And off to one side lay the shells of two
Hurricane MkI fighters, probably damaged in combat and
abandoned when the British evacuated the site. At the far end
of the strip, tall teak and mahogany trees pressed close to the
runway, effectively diminishing its usable area even further.
I judged that, for our G4M and Ki-21 bombers to fly in, we
would need to extend the strip by another 100 meters.

I ordered my chief engineer, Lt. Isao Tajima, to reconnoiter
with his squad and provide me with a realistic estimate of the
time and resources necessary to complete the project. Apparently, the British had demolished the facility before leaving,
specifically to hamper our progress. But Lt. Tajima soon
reported to me that the existing runway could be bulldozed
and partially matted by days end, the extension area cleared
by mid-afternoon the following day, and metal matting laid

over the entire surface by noon on the 23rd. Satisfied, I left Tajima to oversee his task and went to coordinate siting the fuel, ammunition, and maintenance depots with Lt. Tochiro, our construction specialist. He was one of our youngest officers, a proud and pragmatic man whose brother piloted a Ki-43 in the IJAF and would likely to be assigned to the Myatauki fighter group. Tochiro looked haggard, as did most of the men, but his bespectacled eyes still gleamed with eagerness to perform his duty.

"There are several good sites for the depots, sir," he said. "We can use some of the material left behind by the British to supplement our own. And I will have the Quonset hut set up as your HQ within an hour."

"Excellent," I replied, pleased that the men seemed to have been revitalized. As the work teams dispersed to begin their tasks, I went to the Quonset hut with my aide, a stern young captain named Shindo. I admit that I felt somewhat disconcerted by the tenebrous aspect of the structure; its near wall had collapsed, and inside, the ridged metal skin was blistered and blackened. The enemy had probably tossed in a couple of grenades before abandoning the place. I was about to step inside when Shindo paused and called to me, pointing upward at something beyond the hut.

I stepped back and looked in the direction he was pointing. The wooded ridge rose several hundred meters above the plateau; for a moment, I saw nothing unusual. Then I realized that the tall trees near the top of the ridge were swaying and trembling, as if something large and unseen were passing among them, moving from south to north. "What do you suppose that is?" Shindo asked.

There was no wind, and after a few moments, I detected the faintest aural vibration — something I actually felt more than heard. It was an irregular, deep buzzing, almost like the droning of an immense swarm of bees. Shortly, though, the movement amid the trees ceased, and the barely perceptible sound dwindled and died.

"Enemy?" he asked softly.

I shook my head. I did not believe that the sound could have been from engines or other machinery, but neither did it suggest some natural denizen of the jungle. "I do not wish to have our timetable ruined by attack or sabotage," I said. "Send three men to reconnoitre. Have Sgt. Ishida lead."

Shindo saluted and hurried to obey my command. Though our advance brigade had driven the British from the country, I could not rule out an encounter with another regiment of the Burma Rifles. Also, I was aware that even in the remotest jungles of this country, isolated tribes of primitive natives still thrived. Most of the Burmese people were friendly, and up to now, we had only come upon one hostile village. But the inhabitants had been of a strange, physically degenerate type — possibly a result of inbreeding — and were fearlessly aggressive. Regrettably, I had been forced to have them all killed, including the women and children. Lest I be judged cruel, to my mind, the greater evil would have been to spare them to live without their husbands and sons. I took no joy in the extermination of an entire village, but their almost inhuman ferocity made them too dangerous to suffer.

Shortly, my aide returned with the reconnaissance team. Sgt. Ishida was our most capable scout, a rugged man of 33 years — two years older than myself — a veteran of the bitter China campaign. He had selected two younger men: a private named Koseki, about whom I knew little, and another private named Sakai, who had been on the team that executed the natives. He seemed a ruthless, driven young man for whom the war was but a proving ground for his cunning instincts. If he survived his tour of duty, I felt he might become a dangerous man among our peaceful people; but under the circumstances, he was a wise choice.

"Sergeant," I said, "Take your team to the top of the ridge. I believe there may be hostile personnel in the vicinity, but take no action unless you are threatened. Report your findings to me by 1500 hours." Ishida replied affirmatively, understanding that his party was to move unseen. I dismissed the men and watched as they quickly and silently entered the shadowy, tangled rainforest. Even after their long, uncomfortable march, they showed no sign of physical or mental dullness.

Happily, the bulldozers were able to quickly smooth the pitted runway and move the earth off to the sides, where the digging crews began to sculpt it into revetments for our aircraft. True to his word, Lt. Tochiro had scoured the inside of the Quonset hut and constructed a thatched panel to replace the destroyed wall so that I might have a temporary headquarters. Here, I found a single table and chair, and a small, battered file cabinet. The field radio had been placed in one corner of the hut, and outside, I could hear the low grumbling of our portable generator. Seating myself at the table, I proceeded to indulge myself in my one sacred personal ritual: from my valise, I took my small, leather-bound journal, and from it let fall a number of dried, pressed cherry blossoms — a reminder of my home in Okayama. I poured one cup of water from my canteen and dropped the blossoms in. Then, also from my valise, I took the picture frame — its glass cracked — that held the portrait of my beloved Machiko and our three children: my son, Joji, and two daughters, Hiroko and Etsuko. Placing the frame on the table, I offered a brief prayer for the safety of my loved ones to Kamimatsu, the spirit from which, according to ancestral lore, my family had descended.

About 1400 hours, Lt. Tajima reported to me that one of the bulldozers had thrown a tread; it could be repaired easily enough, though it would result in at least a half-hour's delay. Then, as Tajima consulted with me outside the Quonset hut, we heard from the distance the unmistakable crack of a standard issue Model 99 7-7mm rifle. Shindo came running, and we all gazed anxiously toward the ridge, but no more shots came. Then, from a great distance, I heard a high-pitched cry. Shindo gasped audibly.

Tajima asked in an anxious voice, "Colonel, should we investigate?"

I shook my head. "Continue the work. We will learn what has happened when Ishida reports."

"Yes, sir," Tajima replied, his expression sour. I knew him to be fond of Sgt. Ishida, and I sympathized. But he returned to the stalled bulldozer and unleashed his frustration by pushing his team to work harder and faster.

At 1500 hours, when Ishida was due to report, there was no sign of him or his two men. Tajima came again, suggesting that another small team be sent to investigate; again I denied him. As strongly as Tajima, I wished to see this situation

resolved quickly and satisfactorily. But the brutal fact remained that if our work was not completed to the minute,
we would fail in our duty to the Emperor, and to each and
every man on my team, such a humiliation would be worse
than a thousand years in Hell. I knew that, above all, even if
something had happened to Ishida, he would never want the
unit's failure on his conscience.

By 1700 hours, I was forced to accept that we probably
would not be hearing from those men again. But I did not
have the manpower to mount a search party, nor the desire
to place any more men in possible jeopardy. Two hours of
daylight remained, and with the bulldozer now back in op-
eration, I was determined to press on. The crews worked
furiously until the sun dropped beyond the trees; by now all
of them knew that we had lost three of our comrades. Finally,
as the last light faded from the sky, we broke for our meager
evening meal: a few kilograms of rice, dried fish seasoned
with sesame oil, and some fresh peanuts we had gathered on
our journey.

After supper, the men began to set up their living quarters,
and by the time the last light faded from the sky, thirteen
tents had been pitched beneath the sheltering branches of the
tall mahogany trees and coconut palms. A number of camp-
fires burned brightly to dispel the deep shadows of the jungle,
now alive with the sounds of nightlife: chirps, caws, and trills
of unseen creatures that seemed thoroughly ambivalent about
this group of humans that had infiltrated their territory.

I decided to double the watch for the night and instructed
Tajima to lay a strip of landmines outside the perimeter, and
to unroll a spool of barbed wire inside the nearest trees. This
was accomplished quickly and expertly by lantern light, and
once done, a certain sense of relief seemed to spread among
the troops. I had no tent, but intended bed down inside the
Quonset hut, along with Cpt. Shindo. A fatigued silence
pervaded the camp as I made a quick inspection of our
defenses. Tajima himself had taken the first watch, along with
seven of the enlisted men; he stood near the rear of the
Quonset hut, facing the dark jungle, his hands tensely gripping his rifle. At my approach, he lowered his weapon and
snapped a salute.

"It is a hard thing to lose friends," I said softly.

"I have lost many."

"As have I."

From the darkness near the most distant of the tents, I heard a low humming sound, then the voices of several men raised in a soft, melodic song. For a moment, it brought to mind the image of Machiko's face, and a whisper of breeze suddenly swept through the camp, brushing my cheek like the touch of her soft fingers.

The song went:

> *We have traveled far*
> *Each day that passes, we go farther still*
> *I fight beside my brothers*
> *One brother will never see home again*
> *Another will come home broken*
> *I would fly on the wind*
> *To return to you again*

Tajima looked long into the darkness, and finally said, "It is a song of mourning. Ishida is gone."

"Be watchful," I said. "If any of those men come back, they will expect our defenses but will not know which way to bypass them."

"Yes, sir."

I bade Tajima good night and returned to the Quonset hut, where Shindo had laid out our beds of thin rush matting. The warm glow of a single lantern cast long shadows in the close confines of the building. I was weary to my bones, yet I knew that sleep would be a long time coming. To my delight, Shindo surprised me with a small bottle of plum wine.

"I was saving this until our mission is accomplished," he said. "But I think tonight it is more vital."

I had just finished my cup of wine when I heard a sudden rapping on the door of the hut. Shindo sprang up and opened the door to admit a grave-looking corporal named Torohata — one of the guards Tajima had posted. He saluted me and said, "Sir, there are lights in the jungle."

I took my rifle and followed him out of the hut. Indeed, far up the ridge, deep within the trees, I could see a number of flickering lights moving slowly in a southerly direction. It was difficult to determine whether they were descending toward us.

"Torches," Shindo said. "Almost certainly natives, wouldn't you say?"

I listened intently for several moments, but could hear nothing in the distance. I realized that, apart from the soft crackling of a few nearby fires, the night had gone eerily silent. I ordered all fires extinguished and the men to assume defensive positions. Though we were a unit of engineering specialists, we were thoroughly trained in all aspects of warfare and ready to challenge any threat. Torohata slipped away to spread the word through the camp, and soon, our fires were all smothered, leaving us in darkness, total but for the distant flickering torchlight. A few moments later, Tajima joined me, his rifle at the ready.

"I count twenty individual lights," he said. "I estimate they are 400 meters distant and moving toward us."

I nodded, pleased with his expert appraisal. Just then, I noticed a faint tickling behind my left ear and, much like earlier in the day, a low, buzzing hum began to rise and fall erratically, slowly growing louder until it seemed that we were surrounded by a vast swarm of hornets. In the darkness, Shindo and Tajima's eyes darted back and forth nervously. Nothing I saw could possibly account for this almost unearthly sound.

Then, like the concussion of a bomb many miles distant, I heard a low, very deep *thud*, the vibrations of which crept up my legs like a horde of tiny spiders. Several seconds later the sound was repeated, this time louder, more powerful. And it continued — a heavy, almost nauseating pounding that came at regular intervals like the beating of a monstrous *kabuki* drum. Tajima suddenly pointed to the ridge, saying softly, "The lights are gone."

Each of us waited expectantly as the pounding grew louder, more deafening, assaulting our senses like a barrage from the guns of a battleship. Yet these were no explosions. Just as it seemed the unseen source of the thunderous sounds were right on top of us, an overpowering, noisome odor assailed our nostrils, and I heard Tajima beginning to gag. I can liken it only to the singularly foul stench of burning flesh, mixed with the acrid sting of sulfurous fumes.

And then . . . it was gone.

The pounding fell silent, the buzzing faded, and only the faintest lingering echoes served to remind us that we had actually experienced some nightmarish and inexplicable phenomenon. At last, the stench of brimstone began to drift away, to be replaced by the sweet smell of woodsmoke from the extinguished fires. Yes, we were truly awake, not dreaming, for now I could hear the sounds of men coughing and choking, and several exclamations of shock and disbelief.

And then, the most terrible thing of all: the high-pitched, piteous sound of a man screaming, *"Yaieee!"*

Together, Shindo and I rushed into the darkness toward the source of the sound. Suddenly, golden lanternlight burst to life a few meters ahead of me, and I saw Tajima, his face a mask of unutterable revulsion. He lifted one arm and pointed to a sight that, for several seconds, my mind simply could not accept.

Three staves of bamboo sprouted from the earth at the edge of the runway, and atop them, the decapitated heads of Sgt. Ishida and his two men were mounted like bizarre trophies, their eyes open and staring, mouths open as if to scream their agony and disbelief. Rivulets of blood poured freely down the pale lengths of bamboo, indicating these murders had been committed all too recently.

"Ishida," Tajima groaned, shaking his head violently. "He was the son of my father's closest lifelong friend. I have known him since we were children. He was like an older brother to me. Oh, my friend Tadao."

I squeezed Tajima's shoulder as he slowly dropped to his knees. "I'm sorry. I didn't know."

"We never spoke of it," Tajima whispered. "We both knew . . . that one of us might be lost. But not like this!"

At last collecting my scattered wits, I finally said, "We must continue our work. It is our duty to the emperor. But we must defend ourselves. Whatever was in the jungle must still be there. We cannot lower our guards for an instant."

Shindo gazed at me appraisingly, his eyes finally affirming that he understood my decision. I saw several of the men take up their rifles and turn away from the profane totems, their training and solemn devotion to duty overcoming their personal fears. I allowed Tajima several moments to grieve silently before telling him, "You will be in charge of removing these . . . travesties. See that Sgt. Ishida and his men's remains are laid to rest with the utmost honor. Do it now, and then return to your post. Whomever — whatever — is responsible must not be allowed to overcome us again."

In a quavering voice, Tajima replied, "Yes, sir." And he rose, his eyes hard and focused, his body rigid and strong, no longer weakened by grief or uncertainty. He and his men performed the grim task quickly and efficiently, burying the pitiful remains of his friend and the others with whatever personal items he could find. At Tajima's side, I attended the saying of prayers at the gravesite.

The rest of the night passed uneventfully, though I am certain not a single man slept so much as an hour. At dawn, the camp came alive again, but I could tell from the men's lethargic pace that the night's ordeal had taken a dreadful toll on them. Once we had eaten our breakfast of fruit and dried beef, I transmitted a message to Lt. Gen. Iida and informed him that three of our party had been lost, guardedly expressing the opinion that the security of the region was in question.

Gen. Iida's reply came: "Continue with the work as scheduled. XVII Tank Group is 18 hours from your position. A single element will divert to assist."

That our operational commander would offer so much as a small group of tanks to reinforce our position improved the morale of the men so that they worked at a pace belying any deprivation of sleep. At 1200 hours, I was so pleased with our progress that it was almost possible to believe that the horrific events of the previous night were now long passed, and that from this point on we had nothing to fear. Still, at any given time, three men now stood guard at the jungle perimeter, with license to open fire at the first sign of any trespasser. However, if opportunity presented, I wanted any human that might come near to be captured and brought to me immediately.

And so it was that, at about 1430 hours, a commotion

erupted not far from my Quonset hut headquarters. I went out to see Cpl. Torohata emerge from the trees, his bayonet thrust into the back of a squat, bronze figure who was being dragged, struggling, by two other guards. As I approached, followed by a dutiful Shindo, the guards grasped the creature's arms and hurled him to the ground in front of me. I saw at once that this was a native much like those we had executed a few days before. He appeared to be roughly 130 centimeters tall, his features brutish, with opaque black eyes beneath a curiously scaly, bony brow, and an awkwardly protruding lower jaw. He wore only a loose, robe-like garment of tanned animal hide.

"I saw him watching us just beyond the minefield," Torohata said. "I ordered Serizawa and Fuchida to take him alive. Beware, he moves quickly. He almost escaped and I thought we might have to shoot him."

"Excellent work, corporal," I said. Glaring at the evil-looking creature, I leaned close, only to be repelled by the sour odor of decay that his coppery flesh exuded. Even realizing he could not possibly understand Japanese, I growled, "Do you speak, animal?"

Torohata spoke adequate, if not fluent Burmese and spouted a few interrogatives at our captive, who gazed at us with unconcealed hatred, seemingly oblivious to the words. I knew that tribes in the mountains often had languages of their own, and the one this beast belonged to was probably no exception.

With a smile that revealed unnaturally long, sharpened teeth, the man growled, "Mi, byong yi. Eh go me shogo na, byong mi rien."

Torohata shook his head. "It's not unlike Burmese, but it makes no sense to me."

"Colonel, look at his hands," Shindo said.

Leaning perilously close to the hissing thing, I found that the short, clumsy-looking hands were covered in coarse, dark hair and ended in sharp, claw-like nails that glistened like burnished steel. Though he bore a resemblance to those natives we had seen before, his physical degeneration was far more pronounced.

"What came to us last night?" I asked. "Who killed my

men?"

Though the words might make no sense to him, the creature seemed to comprehend my meaning. His lips spread in a malicious smile and, with saliva spraying from his mouth, he hissed, "Go-go, mi ingah eh cho-chiyo gah san!"

And then, like a blazing wind, I felt the arrival of pure hatred. Lt. Tajima strode past the guards and leaned down to regard our fidgeting captive. Almost as if he recognized Tajima, the brute smiled again and said in a wickedly gleeful voice, "Ba-kai! Ong, jin yi tadami dah. Baung shaggat!"

With controlled rage, Tajima raised an arm and slapped one bony cheek with enough force to send the brute reeling backward. The thick lips parted in a gasp as he fell upon his still-bleeding bayonet wound. With an effort, the squat man managed to get back to his knees, and for the first time, I saw a hint of pain in those black, impenetrable eyes.

"Colonel," Tajima said in a somber voice. "We are wasting our time with this . . . beast."

Every officer in the Imperial Japanese Army carries with him a sword, which is a sacred symbol of his honor. I now drew mine, its long blade gleaming before the pained eyes of our captive. Some of his defiance seemed to melt, but his lips curled into a feral snarl. Speaking in a tone that I was certain he would comprehend, I said, "You are useless, animal. Whatever pit you crawled from, you will not return to it alive."

I raised my sword, making clear to all my intention to use it. But then, seeing the dullness of disappointment in Tajima's eyes, I paused and lowered the weapon. Tajima glanced at me in surprise; but then I nodded to him, and he understood. He unsheathed his own sword and drew it back slowly, his muscles coiling. Now, peering straight into the brute-man's eyes, he growled triumphantly, "For Ishida." Then with all his strength he brought the sword down and around, crying, "Aiiee!"

The kneeling creature's eyes flashed with terrible realization, just as the blade bit into the flesh of his neck, sweeping through muscle and bone like a scythe through stalks of grain. The head toppled from the body, and a fountain of blood spurted from the gaping wound. We watched with grim satisfaction as the headless body struck the ground with a thud, the purple blood mingling with the dust until it formed a vile-looking pool of thick black mud.

Lt. Tajima took a white handkerchief from his coat pocket, wiped the blade, and with a smooth motion resheathed his sword. Then, with cold deliberation, he picked up the head by its long, coarse hair and carried it to one of the blood-drenched staves that still stood nearby. He lifted his trophy and firmly forced it down onto the sharpened bamboo tip, stepping back to regard his handiwork. With a hiss, he spat at the unseeing, coal-black eyes beneath the bony brow; then, unleashing a heartfelt sob, he turned and walked away, his thoughts all too clearly focused on the memory of his lost friend.

And now, knowing my duty, I ordered the men back to work, including Tajima. While this unpleasant episode had been unavoidable, we had lost precious time. There were clearly more of these debased tribesmen in the jungle, and I expected some sort of retaliation. And not a one of us could forget the indescribable horror of the night before, of the monstrous pounding of the earth, of the gut-wrenching odor that had swept over our compound. My greatest fear was that, whatever otherworldly evil reigned here, it might be somehow allied to the subhuman children of this dark country.

We had only been back at work for a short time when Cpt. Shindo approached me, his demeanor uncharacteristically furtive. In a near-whisper, he said, "Colonel, there is something up on the ridge. I have been unable to get a clear view of it. But I know that it is there."

He led me past the line of new revetments to the edge of the runway, where we had a clear view of the ridge's crest. Without pointing, he said, "Look toward the top, just to the right of its highest point."

I did as he suggested and, at first, saw nothing unusual. But as I started to look away, something at the corner of my eye turned my head.

It seemed little more than a heat haze rolling from the jungle. When I looked straight at it, it disappeared. But as I focused my gaze to one side of it, I could see an indistinct, blurry mass, almost like the illusory dark pools that sometimes appear on a road beneath the hot sun. But from this

202 Stephen Mark Rainey

patch of discoloration, I could see what appeared to be thin tendrils of shadow wriggling and creeping down the mountainside. Above, a few cirrus clouds crept across the sun, their wispy shadows undulating over the side of the ridge to mingle with those unnatural, barely visible streamers.

"Shindo, have Sgt. Hikaru order up his gun crew."

Shindo replied in an equally low voice, "Yes, sir," and left to fetch Hikaru, who would be working on the revetments. Our unit, like most of similar size and composition, was equipped with two 70mm Howitzers, which were ideal for shelling over ridged and mountainous terrain. I found my mind clouded with doubt, for how could I be certain that we would not be firing at a mirage? But Shindo had seen it; if I looked away from the crest of the ridge, I could still see it. And the more I tried to view this thing that had no place in the rational world, the nearer I came to breaking into wild, panicked flight. Only my well-honed sense of duty and years of military discipline kept me rooted to the spot.

The four gun crewmen reported within moments, each eager to have a shot at whatever target I might order. Some of them scanned the ridge with questing eyes, but none apparently saw what Shindo and I had seen. When I glanced back, I confirmed that the wavering blur still hovered menacingly above the tallest trees. But from the disturbed expressions that suddenly stole over the men's faces, I judged that they, too, perceived *something* awry.

"Men," I said, "I want you to lay down a series of shots along the very top of the ridge. North to south, starting there" I pointed to the steeply angled summit, off to my left, "and finishing about twenty degrees to the south."

The heavy Howitzers required both of its crewmen to wheel it out to the edge of the airstrip, which afforded a clear shot at the ridge crest. Hikaru ordered four more men to bring up the crates of ammunition. Though the men still working the field were curious about this new flurry of activity, they continued without breaking their pace. At the southern end of the field, the crews were laying down the metal matting, which meant we were maintaining our schedule.

Turning to Hikaru, I pointed at the ridge. "I estimate it's 450 meters to the summit. Lay down your fire within ten to thirty meters of the crest."

As the crewmen cranked the stubby barrels into firing position, one of them, a private named Gondo, began peering at the summit with an apprehensive frown, as if doubting his senses. He glanced at me questioningly, obviously hoping I might confirm or deny his vision. I merely nodded thoughtfully, and his face grew pale with the realization that we were surely challenging some ominous unknown. I was certain that we must have shared the same unspoken thought: that by unleashing our weaponry upon this thing we might be inviting our own doom.

Casting aside that unseemly notion, I stepped away to let the gunners do their jobs. Hikaru made a quick calculation on a small notepad, then called out, "Number one, set your target bearing 74 degrees, trajectory 40. Number two, set target bearing 79 degrees, trajectory 38. Lock and prepare to fire."

The first crewman waved to signal his readiness. Hikaru's arm rose, hovered for a moment, then fell. The cannon erupted with a *boom*, recoiling angrily on its locked wheels. I heard the scream of the shell as it arced over the ridge, where it exploded violently, just a few meters to the left of the lurking, phantom watcher. A moment later, the second Howitzer unleashed its shell, which threw up a pillar of black smoke and the debris of several trees. But this time, as the smoke rolled upward, I saw it curling around a previously unseen contour, defining a strange, alien figure that now could be viewed by all.

It was a vaguely mushroom-shaped mass that I judged to be at least forty meters tall, from which sprang dozens of wavering, curling streamers that seemed to flicker and dance like filaments of black flame. As the smoke cleared, the silhouette once again became an indistinct blur that dared me to pinpoint its location. But I pointed to where it had materialized and called to Hikaru, There! Concentrate your fire on that spot!"

The Howitzers spoke again, hurling their lethal loads unerringly to their target. This time, as the explosions shattered the air, I saw something rising above the smoke and flame: a questing, unfurling arm of shadow, the tip of which widened like the mouth of a trumpet. Suddenly, above the ringing echoes of the explosions, I heard the hornet-like buzzing that had previously come down from the ridge, only this time with such volume that I could actually see the limbs of the nearest trees quivering with the vibrations. Swarms of ants seemed to rush over my skin, and my ears felt as if spikes were being driven into them. I could not suppress a pained cry, and Hikaru gasped with shock, but he immediately cried out for the guns to fire again. The cannons loosed another volley and the shells struck home, hurling huge pieces of the ridge into the air that rained noisily into the jungle like black hail. The buzzing began to soften and moved into the distance, and I knew that any further shots would be futile. I ordered gun crew to cease fire.

We watched with a feeling of grim helplessness as the smoke began to clear and silence returned. I knew that, whatever was up there, our weapons had not touched it. Worst of all, I felt that, if this thing behaved in any fashion like the higher denizens of our world, it might return with a new, vengeful purpose when we were the most vulnerable: with the coming of night.

I knew that, somehow, I must persuade Gen. Iida to relinquish this particular airfield and reassign my unit to another location. *Any* other location. At the same time, I knew the chances of such a feat were nonexistent. No matter that I might argue that the British were gone, that the Myatauki airfield could not possibly be used against us, I would be accused of insubordination and cowardice — the most heinous offenses of which an officer might be found guilty. Yes, I — as well as every man in my outfit — had pledged my service and my life to my country, to my emperor; but where, I wondered, was the honor in sacrificing our lives to complete a task that would simply open the way for more of our comrades to be destroyed?

Inside the Quonset hut, I found Cpl. Okada, our radio operator, at the set, speaking into the transmitter. When he saw me, he called out, "Colonel, it is Lt. Gen. Iida for you."

I sighed deeply. The timing could not have been more — or less — propitious, for I had no time to consider my options further.

"This is Col. Terusawa," I said into the microphone, taking

the headset from Okada. "Go ahead, General."

The voice on the other end sounded a million miles away, reminding me of the vast distance between this haunted plateau and the disciplined, regimented world beyond. "Col. Terusawa," Gen. Iida said, "Fighter Group IV is to arrive at 1100 hours tomorrow. You will be ready for them?"

"We are on schedule, General."

"What of the difficulties you reported earlier?"

I hesitated. I knew I must speak now, or not at all. "We have engaged an enemy," I finally stammered. "We've suffered no further losses, but at this time I believe our position is not secure. We do not have the manpower or weaponry to repel an attack, should it come."

Several seconds of silence followed. Then: "And this enemy? Who is it?"

I swallowed hard. "Its true nature has not been ascertained, General. There is something . . . deadly . . . in the jungle, sir."

"I do not follow you, Colonel." Iida's voice had a harsh edge.

"Sir, I ask you to trust my word that an air group will not be secure at this site."

I heard a muted voice speaking to Iida, and silence followed for several moments. Finally, he replied, "You are an excellent soldier, Colonel. Your record is exemplary, and I am sure I made the right choice in assigning you this mission. An element of tanks arrives in the morning to assist you, does it not?"

"Yes, sir."

"And do you feel this is insufficient for you to complete your assignment?"

"I am certain I can complete my assignment, sir. But I believe that to do so is ill advised. This is my most prudent military judgment, General."

Iida seemed to ponder the point briefly. But then he said, "Col. Terusawa, your orders are to complete the renovation and be ready for Fighter Group IV to arrive as scheduled. Do you have any other questions or comments?"

My heart sank. His decision was final. "No, sir. I do not."

"Very well. You will be pleased to know the campaign in Malaya is succeeding beyond all hopes. Gen. Yamashita has routed the British to Johore, and expects to occupy Singapore within ten to fifteen days."

"That is excellent news, sir."

"I anticipate similarly excellent news from you tomorrow."

"I understand, sir."

"Until I hear from you, then." The receiver went dead.

I turned away and dismissed Okada, telling him to spread the news about our victories in Malaya, which would hearten the men somewhat. I was truly pleased for Gen. Yamashita, whom I had met before. He was considered by many to be a somewhat neurotic, but highly capable officer.

As I went to fulfill my duty, a new, numbing fear began to overcome me, nearly trivializing all that I had experienced up to now: that, officially, I myself might have just been labeled "neurotic" by none other than Gen. Iida himself.

*F*or the rest of the day, I pushed the men almost cruelly, and, though fatigue showed on them like a cerement, they obeyed my orders with a quiet desperation, aware of the fate that might await us in the coming night. The tractors had laid matting over the existing runway, leaving only a portion of the newly extended strip yet uncovered. I knew that we would be finished well in advance of the fighter group's arrival. As the sun touched the treetops in the west, Cpl. Okada brought me the report that, less than a hundred miles to the north, 55 Division was streaming across the border from Thailand at Kawkareik, bound for Moulmein on Burma's western coast. The news of our advances should have brought us reason to rejoice, but faraway victories could scarcely assuage the dread that simmered in the aging afternoon.

Once the purple and gold streaks that mourned the daylight began to dim, we went to our evening meal. We had so far been frugal with our rations, but tonight I ordered extra portions of sesame-seasoned rice and dried beef for all. The guards rotated, and fires began to spring up among the trees, creating a bastion of light against the menace that lurked somewhere beyond. But the camp was unnervingly silent, for not one man called to another, no one spoke above a whisper;

even the jungle's nightsongs seemed muted, as if its creatures shared our fear of what the Burmese darkness mirthfully hid.

At about 2030 hours, as I sat with Shindo before a reassuringly bright fire, I heard the erratic jungle rhythms falter and cease. We immediately took up our rifles, as did every other man within our sight. I almost regretted having allowed the fires, for they blinded us to anything beyond their short range of illumination, but presented us to our enemy with merciless clarity.

It seemed ages we remained frozen, thwarted by the stillness that mocked our vigilance. And then, with a terrific *boom* and a blinding flash, a landmine exploded some fifteen meters away, its light revealing *something* that stretched out of the jungle like an onyx serpent: a thin ribbon of uncoiling, solid shadow. I heard screams far to my left, from the northern end of the camp, and another landmine blew up with a dull *thump-crack*, followed by another, and then another. A volley of rifle fire came from my left, their muzzle flashes creating a strobing effect by which I could see an ambiguous thrashing among the trees. Another landmine exploded, and in that moment of brilliance, I saw three or more men being dragged, struggling and screaming, through the barbed wire into the void beyond the minefield. I lifted my rifle and blindly emptied its five shots, lamenting the futility of the gesture even as my finger squeezed off the rounds.

Near me, I saw Lt. Tajima unsheath his sword and run, crying defiantly, toward our useless barricade. His sword swished back and forth as if in battle with some invisible assailant, but suddenly he was cut down. As more gunshots lit the night, I saw his body being pulled across the ground and through the coil of barbed wire. He screamed shrilly as his flesh was shredded; then his voice was stifled, and he was gone.

Something small followed Tajima's figure into the darkness: a grenade. Seconds later, it exploded with a muffled *thump,* as if its force had been absorbed by something solid. The now-familiar hornet's buzzing suddenly swirled angrily out of the jungle, again assaulting my eardrums like stabbing needles. But seconds later it ceased again, and I detected no further movement amid the trees. I lifted a hand, signaling the nearest men to hold their fire.

We stood like frozen Noh-players until, finally, a single insect somewhere to my right chirped for a mate. From my left, one answered tentatively. And the jungle came to life again. I ordered Shindo to take a head count, and he rushed away to comply. When he returned two minutes later, his face was stricken with disbelief.

"Eleven men are gone," he said.

I choked back a sob. Never in my entire career could I have witnessed such useless death. "Every man will remain vigilant tonight. There must be no sleep," I said.

Shindo said softly, "None of us will close his eyes tonight."

I nodded and began to walk among the men. They were dutifully gathering spent clips from the ground, reloading their empty rifles, picking up the dropped weapons of their lost comrades. Though each man's hands shook, and each face bore the ghastly pallor of fear, they performed their duty like soldiers. A small tremor of pride passed through my body, for, in spite of the horror we had just faced, my men remained steadfast and valiant.

I finally returned to the dim interior of the Quonset hut, fully aware that tonight's ordeal might have only begun. I looked at the radio set — our one link to the proper world we had left behind. It seemed a pitiful, laughable device that had no relevance in this haunted place. Without pausing to consider what I was doing, I lifted my rifle and fired, and the radio set exploded, its components clanging loudly against the sides of the hut.

A second later, Shindo rushed through the door, his eyes wide, jaw agape. He paused to regard the damage I had done, and for a moment I thought he was actually going to strike me. But soon, the burning in his eyes cooled, and he lowered his head, shaking it uselessly back and forth.

"So, you think we are finished?" he asked in a hoarse whisper.

"Not finished. Lost."

Shindo turned up the lantern so that its golden glow threw hideously foreshortened shadows on the walls. I sat down at the table and, as before, he brought out a bottle of plum wine. "It's the last," he said.

He took two small cups from his personal kit and filled them for the both of us. We drank silently, watching our movements mimicked by the unnaturally long, thin black shadow beings on the wall.

"Whom did we lose?" I asked.

"Tajima. Okada. Torohata. Adachi. Gondo. . . ."

"The men we most need to complete the work."

Shindo nodded, unable to continue. Finally, he whispered, "What kind of world does such a thing come from?"

"A dead, black world," I said. "It must have a black sun, that burns horribly in the night. And the sounds . . . the very air must be forever filled with its evil song."

"Why is it here?"

"It is somehow connected to the people here. I regret destroying that village, for the ones on the ridge are surely their cousins. But more than that, I only regret that I cannot kill each and every one of them myself."

"But sir, if we can hold out until the air group arrives, we may get reinforcements, and then we can destroy them utterly."

I shook my head. "Shindo. Do you believe that any number of our men could do more to that black-hearted thing than we have already done?"

He sighed. " No, sir."

"Shindo," I said. "Have the men move to the edge of the runway. We are too near to the trees."

"Yes, sir."

He left to do as I ordered. And I watched the lamplight, the little caged star with the power to spell the difference between courage and cowardice. Take that little star from the night, and what did we have left? I twisted the knob and doused the flame. The darkness came complete, and I laid my head on my arms on the table, aware that my body was a spent ember. I did not dare close my eyes. But I could not keep them open.

Sleep washed over me like an ocean tide, tugging me far away, so quickly I could not even realize what was happening.

I opened my eyes to a darkness so pure I that might have

been closed within a coffin. My muscles were frozen, and I could not even move a finger. After a few moments, I realized that my head lay on the tabletop, cradled by my arms. Something was tickling my left ear; an insect, perhaps. I wanted to bat it away, but I could not move.

A sharp buzzing sound began, like the whirring of a beetle's wings. But it rose steadily in volume until it became far louder than any insect. And then the buzzing took on a strange, articulated quality, rising and falling in a terrible imitation of speech. Eventually, I could make out words, though they had no meaning to me:

"Michi kyong mi, ghia da cho-chiyo. . . ."

A stab of sheer terror broke my paralysis, and I bolted upright, batting frantically at my left ear, certain there must be something resting there, but my fingers touched only air.

And the sound continued.

"Kyo-gha baung, balah-kai . . . We . . . we . . . watch . . . we . . . win."

I cried out, hands flailing. One of them struck the lantern, and it fell to the floor with a crash. As the echo died, the buzzing voice also went silent. The tickling behind my ear remained, though, as if legs of chitin had grasped the flesh of my earlobe. I called Shindo's name, but received no reply. Stumbling blindly toward what I hoped was the door, my hand struck the ridged wall of the hut so fiercely that pain charged up my arm like an electrical shock.

Finally, my questing fingers found the door, and throwing it open, I lurched outside, desperate even for starlight to break the terrible blackness. I could see the dying coals from several fires, and above, a few stars twinkled in a hazy sky. There was no moon. None of my men was in sight. I wanted to call out, but now I feared to raise my voice — for again, the night was bereft of sound. To my left I could see the dark hulk of a bulldozer, and I went toward it slowly, picking my steps carefully over the rutted earth.

When I reached the machine, I glanced up at the ridge, only to see a single, flickering point of flame near the darkened crest. The light was stationary, as if the torchbearer were simply watching and waiting, knowing that it had nothing to fear. Had I brought my rifle with me, I would have opened fire, though it was far beyond the range of my puny bullets. Instead, I merely rested my weight on the cowl of the bulldozer and glared defiantly at the torch. I sensed that whoever held it was laughing.

At last, I turned to gaze upon the runway we had labored so diligently to complete. In the pale starlight, a few meters away, I saw *something* that struck me as out of place. As I went toward it, fingers of cold nausea began to wriggle up from my stomach. It was a tall and spindly thing, with something large and bulbous perched atop it. Taking a few steps closer, I peered closely at it, trying to establish the identity of the dead.

It was Shindo. His eyes were closed, the mouth open and tongue lolling from slack lips. Black blood still dripped from the torn neck, pooling like oil on the ground at the base of the bamboo stave. I groaned miserably, no longer repulsed or sickened; simply finished. How long had it been since we had shared the last bottle of wine? A few hours? Only minutes, perhaps?

Suddenly, Shindo's eyelids flew open, and the dead eyes turned to look at me, shining with terrible cognizance. With a gasp, I backed away, unable to tear my gaze from this sickening desecration, unwilling to accept the indisputable proof of my own sight. The living eyes followed my every movement, their gaze horrified and pleading. *No! No awareness could possibly remain in that ruined case of flesh and bone.*

I turned and ran toward the row of tents that now lined the earthen apron beside the airstrip. I tore open the flaps of the first one I came to and poked my head inside, only to find it empty. I ran from tent to tent, rewarded with the same result at each and every one. *Where? Where were they? Every man in the camp could not have disappeared. It was impossible.*

But I was alone.

I cried out to the night, to the burning light at the top of the ridge, to the unseen horror that I knew lay in wait somewhere in the vast darkness. I cared little that it might reach out to take me, for at least I would be where I belonged: with the men of the 212, who had lived and worked — and died — in my charge. I screamed until my voice faltered and went silent, my throat raw and tortured. On the ridge, the torchlight continued to burn indifferently.

At some point, I stumbled back to the Quonset hut and in the pitch blackness settled myself in the chair at my little table. My fingers found the framed photograph of my wife and children, and I squeezed it to my chest with such strength that not even the hideous clutches that had pulled my men through barbed wire could have loosened it from my grasp.

The darkness held its breath, and I wept.

*T*he sun could have been up for moments or for most of a day before I became aware of its light creeping through the still open door of the hut. It was not the light that had drawn me from the secret place where I had retreated and that I could not recall; it was a sound: the low whining of distant engines.

My first thought was that the tanks had arrived, for they were scheduled to precede the fighter group. But the sound I heard was not the deep grumble-clank of motors and treads. This was the distinctive drone of airplane engines. I rose from the chair and crept into the daylight. The sun had risen halfway to its zenith, which meant the fighter squadron was arriving on schedule.

But where were the tanks?

Stiffly, I walked down to the airstrip. The first thing I noticed was that Shindo's piteous remains had somehow been removed, with only a repugnant dark stain left behind. Looking skyward, I could see no sign of the planes as yet; but the sound of their engines grew steadily louder, echoing through the jungle so that I could not determine the direction of their approach. They would have been trying to contact us — unsuccessfully, of course.

At last, I saw a trio of dots veering in from the east. They quickly grew larger until I could recognize the graceful profiles of the Ki-43 Hayabusas. They roared low overhead, dipping their wings as the pilots regarded the airfield curiously, the brilliant red balls of the rising sun gleaming from their forest green fuselages and the gray undersides of their wings. One of the pilots saw me, and I raised a hand in greeting, for a moment feeling a strange sense of normalcy, as if all that had happened here had been swept away by the arrival of my countrymen.

Five more vee-shaped formations followed, and behind them, a trio of Ki-57 transport planes appeared, carrying the squadron's supplies and ground crew. The lead Hayabusa swung back to the east to set up its approach, and the other fighters fell in close behind. A lump of joy and relief rose to my throat, though some whispering voice inside warned me that my most difficult task might yet lie ahead — once the pilots discovered the awful truth of what had happened here.

Despite a conscious effort to avoid doing so, I chanced a look toward the top of the ridge. Suddenly, my blood went frigid and my heart began clanging like a gong in my ears. There, as on the previous day, a wavering heat haze marred the sky above a cluster of swaying trees. I could feel the thing watching me.

Then, as the fighters began to descend, I heard a deep, buzzing sound, like a swarm of mad hornets. Yet this was different from the sound that had become so horribly familiar to me; this had a deeper, more mechanized timbre. And then, when the truth of this new reality began to dawn on me, despair again gripped me and I ran out to the runway, waving my arms frantically, trying to make the fighter pilots understand and veer away.

From over the top of the ridge, a swarm of dark, roaring silhouettes appeared, buzzing rapidly toward the descending fighters. The lead Ki-43 had already dropped its gear and was only a few hundred meters from the end of the runway when it disappeared in a ball of flame, accompanied by a deafening *boom*. The wreckage hit the ground and splattered like liquid fire, sending debris spiraling into the nearest trees. The pilot of the Hayabusa behind it firewalled the throttle, and barely avoided dropping into the inferno itself. I saw the plane's gear starting to raise and heard its engine straining to lift it out of harm's way.

But even that heroic effort gained the pilot nothing. An olive drab Tomahawk dropped onto the Ki-43's tail, its .50-caliber machine guns blazing, tearing chunks from the Ki's wings. The stricken plane rolled slowly onto its side, and I saw something — an aileron, perhaps — whirl into space. The Ki-43 suddenly nose-dived and smashed into the ground a mere hundred meters from where I stood, the horrendous impact knocking me onto my backside.

Looking up, I saw at least eight P-40s, their noses painted with the distinctive fanged maw and glaring eye insignia of the so-called Flying Tigers. The AVG — American Volunteer Group — must have retained a squadron at Toungoo or Rangoon, which were the only remaining Allied airfields close enough to accommodate the fighters. With deadly, unified purpose, they swung around to pounce again on the low, slow Hayabusas, who, in preparing to land, were at their most vulnerable. I saw a few of the trailing Ki-43s pulling up into desperate climbs, their pilots hoping to gain some advantage on the enemy fighters; but it was to no avail, as four of the P-40s banked away to pursue. Within seconds, three more of our fighters had been blown from the sky, and I saw one of the Ki-57 transports totter in the air and spiral down as it attempted evasive action. The pilot had turned too sharply and stalled the plane, too low to recover. It disappeared behind the nearest trees, and a moment later, another thunderous *boom* shook the ground. A column of black smoke rolled skyward from the site.

Our Ki-43s were far more maneuverable than the P-40s, and at least two managed to swing around to attack the Tomahawks. My heart leaped as I saw one of them open fire at the trailing P-40, causing a plume of smoke to erupt from its engine. But no sooner had he taken his shots than two more P-40s dove onto his tail and, in an instant, sent him whirling to his death. High above, atop the ridge, the roiling heat haze seemed to regard the tableau as a cold, calculating monarch might watch two enemies struggle to the death for its own amusement.

A few moments later, I heard two more deep explosions in the distance: two more Hayabusas lost. I saw the single, stricken P-40, trailing smoke, climbing toward the ridge, finally disappearing over its crest as it retired from the fight. And shortly afterward, the remaining enemy fighters reappeared from the southwest, seemingly all intact, with nary a Ki-43 in pursuit. Then, to my horror, the lead P-40 banked toward the runway — and me. I saw bright flashes from its wingtips as its guns opened fire; before me, twin rows of earthen splashes homed unerringly on me, and I felt a stab of indescribable agony as my left leg was hit. My lower leg buckled at an awry angle, blood spurting through the fabric of my trousers. I toppled to the ground, seeing white bone protruding from a jagged rip in my skin. For a brief time, I went completely numb, feeling only surprise and disbelief at the sudden strike against me.

All I could do now was shout and point to the devilish haze atop the ridge, praying that one of the enemy pilots would notice it and initiate an attack. At least one of the Americans saw my frantic waving, but he merely offered me a mocking salute; then his plane disappeared over the ridge on its way back home. Pain began to creep up my leg again, and a disturbing amount of blood was pooling on the dusty ground beneath me. I could not last much longer. But at least I could now be satisfied that I had died in combat, in defiance of an enemy who had insidiously attacked our hapless fighter group.

After a time, I again heard the buzzing of hornets from direction of the ridge. The heavy pounding began, as on that first night, so deep that it shook my body to the point of nausea. And as the horrid buzzing rose in volume, it once again articulated itself into some language I could not understand. But finally, the syllables began to become clear to me: *"Cho-chiyo ich byong mi . . . Remember . . . Remember the children."*

I lay back on the ground, all my energy spent. I expected now to simply fall asleep and not wake up, for the pain in my leg was simply a dull, distant thing with little meaning. The persistent buzzing no longer frightened me. It seemed an almost soothing, lulling background voice to accompany the final release from my pain.

But sometime later, I heard the deep, droning whine of airplane engines. Craning my neck backward, I saw a lone Ki-57 slowly lowering itself to the runway, barely avoiding the wreckage scattered along its edges. As the plane slowed to a stop, its doors opened, and a pair of frantic-looking crewmen came running toward me. I realized that one of the transports must have survived the attack, and its crew had come to render whatever aid they might.

I recall being carried to the plane by four able-bodied men.

But though their limbs were strong, their movements well-practiced, I could see in their eyes the unmistakable look of confusion, and in some cases, outright horror. Even if they could not actually see the thing that watched from somewhere on the ridge, I knew they felt its presence as profoundly as I did. By the time they carefully loaded my near-ruined body into the cargo hold of the transport, I could again hear the distant hornet's buzzing from the ridge. Glancing out the door, I saw the trees swaying and bending as the thing began to descend steadily toward the field. I cried out for haste, and though the pilot and my attending rescuers probably misunderstood, it was my fear for *them* that drove me to fitfully scream, "Get us out! Get us out now!"

After that, I recall nothing until I woke in a hospital in Bangkok, and even then I had only a few lucid moments. The doctors were able to save my leg, though the damage was severe enough that I will never regain full use of it. My physical condition improved rapidly, but I remained in a kind of mental fog, the memories of which are disjointed and often frightening. Throughout this experience, I could never explain to the doctors, or to the officers who came to debrief me, exactly what had happened at the Myatauki airfield. But through them, I learned that the tank group that had been sent to assist my unit had simply vanished as if it never existed. Furthermore, when army investigators arrived at the airfield, they could find no trace of anyone from the 212 Engineering Corps, either alive or dead. Though I cannot recall saying it, I understand my explanation was simply, "They were taken by the children."

The wreckage of the air group showed all too plainly that we had been attacked by the AVG, and my "valiant resistance" earned me a meritorious discharge, despite the unexplained loss of my entire unit. I was questioned personally by Lt. Gen. Iida, who pointedly asked me if the catastrophe was related to the "unexplained threat" that I had reported on more than one occasion. To this I could only answer, "It must have been," and no amount of interrogation could draw from me any elaboration.

Finally, after two months, I was sent home. And though my memory of the events in Burma has finally returned to me unclouded, under no circumstances could I reveal to the army, or to my family, the extraordinary truth of my experience. To do so would undermine whatever honor I have remaining, and subject my beloved wife and children to undeserved disgrace. Here, in the security of my home in peaceful Okayama, I have been able to bury the horror of those days beneath the support offered to me by my loved ones. My sweet Machiko has always been unquestioningly faithful, but even to her I could not speak of the things that happened in that dreadful place. It upsets her that I am silent about this matter; she loves me and knows me well enough to understand that some secrets must be held in a man's heart until the day they are released by his death.

Though the army has publicly maintained that I was released from the service with honor, I shall never forget the look of contempt on Lt. Gen. Iida's face as he presented my discharge papers to me. I am certain he felt that I am to blame for the disappearance of my unit. Indeed, I *am* shamed at having been overcome by that awful thing and its brutal minions, yet I am confident that I fully and honorably performed my duties as a soldier. Despite the grievous loss of the 212 Engineering Corps, the task of renovating the airfield was completed, under my leadership, to the exact specifications of the operational commander.

Sadly, I have been informed that a second regiment sent to the Myatauki airfield to insure the security of the region vanished under similarly bizarre circumstances. But due to the minor strategic value of that particular airfield, and now that the Allied bases at Mergui, Tavoy, Moulmein, and Toungoo have fallen to our forces, I have been informed that further efforts to hold the Myatauki region have been abandoned. Yes, I am relieved that no more of my countrymen should perish in that forsaken shadowland; but I am also galled that so many men's lives were wasted in pursuit of a meaningless goal.

Now, as I write, the Burma Road is in our hands. Rangoon has fallen. Burma belongs to the emperor. It is a day to rejoice, and to forget the dream voices that have followed me for all these months.

How I love to sit beneath the cherry blossoms of my home

in beautiful Okayama. Machiko tends to me when my injury precludes me from even the simplest tasks. I enjoy watching over my children, who are half-oblivious to the dark lines and shadows that mar my face. They are old enough to understand that war changes men and have accepted that I returned a different person than they knew before.

Yet, they still love me with all their hearts and know that I am, forever and always, their father. And they will always be my children.

*A*dministrative note: The preceding manuscript was discovered among the belongings of Colonel Kenjiro Terusawa, formerly of the 212 Engineering Corps, XV Army, and forwarded to Operational HQ, Rangoon, for investigation following the slaying of his young son and two daughters. The details are particularly brutal, for the once-honored officer had apparently decapitated all three of his children and mounted their heads on bamboo pikes in front of his home. The only words that the subject has since uttered are, "Remember the children."

Terusawa's wife, Machiko, was reported to have committed suicide shortly after discovering the murders.

Col. Terusawa has been confined for the remainder of his life to an institution for the criminally insane in Hiroshima.

— Gen. Shibata Ryuichi
Operational Commander, XV Army
June, 1944